The Beauty In Darkness

By Leah Reise

Leah Reise

A New Race
Book 2

Edited by Kevin Miller
Cover design by Dane Low at Ebook Launch

ISBN: 978-1673301557

Printed in the United States of America

First Edition

Acknowledgments

To my sister, Flo, the animal protector who always follows her dreams.

A special thanks to my husband, Benjamin, who always supports me no matter what life brings our way. You are my refuge from the storm.

Contents

1

Long-lost Friend

The buzzing in my ears woke me. Sometimes it was there, sometimes not. I still didn't quite understand it. All I knew was it didn't come about until I first awoke as a vampire.

I lay quietly in the dark, my mind spinning as it always did until I realized something. As time went on, the endless night, as still and beautiful as it was, was harder to adore knowing it was all I would ever have.

I cast the thought away and imagined I was human again, traveling the world the way I would have been if I hadn't become a clairvoyant blood-drinking creature of the night.

I laughed softly to myself, and my eyes found the stars through the slightly opened curtains. I imagined the flickering lights amidst the blackness slowly eclipsed by the rising sun and a clear blue sky. I imagined I was on a trip somewhere—a small beach pueblo in Mexico, the sound of ocean waves in the distance, children running and cackling, men riding by on horses wearing sombreros and chattering in Spanish. I smiled as I felt the burn of desire for the life I could never have, but it was a good kind of burn. Then I imagined I was in a coastal town of Greece, my room paved with round white cement walls, an old man walking outside my window with a donkey . . . were there donkeys in Greece?

I sat up, shaking my head and giggling to myself. I'd had too much time alone. One would think time moved quickly in the vampire world. Not to me. Not as my mortal family lived. Every day that passed meant one more day to worry about them.

Jule, my vampire roommate, who had a budding mind ability of her own, had been gone for two weeks on a trip to England. With my Uncle Uri's help, that was where she discovered relatives who shared her gift. The cottage was quieter without her thoughts, though she had learned to shield her mind most of the time. I was pretty sure it bothered her that I could hear her mind. I didn't want *my* thoughts heard. In fact, I'd been attending sessions with Uri to learn mind-blocking as well. It made me uneasy to know he could read me. My thoughts were not always what many would call "pure." I'd say I was only human, but, well, you know . . .

The glow of moonlight drew me toward the bedroom window. I pulled back the brown velvet curtain to inspect the night. In the garden, Mikale, our immortal Hawaiian guard and a close friend of mine, sat amid a circle of flowers tending to the soil. His white T-shirt was slightly dirty, but his black cargo shorts weren't. It must've been the way he sat on his heels and wiped his palms over his chest. I focused on the smudges of dirt on the fabric, which defined his pectoral muscles. They were hard to ignore. His blue-eyed gaze met mine, and he smiled, his pale skin accenting the moon. I smiled back. I couldn't help it. My cheeks ached every time.

I still found it so odd that I had all the same human sensations, just more intensely. Uncle Uri had educated me all about the infection that caused vampirism. The immortal bacteria, Bacillus F, allowed a vampire's body to function via some weird symbiotic partnership. Even though my human body had died, the bacteria remained, using my body as a host and coalescing with my cells and organs. The bacteria governed my very being and allowed me to "live" in this immortal form, although without the need for a beating heart and working lungs. Apparently, the bacteria maintained the oxygen level needed in any environment as well as the flow of blood as long as I fed and didn't go out in the sun. Frankly, it still creeped me out.

I threw on my white robe and made my way out the side French doors of the cottage. Mikale, still sitting on his heels, looked up at me and smirked playfully.

"Getting dirty as usual," I teased.

"You know me, Edrea," he said, his eyebrow raised in his coy, sexy way.

I rolled my lips inward to prevent myself from smiling widely. "Weren't we going for a stroll in the city tonight? I haven't fed on an actual person for a few weeks now."

He laughed. "That's right. But you'll have to accompany me home, so I can clean up and change clothes. You know Uri doesn't want you home alone without a security guard on duty."

"Yeah, I know. It's not safe. I have the feeling it never will be," I said, shrugging with frustration. "I just need a moment to get dressed."

Mikale nodded, his gleaming blue eyes watching me. My lips turn up, and I pressed them into a tight line, feeling my dimples cave as I turned for the door.

Once inside the closed French doors, I fleeted back to my room and threw on some jeans and a gray tank top that had white, dainty images of Fior di Liz, the Eiffel tower, and cursive French words about travels and Paris. I slipped into some black flats. I could never be too comfortable. I swung my long gray hooded sweater around me and headed for the front door.

Mikale was waiting there patiently, stern and professional, as if this leisure trip were part of the job. As soon as I stepped onto the black doormat, he locked the door and took my hand. It seemed natural to him, the way he held my hand. I wasn't sure it was for me quite yet.

As we walked down the cobblestone path, I gazed up through the canopy of whispering trees. I loved how the stars twinkled through the twisted branches and fluttering leaves. My ears tickled with the sound of dancing granules of glass as the light breeze swept through the gazebo and its Zen sandbox, one of my favorite features of the midnight garden. Perhaps that's what I would call it, "The Midnight Garden." Something so beautiful should have a name, after all.

We made our way through the back French doors of Uri's house, which was only fifty feet or so from my little cottage. We walked into the large family room—I called it the astronomy sanctum. Between the assortment of colorful couches was a telescope pointed at the cosmos through a glass dome. Around it was a donut-shaped coffee table.

I felt Uri's tension in the adjacent den. He had been anxiously following the movements of some crazy Russian scientists who had discovered the bacteria, Bacillus F. Uri came across some of their studies online and suspected their experiments could be more dangerous than he'd originally thought. He had spent the last few days in his den reading their recent findings and documenting any future conventions the scientists might launch.

"Sir," Mikale greeted him as we stepped into the warm light of the den.

Uri's eyes found us from above his glowing computer screen. "Hello, kids. Going out tonight?"

"Just for a stroll," I replied. I couldn't help but feel concerned for my great uncle. I had never seen him so fixated on something. It worried me.

"Hmm . . . a stroll, eh? You behave yourselves now." Uri raised his eyebrows and smirked. *Be easy on him, Edrea*, he concluded in my thoughts.

I rolled my eyes and nodded, then nudged Mikale with my shoulder to follow me to the hallway.

"What was that about?" Mikale asked, a tint of excitement in his eyes. I shrugged and turned my back to him so he wouldn't catch the embarrassment on my face, and then quickly opened the front door.

We fleeted toward Twin Peaks, where Mikale lived, one of the many homes Uri owned in the city. As long as Mikale worked for my uncle, he had a place where he could stay rent-free. We followed the Lands End Trail to the Great Highway along the shore, then onto Sloat Blvd., where the streets bustled with cars and people. The streetlights zipped by our eyes, the familiar oval window of sight curving around us. I couldn't help but think of Alexio, my late love. My dark guardian who had given his life to save my sister's. Not so long ago, it was Alexio's hand I felt squeezing mine as we soared through the streets at night.

Mikale and I reached the pitch-dark base of the grassy peaks, and I withdrew my hand from his, stopping abruptly on the dry crunchy earth. He looked at me as if I had done something strange. I strained a smile that didn't reach my eyes.

"Are you okay?" There was a softness in his voice. On top of his island accent, it made my stomach tingle. The gleam of his blue eyes took me, and finally my eyes smiled too, following the ache when my dimples caved.

"Of course . . . just a sad memory."

He took my hand delicately and led me off the bare earth and across one of the sharp loops of Twin Peaks Blvd. We hopped over the guardrail, and our feet found grass again. There, right below us, down at the bottom of the flower-peppered hill, was a large gray house.

"Come on," Mikale urged. He ran down the slope like a playful child. I giggled and followed close behind. I couldn't help but notice my mood felt lighter in the company of the peppy Hawaiian.

We cut around the back of the home and scurried down the side of the hill, which met a narrow street. "Well, this is it," Mikale said, his palm open and a charming smile on his face. I pressed my lips together into a tight smile, noticing he may have looked a little too happy. We walked up his driveway and around the side of the garage where a black door was set in a decorative concrete wall. He pulled keys out of his pocket and let us inside. We ran up the stairs of the front porch, and he opened the front door.

Inside, my eyes were drawn to the corner of the living room, where the glow of a small lamp sat on a wooden side table with three books. Beside them was a blue padded chair. The lights flickered on above where dozens of glass balls hung from the high ceiling. My gaze fixated giddily on the bright little spheres, which looked like galaxies in the night sky. "That's beautiful," I breathed, gaping.

"They are, aren't they? I've always admired Uri's eye for interior design," Mikale said. "Have a seat anywhere you like. I'll be out in a moment."

He disappeared up a dark stairway, and I walked around the L-shaped grayish-brown leather couch. Against the wall was the largest fireplace I'd ever seen, gray stone tiles surrounding it. On a short coffee table in front of me, which looked to be made of petrified wood, sat several more books, spread across the surface. It appeared Mikale enjoyed reading. We immortals *did* have unlimited time for that.

Just as I picked up one of the fantasy novels about druid wars and dragons, Mikale skipped down the stairs in his famous black cargo shorts and black shirt. "Original," I teased and then laughed at his goofy expression.

"Should I slip on my leather onesie instead?" he asked.

That was when I lost it. He joined in shortly after when he couldn't maintain his ridiculous poker face.

"Speaking of leather, what do you say we hit up a vamp bar in the Castro tonight?" Mikale said.

"There's one in the Castro?" I hadn't given much thought to how many vampire bars existed in the city.

"Right under the Castro Theater. Actually, it's more of a cellar that gets rented out now and then." He smiled and lifted his eyebrows.

I raised an eyebrow and smirked. "Oh, so you're expecting me to woo a gay man?" Few straight men were comfortable enough with their sexuality to go to gay bars, and I didn't feel comfortable pretending to be attracted to women either.

Mikale laughed, and even in his laughter I could hear the sexy Hawaiian coo in his voice. "Actually, the bar is hosting some kind of after-hours party tonight. That usually draws in all types."

"The Castro it is," I said. "What's this place called?"

He smirked. "Promise not to judge me." Then he fleeted to the couch and extended his hand. I took it and stood up, then cocked my head slightly to the side. "What's it called?" I pressed, tugging playfully at his hand.

"Well, the mortals know it by the name of . . . Tailspin," he said, pulling me toward the front door.

A burst of laughter escaped my lips. "Not surprising."

Mikale grinned as he searched for his keys. "The vampires, they call it Under The Rainbow, from what I'm told."

I laughed again. "That's not surprising either."

Mikale smirked. "Well, let's go get our late-night snack."

Outside, the night air had crisped by at least a few degrees. It was nice never to have to worry about catching a cold. I looked up between the clouds and admired the glimmer of stars that competed with the city's glow. The view had a certain polarity from up there.

After Mikale locked up the house and the outer-wall door, we made our way down the street. I noticed the sign at the corner read "Midcrest Way." I stopped there for a moment and lifted my large hood over my head.

"That's not going to stay on while we're fleeting," Mikale said. "You know that, right?"

I pressed my lips together and raised my eyebrow at him. "You don't say?"

We laughed as we reached the corner of Twin Peaks Blvd. Then we stepped under some trees that shielded us from any streetlight.

"I just realized that I know a few people in the Castro," I said, a slight tone of concern in my voice. "I need to stay concealed at all times."

"We'll be careful," Mikale promised. "Ready?"

"Yep."

We took off and fleeted toward Tailspin—or Under The Rainbow. The names for the cellar club had me smirking on the journey.

I focused on the nightlife streaming by my window of sight. The strange tunnel view of ribbons of streetlights, cars, and houses fascinated me a little more every time I fleeted through the city. It was exhilarating.

We stopped moments later in the darkness of a building where Market St. meets Castro St. I kept my face under my hood, feeling a little nervous.

Turning on Castro St., we walked across from my favorite little diner, Pinky's. Mikale strutted with ease. I, on the other hand, felt like a freak hiding under my hood. My eyes moved erratically between the pavement and whatever I could see around me. I wasn't sure what made me more uncomfortable: my oversized hood or the fact someone who knew me might see my face. It was still unsettling knowing I'd have to hide my identity for decades to come.

Right ahead of us a middle-aged man wearing nothing but a translucent neon-green speedo cut across the street. "Close your eyes now, E," Mikale teased. I grimaced, glad he didn't use my real name in public—there of all places.

I tugged slightly on my hood, trying not to appear too suspicious, and we hurried across the street between passing cars. I caught a whiff of the little cookie shop a few doors down from the theater. The sweet aroma was strangely different now; it didn't trigger hunger pangs. As usual, the window displayed large cookies in the shape of male genitalia.

"Are you sure this isn't the 'late-night snack' you were referring to?" I asked, grinning.

Mikale glanced in the window of the cookie store and laughed. "Very funny."

When we reached the theater, Mikale held his elbow up invitingly and twitched his eyebrow. I took his arm. "Why, thank you, sir."

We made our way around the side of the building toward its little rear parking lot. At the back of the building were two short lines behind a red door. A finely dressed bouncer stood at the entrance, his expression blank.

"Come on," Mikale whispered by my ear. "All vampires enter in the VIP line."

Still nervous about someone recognizing me, I held my head down and followed Mikale into the vampire line. Ahead of us were several immortals, none of whom I'd seen before. The brunette lady vamp in front of me wore a loose-fitting black dress made of fine linen and brown leather booties. She looked like she was dressed for a country music event, complete with line dancing. Her rubber-soled booties were a brilliant choice though. I'd have to get some of those. Stylish and perfect for fleeting.

The longer we waited outside, the more anxiety prickled beneath my skin. I fidgeted with my sweater, tugging on it from my hips and continuously pulling my hood down to ensure it properly shadowed my face.

I bet there's a pretty face to go with the curvy little body beneath that gray sweater.

I stiffened at the surprisingly loud words in my head, heard above all the rest. I glanced to the human line on my left where the intrusive thoughts came from. Sure enough, there stood a young man staring with engrossed blue eyes and buckteeth. The moment he saw my glare, I looked away.

Mmm . . . she wants me. I'll have to get a piece of that later.

I quivered at the lewd and clearly delusional assumption. And yet . . . he'd be the perfect prey.

Mikale caught me giggle under my breath and nudged my shoulder. "What's so funny?"

"Oh, nothing. Just found my dinner." I motioned slightly to the left with my head.

The moment Mikale peered in that direction, he chuckled knowingly. "Oh, he's definitely been a problem around here. You sure seem to attract the winners."

I wanted to laugh, but a thought flowed through me with a chill—the memory of the sick man who ended my life. The man who raped me when I was human.

"I'm sorry, Edrea . . . I didn't—"

"Don't worry about it. It's okay, really." I smiled and looked into his wary eyes, so he could see I meant it. I nudged him. "Let's have some fun tonight, huh?"

As if on cue, music from the midnight movie playing within the theater walls made itself known—none other than the *Jaws* theme. Everyone in line, both human and vampire, burst into laughter. Of course, we vampires shared a secret dark humor in our eyes.

I looked up at Mikale and caught his penetrating gaze. It was the same gaze I remembered from the first night I ever saw him in the interrogation room when he was posing as a Décret guard, though he was secretly loyal to Uri and the Shevet coven. The intensity in his blue eyes made my body tingle. I shifted uncomfortably, a tight smile forming on my face.

The red door opened a crack, and the bouncer turned his ear to the dim glow behind it. He nodded. "IDs out, please," he said as a group of people pushed their way out the door. One of them was a pretty blond mortal staggering with bent knees as she hung giddily on the sharply dressed vampire at her side. His coat covered the soft, fair skin of her neck. The humans surely thought intoxication was behind her behavior. I, on the other hand, knew she had just been fed upon.

We neared the door, and I realized how monstrously large the immortal bouncer was. I wouldn't want to get into a brawl with him, superhuman strength or not.

I stepped to the front of the line and held my ID above my head, smiling. The bouncer was *that* large, especially since I was wearing flats. He glanced downward, probably wondering if I was a youngblood. He eyed my brilliantly fabricated ID and then looked back at me. Then he returned a genuine smile, and I decided I liked him, just like that.

"Thank you, sir."

The red door opened again, and I walked inside a tiny room lit with a soft yellow hue. As expected, a stairway led down into a darker area where trance music buzzed through the ground. The music was a lot quieter than it should have been, which probably meant the walls were reinforced with extra insulation. I couldn't help but wonder if the cellar was used for more than an after-hours nightclub. The possibilities made me cringe.

I peered over my shoulder as I continued down the basement stairs to make sure the footsteps at my heels were Mikale's. He smiled and lifted an eyebrow and then jumped down the last few steps. He propped open a large metal door, gesturing his hand in a circular motion and bowing for me to enter. Shaking my head, I walked into a short dark hall, the bass pulsing loudly. I pushed open a pair of double swinging doors that appeared to be borrowed from an old western saloon. They squeaked as they swung back and forth behind us.

I took in the scent of blood that permeated the air despite the smell of sweat and the moldy walls. The small room's purple paint job did not do it justice. Beneath me the coolness of the concrete seeped into my feet just like the scent of human blood oozed into my skin and senses. I was glad I hadn't wandered in there the first night after revamping. The confined, insulated club would be the worst place for a youngblood. One whiff of the air down there was like crack for a vampire. I almost couldn't take it. Was it where immortals went to be stripped of their humanity?

I looked back at Mikale, unease gathering in my gut. I wasn't sure being there was the best idea. I was surprised to see a dark excitement in his eyes, a shade of my Hawaiian bodyguard I wasn't sure I'd seen before. Perhaps it was something I had ignored. His impassioned eyes scanned the room and landed back on me, on my lips. I saw a hunger in him. He was not the same Mikale I'd known.

He must have noticed the concern on my face because he adjusted his posture, as if turning his "inner beast knob" down a few notches. I realized he had plenty of practice with this. I found myself staring at him, at every movement he made. His hunger tickled me in just the right way. Once again I was faced with a man with a delicious combination of tenderness and darkness. At that moment, I realized our friendship had shifted. He had the kind of passion that drew me in. I couldn't turn away from it no matter how badly it burned. Realizing this also saddened me because I knew a love affair wouldn't last. And yet knowing that also felt safe. Unshackled. Wild.

"Mikale!" An excited female voice traveled from a small bar on the left. A tall olive-skinned brunette in a black dress tight enough to choke a human hopped off one of the six red shimmering barstools. A dark-skinned woman in black skinny jeans and an emerald-green shirt followed behind her with a smile to die for. Neither of them even bothered to look at me. *Ugh.*

When the buoyant females were halfway to us, I knew they were both immortals. The moment the brunette reached Mikale, she threw her arms around his neck, and her bright-red lips smacked into his with an obnoxious moan of pleasure. The second female greeted him similarly. Mikale embraced them in a big "friendly" hug, only they stayed attached after the release, dangling like jewels at his sides. "Chelsea, Brooklyn, I'd like you to meet Edrea," he said, his hands on their waists.

The giggly females shot me a glance. "Hey," they said in unison and a similar tone of disinterest.

I raised both eyebrows and smiled widely to mask my

13

sudden nausea as the term "vamp tramps" reeled in my head. "I'm gonna see what they have at the bar," I said as I swiveled on my heel. I laughed to myself softly as I walked away. *I should have seen this coming.*

I tried not to slump over the now-empty bar, purposely holding my shoulders straight. I wasn't sure why the two ladies bothered me so much. A man—a vampire man—like Mikale had the kind of passion and charm that couldn't possibly remain hinged.

"What will you have, sweetness?"

The words that came in a thick French accent from behind the bar tore through my body with sudden anguish. As if breathing were still part of my nature, I sucked air into my lungs to catch the pain. That word, *sweetness* . . . that was what Gustav, the man who defiled and murdered me, called me the night Rena was kidnapped. Even in death his memory still broke free now and then. Sometimes in a dream. Sometimes in a word. It reminded me of the darkness in the world, the darkness that would always exist.

I quickly loosened my posture and looked into the bartender's curious gaze, which belonged to a familiar face. *My little mind reader,* he said to me in his thoughts. My chin dropped as I sucked in air again. I knew who he was. The French vampire who had served as a Décret interrogator that night in the tunnels. The immortal who interrogated one of Uri's spies, the spy I was meant to read.

Tonight just keeps getting better and better, I thought sarcastically.

I scooted onto one of the barstools. It wiggled and squeaked beneath me. I leaned slightly over the bar and smirked. "You practice many trades, don't you? A bartender and an interrogator. Do you interrogate drunk humans now? Is that a new thing?" I smiled widely.

The French immortal smirked deviously and leaned over the bar until his face was only an inch from mine. "I don't think we've been properly introduced. My name is André. You're Edrea?" As my name left his lips in a whisper, his eyes searched the room for anyone listening.

"That's right. The one and the only," I said, rolling my eyes.

My eyes found their way over to Mikale. Amidst the storm of vivacious curls, bosoms, and wide-mouthed laughter, his gaze somehow met mine, and he winked to acknowledge me. I shook my head and laughed under my breath, swiveling back toward the bar.

"Are you two a thing?" André asked, glaring at Mikale.

I realized André must be aware Mikale had worked for the Décret as a Shevet spy. And yet, before I became Shevet, I had been Décret too. They were the ones who turned me. It was strange that there was an ongoing war between the covens, and now there we were, having a normal conversation. Maybe it wasn't so strange, seeing as we were partly human.

"No," I answered, furrowing my brow as if Mikale and I weren't even a possibility. "Mikale has been a good friend to me during some hard times."

My eyes narrowed at André. I felt protective of Mikale. I also knew deep down that I had feelings for him. That was why his behavior with the ladies was a disappointment. Oh well. I couldn't hate him for being a ladies' man.

At that moment, one of the two lady vamps burst with obnoxious laughter, and I glared in her direction. Oddly, it pleased me to see Mikale as happy as he looked then, and I couldn't help but smile at him. He had put his life on the line for me and Rena, and I could only love him for that.

Behind the nauseating show that the floozy lady vamps put

on for Mikale, a few people came through the swinging doors, and they were definitely human.

"This one's on me," André offered as he slid a chilled metal shot glass in front of me. "B positive. It's one of our best. Make sure you shoot it all down and hand it back to me afterwards." He raised an eyebrow at me and waited.

"Oh . . . thanks." I put the cool metal to my lips and threw my head back until every last drop was in my mouth. While the silky chilled blood flowed down my throat, I tasted accents of cherry and orange. I licked my lips clean with a soft groan. It was so amazing that I forgot André was standing there watching—salivating, actually.

I smacked the shot glass down on the counter, waking him out of his temporary fixation. "Very nice, André. Do you infuse your blood here?"

"You've never had infused blood?" he asked with a look of disbelief.

"Apparently not." As I spoke, a human sat to my left, the bucktoothed guy from the line.

"What will it be tonight?" André said, his lip curling in disgust as he turned to face the newcomer.

I laughed through my nostrils and then rolled my lips in to stop myself. The guy was clearly a regular.

The bucktoothed man turned to me and smiled as he rested his elbow on the counter and stroked his poorly shaved chin with his thumb. "Give me some Jack on the rocks," he said, his eyes never leaving me. After an awkward ten seconds of gawking, he finally spoke. "I've never seen you around here."

"That's because I've never been here." I pressed my lips together but didn't quite smile.

"I know that. I always remember a pretty face."

André snickered to himself with his back turned. All I

could think was, *Really*? I almost felt bad for the guy. I would have if his thoughts weren't filled with pure filth that made my shoulders roll in repugnance. The man's obsessed eyes found my breasts, and he bit his bottom lip. *I would do such dirty things to those perfect ti*—

"Listen!" I snapped, turning to address the ridiculously aroused man straight on. "I'm here with someone tonight." I couldn't think of anything else to say.

He laughed, snorting between breaths. "That's funny. Your friend appears to be with everyone but you tonight, honey."

"Ugh," I sighed in annoyance. I should have thought that one through.

I was about to tell my new stalker it would be best if he left me alone when I caught a glance of someone coming through the door. My body froze when I realized who it was. Jojo. I stared at my long-lost friend, finding it hard to think. The bucktoothed man slurred something else at me, but as far as I was concerned, he no longer existed.

Jojo, one of my closest human friends, was wearing his favorite white-and-red leather jacket and fitted jeans, his light-brown hair loosely styled and gelled. My body filled with overwhelming sorrow, and I couldn't move. The ache in my chest burned as every bit of our past came back to the surface at once. All I could think about was how much I missed him.

He looked in my direction, and I threw my hood over my head, jumping to my feet. I couldn't let him see me. The results would be devastating. I walked nervously across the room, so I could loop around him. I passed Mikale and his lady friends, who had taken their party to a booth against the wall. Mikale leaned over the table with his back turned, four breasts and eyes looking up at him. I couldn't risk stopping to tell him what had happened.

Nearly to the door, I heard my name in Jojo's thoughts.

Edrea?

I gasped in horror. *Shit. He didn't see me. He didn't.*

I burst through the swinging doors and pushed open the heavy metal door to the stairs. It closed behind me with a bang, so loud the soundwaves almost knocked me off my feet. I focused on the front door above where an immortal sat on a stool. His eyes inspected me as I ran up the stairs as calmly as I could, but only turbulent unease flowed through me. Then his eyes looked behind me. I hadn't heard the steps below until then. *Edrea . . . it can't be her.* Jojo's thoughts sounded again like an alarm.

I didn't wait for the doorman to let me out. I shoved the door open instead, desperate to save Jojo from what could only be death if he confirmed it was really me. I moved swiftly around the bouncer and nodded goodnight.

Hustling around the side of the building, I neared Castro St., walking as quickly as I could while hiding my face under my hood. I heard steps quicken behind me. I cut a sharp left from the long parking lot onto Castro St. and hurried toward 18th Ave. Halfway down the block, I heard it.

"Edrea!" My name cut through my chest like a knife, and I wished I could cry.

"Oh, fuck," I cursed under my hood, hoping Jojo's yelp wasn't heard by any immortals who knew me.

Finally coming to the corner of Castro and 18th, I ran toward a familiar dark alley a few houses down. I could have sworn my heart pounded, but that was impossible, just like imagining Jojo harmed was impossible. I darted inside the dark shadows of two Victorian houses. Pressing my back against the cold wooden panels of the wall, my eyes searched the alley for any wandering humans. I squeezed the fabric of my sweater over my heart, and my gaze found the stars. I blew out a heavy breath that I wished was a scream. The moment my ears attuned to rapid footsteps rounding the corner, I fleeted off.

2

Different Shades of Blue

After fleeting for a few seconds, which probably carried me for a few miles, I remembered I hadn't let Mikale know I left. I pulled my phone out and, sure enough, I had a missed message.

"Where'd you disappear to?" Mikale's text read.

I was actually surprised he noticed so soon, what with the whirlwind of female vamp fans hanging on his every word, not to mention on him. Still bothered by his diverted attention span, I stuffed my phone back into my jeans with a scowl.

My thoughts traveled back to Jojo, and a chill coursed through me. I'd have to watch him closely to make sure he remained safe and to ensure he didn't start some kind of search. I'd also have to tell Uri about this. For the moment I buried my worries inside the darkness of my core with a deep sigh.

I looked around the street, not really sure where I had ended up. I figured I was near the Mission District because I could smell the late-night Mexican food. I used to love a good quesadilla after a night of dancing.

I started walking east on 18th toward Mission Street. The smell of meat, oil, and corn tortillas burned through my nostrils with past adventures and the delectable pleasures I'd never experience again. I had no desire for food, but I still remembered it fondly.

I passed a taqueria on my right. People inside stuffed their faces with burritos the size of their heads. Others stood outside devouring tacos. My nostrils flared at the scent of intoxicated blood. I wondered if I should ever try it.

I stopped abruptly on the corner of San Carlos St.—or rather, my body stopped me. Down the street on the right, two firefighters hovered over an immobile homeless man who lay on the pavement.

"Sir, can you hear me?" a young paramedic asked with concern. I found myself staring at the auburn-haired man in uniform. I wasn't sure why. It may have been the way he handled the decrepit old transient, the way he touched his arm and spoke to him firmly and yet with tenderness. Of course, even in immortality, the way a firefighter wore his fitted blue uniform on a medical call . . . well, let's just say it never loses its appeal.

The firefighters lifted the moaning transient onto a stretcher and loaded him into the ambulance. Shortly after, one of the paramedics ran around to the driver's door up front. The auburn-haired medic stepped outside the back ambulance doors and eyed the vehicle's perimeter for some reason. Perhaps it was protocol, or maybe just a customary personal precaution. When his square dimpled face looked in my direction, his light-blue almond-shaped eyes found me standing there watching him.

His beauty took me by surprise. Something about blue eyes got me every time, but his had a kindness and intelligence that sank deep inside my being.

He stalled for a moment as he studied me. I couldn't pry my eyes from his gaze. Snapping me out of my stupor, a shadow of wind flew by my face into a dark indented doorway across the street. Mikale stepped out of the darkness of the brick building with his hands in his pockets. The paramedic peered in his direction. Mikale ran across the street toward me, and the paramedic watched him intently.

Should I leave her alone? Does that man know her? the paramedic asked himself, clearly concerned for my safety. If I were human, I would have blushed.

"Mikale," I called out and smirked, my tone revealing a hint of annoyance.

The paramedic glanced back at me, flashed me a smile, and nodded. His large dimples deepened on his chiseled face. I smiled back, and he disappeared inside the red ambulance. Mikale approached me as the ambulance pulled away. He wasn't wearing his usual charming smile as he watched the red vehicle drive off down the street.

"Why'd you leave so soon? And why didn't you tell me you were going?"

From above the seemingly sudden cluster of dark clouds, droplets fell and wet our faces. I hadn't realized it was going to rain. Usually, I sensed it in the air's humidity. Even as a mortal when I lived with severe rheumatoid arthritis, my joints seemed to know it would rain before I did. But my mind was attuned to other matters.

My gaze traveled from the clouds to Mikale's confused countenance. "An old friend was there. I couldn't risk him seeing me. And let's just say you looked . . . consumed," I said, raising my right eyebrow.

Mikale smiled, amused by my obvious streak of jealousy.

He lifted his hand and brushed a wet lock of my hair behind my ear. I blinked as the rain tickled my eyelids. He stepped forward, his nose almost touching mine, his lips inching closer. A wanton fireball spun within my chest when I saw the blues of his eyes churning. I didn't move away. I knew I should, but I didn't. His eyes watched my mouth as his lips parted slowly, as if awaiting my approval. The anticipation was too much to bear any longer. My hands moved up his torso with a mind of their own.

Mikale pulled me against his firm body. His lips crashed passionately into mine, his tongue slightly tasting me. I let him take me; I couldn't help it. I embraced him equally and deepened the kiss. The spring rain pattered around us, the wind swirling through our bodies with whispers of the pleasures I knew awaited.

It felt like it was only moments later that we were standing on Mikale's porch, caressing and kissing with the kind of passion I'd experienced only a few times in life and the un-death.

My back pressed against the front door as he lifted me, and I wrapped my legs around his body. Our clothes clung to our skin, wet from the rain and dripping below our feet with soft echoes. His forearm curved around my stomach, and his hungry hand squeezed my waist. His body pressed into me, his lips caressing mine as his tongue explored my mouth in a way that made me moan for more.

With his free hand, he searched for his keys. They jingled from his pocket and fell to the wooden porch. To my vampire senses in such a moment of heightened pleasure, it sounded like thunder. Every sound, however loud, only added to the intensity of my pleasure. We moaned almost simultaneously as we caressed each other. The front door creaked behind my back, warning us it had endured enough pressure.

Forgetting about the keys, Mikale pulled my body against his, my legs linked around his back. In a blink of time, he had fleeted to the side of the porch, pulling me on top of him as he sat in a low wooden chair. My knees pressed into the wood as my hips moved in whimsical circles atop his jeans. His mouth released my lips intermittently and opened with bursts of cool air. He leaned against the backrest and chuckled, watching me for a moment with fire in his eyes. His hands worked up my arms in circular massages and then drew my sweater down from my shoulders to my hips. I arched my back and removed my wet shirt, throwing it to the floor. The thud pounded with sonic waves into the distance, brushing through our bodies. The rain poured harder around us, adding to all the vibrations that tickled through our flesh and heightened our pleasure.

Mikale followed my lead, pulling his black shirt over his head and dropping it to the floor. He clenched my hips in his hands and massaged my sides, demanding I continue the dance. His pectoral muscles flexed with every surge of ecstasy my movement brought him.

When he unbuttoned my jeans and tugged them over my lower hips, his ocean-blue eyes darkened into two kyanite stones. A deep groan escaped his mouth that made me exhale with desire. I jumped to my feet, dropped my jeans to the floor, and crawled back on top of him. I undid his buckle as well, and he clenched the armrests. Staring into his eyes, I extended my hand into his boxers and withdrew his hardness into the open. My eyes found their way down to admire the temptation, and I took it inside me with haste, arching and swaying with shocks of pleasure. Mikale growled as the hunger in his eyes met mine. His hands squeezed the armrests until they split in two with a sharp crunch. A growl rumbled in his throat, and his hands traveled up my hips to my ribs, feeling how my body pulsated in and out of slow time. I moaned in a high-pitched plea, and Mikale covered my mouth with his palm, squeezing my cheekbones and pulling my mouth to his. We laughed as I continued to push into him, his groin thrusting into mine in reciprocation.

A light flickered on in the house above us, and we halted our movements with defiant smiles on our faces.

"We should take this inside," Mikale warned. "We don't want to call any more attention to ourselves." He sucked air through his teeth, his upper lip twitching over his canines.

Through the window of the adjacent home, a shadow neared. I jumped off the chair, and Mikale and I grabbed our clothes and fleeted to the door. We giggled as he picked up the keys and opened the door.

The moment we stepped inside, our lips and bodies reconnected, as if to be apart would cause pain. The keys fell to the floor again when he wrapped his arms urgently around me. The door closed behind my back when he lifted me against it. My legs tightened around him, and he filled me once again. We moaned with pleasure.

Mikale's phone rang piercingly in his pocket. He continued to grind into me, causing the door to thud against the frame. He held my waist with one arm and pulled the relentless phone out of his pocked amidst our thrusting and groans.

His body stilled when he saw the blinking screen. "It's Uri." Our moans drew out into a sigh of frustration, and my feet met the cool floor. Perfect timing.

"Hello," Mikale greeted my uncle. My body relented against the door. I chewed on my lower lip in awkward silence and ran my fingers through my hair. "We'll be right there, boss," he said. He ended the call and grabbed his clothes from the floor.

"What's going on?"

"I'm not sure yet, but when Uri says to get to headquarters right away, it's usually serious." He stroked my cheek tenderly and then sucked my lower lip into his mouth, as if to taste me one last time.

"I'll need to leave my sweater here," I said. "It's soaked. Do you have a sweatshirt with a hoodie I can borrow?" I looked up at his impassioned blue eyes and sucked on my bottom lip to savor his last kiss.

"Which color do you prefer?" he asked with a smirk. "Black . . . or black?"

I laughed and went to retrieve my clothes by the front door. Mikale disappeared up the dark stairs. I worked my damp jeans up my legs and over my hips and pulled my wet gray shirt over my head. Mikale came down the stairs fully dressed and still smirking. He watched me try to unstick the wet shirt from my stomach.

"Thankfully, I can't catch a cold," I joked.

He walked over to me, laughing in his charming way, and handed me a large black sweatshirt.

"Black it is," I said, throwing it over my head. "Fits me like a muumuu."

"Sure does," Mikale said. "Let's get to headquarters. It's been a while since Uri sent for us so urgently." Concern flashed on his face. He opened the front door and stepped outside. I followed.

"What do you think it is?" I asked, tension creeping between my eyebrows.

"Not sure. Hopefully nothing."

As I fleeted toward China Beach, Jojo kept impeding my thoughts. What if it was about him? What if someone heard him call out to me in the Castro? What if he had been taken? The thought needled through me with worry.

When we reached Geary St., the ocean called in the distance with bursts of wind. We continued fleeting, only stopping before the tall dewy gates of Uri's home. The thick fog seeped toward us from over the cliff at the end of the driveway, bringing worry and coldness.

The moment the black-suited guards opened the gates, we fleeted to the front door. Once inside we followed the warm glow down the hall that came from Uri's office on the left. We entered the quiet den, both of us ready to adhere to whatever my uncle needed. Uri sat in front of his computer screen, deep in thought. He didn't look up until we were standing in front of his desk.

"I've received intelligence that two unidentified immortals appeared to be following Rena's car through the city tonight," Uri stated. His eyes dropped down to his clasped hands and twirling thumbs.

I stepped toward him and grasped the edge of the desk. "Is she safe?"

Uri's eyes met mine with less unease than I felt the situation warranted. "She's on her way home. My guards will make sure she gets there safely. There's no reason to be alarmed yet, Edrea. However, for extra precaution, I have additional Shevet guards shadowing your sister." Uri's eyes dropped again before he lifted his head to address Mikale and me. "What concerns me more than the possibility she was followed is that the suspects were too fast to be followed themselves. My guards could not keep up with them."

Mikale stepped forward. "What does this mean, Uri?"

"I'm not sure yet. What I do know is we need to take certain measures in case someone is after Rena. If that's the case, we need to find out who they are. We expected something like this would occur. The Décret has had knowledge of Rena since they kidnapped her and attempted to turn her over a year ago. We just can't be certain they are behind this—although I do have my suspicions." Uri's eyes wandered, as if holding something back.

"Uncle, you said the immortals following her were too fast to be followed," I said. "How fast do you mean?" I figured some vampires could run at slightly different speeds, but something seemed odd about this.

Uri stood up and leaned over the desk, supporting himself on his hands. "As I said, it may be nothing to worry about, but I need you two to keep an eye out for anything peculiar around the city. If you have the slightest suspicion of being followed, I need to hear about it immediately."

Mikale and I nodded in unison.

"As for now," Uri continued with his usual soft tone, "I need you two to locate my old friend, the one who is particularly computer savvy."

I raised an eyebrow. "Does he not have a name?" I had the feeling Uri wanted to preoccupy me in case I thought of shadowing Rena myself.

"Actually, there's a funny story behind that," Uri said. "I have no idea what his real name is, nor does anyone else, and he prefers to keep it that way." Uri shrugged and smiled. "I imagine it's the only way he knows how to protect himself and those he loves."

Mikale chuckled. "Doesn't he live somewhere? He would need a name for that."

"I'm not sure if he lives anywhere at all. He's a bit of a nomad, this friend of mine," Uri said. "I do know of a few spots in the city that he frequents now and then. I've heard rumors he's around the city for a little while. I'm hoping he is because I'm in need of his expertise."

I sighed and bit my thumbnail, still not entirely sure how worried I should be for my sister.

"Edrea," Uri said, "Rena is under close watch, I assure you." The man could read my mind, even though I'd learned to block my thoughts.

Another sigh left my chest. "Thank you, Uncle." I stiffened again the moment Jojo came to mind. "I almost forgot. Speaking of old friends, I think one of mine saw me tonight in the Castro. I . . . I heard him yell my name."

Uri's usual soft expression hardened a bit. "Are you certain?" He glanced at Mikale, as if cross-examining his involvement in the matter.

Mikale's face clouded with a guilty look. "I'm sorry, Uri. I am to blame. I brought Edrea to the bar. She warned me she might know people there."

"Alright," Uri said, as if this was a usual thing. "I'll have Samuel shadow him. Give me your friend's address."

It had been a few weeks since I'd seen Samuel. The African vampire, who was a few millennia old and family to Uncle Uri and me, had gone to Russia to spy on the scientists studying Bacillus F. Apparently, he was back. I was glad. I missed his kind face.

"I promise to be more careful, Uncle." I smiled and jotted Jojo's address and job location down on a notepad and slid it across Uri's desk. He tore the notepaper from the pad and folded it into his shirt pocket. I hoped I wouldn't become a burden to him.

I looked at Mikale, who was typing something into his phone. Our hot yet brief sexual encounter flashed through my mind, bringing a feeling of guilt. Not because I didn't care for him but because I didn't want to taint our friendship or his relationship with my uncle. I had given Uri enough to deal with. I concentrated on keeping that bit of information shielded from Uri's mind.

"Okay, kids, back to business," Uri said, returning to the reason he had called us to his office. He gave Mikale the information on the unnamed computer genius and his supposed whereabouts. Successfully forcing my secret thoughts into the blackness inside, I refocused my attention on the conversation.

According to Uri, there was a private underground venue called the Wave for more intellectually inclined vampires. It was located within Fort Mason Tunnel not far from the Golden Gate

Bridge. This was news to me. Naturally, I needed to learn how to become a member of this sophisticated society.

"Why haven't you told me about this place, Uri?"

Uri's brow wrinkled in amusement. "I thought you would like that." He had an amazing way of lightening the mood. That was what I loved about him. Even though millennia-old vampires would consider him a young immortal, he was probably wiser than most, though he was only one hundred years old.

I smirked, and our eyes met to share a warm smile. "It means so much to me that you watch over my friends and family. It really does."

"Come now," Uri said, his eyes gleaming. "They're my family too, remember?" He winked and swiveled around in his chair to face the crackling fireplace.

He was right, of course. Sometimes I forgot he was my late grandmother's brother, supposedly the third and last immortal in our family to exhibit mind abilities. Well, until me. I was the fourth. I hadn't learned that until recently, my actual place in the family line of vampires. I did know he had mapped our family tree of mortals and immortals, linking the family members that had a form of clairvoyance. Mysteriously, all of them had type O positive blood. He had sketched it onto parchment to keep it safe. I didn't give the phenomenon much thought until the Décret went after Rena, who happened to have the same blood type. Unfortunately, my immortal father, Pierre, a Décret vampire, gained my uncle's trust and stole the map. That was how they learned of my sister.

I had received a letter from Pierre a few days ago, an apology. I wasn't ready to forgive him, let alone trust him. Even if indirectly, he was an accomplice in my death and revamping. He had been sent to turn me, knowing I would be left nearly dead for him. Nadine, a Décret superior and a horrid woman, had recruited a human monster to do her dirty work, one who had decided to rape me first. I know Pierre didn't have any part in that. As he put it, he "was only following orders." He had been told where to be and when. He claimed he didn't even know who I was until he realized I could read minds. But he was still a coward, their puppet. He had betrayed Uri and allowed Rena to be kidnapped and would have turned her too. Now he was asking for my forgiveness? Apparently, he had left the Décret with Angelique, Jule's immortal maker. As if that was enough to redeem him.

Mikale's fingers slipped clandestinely under my palm. I snapped out of my dreary reminiscence and glanced at Uri, who was still watching the flames dance in the fireplace. I pulled my hand from Mikale's before my uncle noticed and shot the island vampire a look of warning. "You ready to go then?" Mikale asked giddily.

"Sure thing."

Off we went to track down the vampire computer whiz who had no name.

3

Rena: A Night to Forget

The Golden Gate was finally in view through the heavy San Francisco Bay fog. Rena's fingers tightened around the steering wheel as she waited for traffic to ease up. There was an accident ahead on the bridge, allowing only one car to pass at a time. She nervously searched the dark street for any sign of the two men who appeared to be following her.

Vampires. She knew this for sure because she had seen them walking on both sides of 19th Avenue and when she drove through Golden Gate Park. That was only ten minutes apart but a five-mile distance. Not even a bus could have made it past her, especially because there hadn't been any traffic on 19th. It was almost 11:00 p.m. She had caught one of the peculiar men in black looking right at her. Her skin had crawled ever since.

She considered driving straight to Edrea's home but realized that wasn't a good idea either. She wasn't supposed to know about vampires. She had promised her immortal uncle and sister that she would pretend nothing had happened a year and a half ago—pretend she had never been kidnapped by sadistic vampires who wanted to kill her, make her a vampire, and use her for her inherited mind abilities that would magically activate when she was turned. Uri promised Shevet vampires would be shadowing her and her family, but she hadn't seen anyone. Maybe they were good at keeping hidden, but she wasn't sure about anything anymore. She even began to wonder if any of this had truly happened at all. Could she just be going crazy?

No. It did all happen. She had found her missing sister. Edrea had been murdered and turned into a creature of the night that preyed on human blood. The human monster that the Décret sent to end her had raped her first. The thought made Rena tremble in her seat, tears stinging her eyes. She couldn't have imagined all that. She had the burn scars to prove it on her legs and arms, the ones caused by the firepit when a Décret vampire held her over the flames and dropped her. Alexio had saved her, threw her out of the way, giving his life to those same flames. The man with whom her sister had fallen in love. There was a vampire world out there, a vampire war, and somehow she knew it wasn't over yet.

Rena's attention shifted to the cellphone that blinked and vibrated on the dashboard. It was her mother. Rena sighed, throwing her head back and forth. Her mom's calls had become relentless since Rena had disappeared for three days during the vampire battle. Rena had tried to explain it was all a misunderstanding, that she'd forgotten to tell her mom about a short road trip. Her mom knew Rena wouldn't just go on a trip without telling her, so she didn't buy it.

The longer the screen blinked on and off, the more irritated Rena became. She had worked on positive self-talk quite a bit since finding her sister, hoping not to return to her previous state of constant frustration. Lately though she could feel the burn of her old ways in the pit of her stomach, crawling slowly to the surface.

With a sharp groan, she snapped her finger to the cellphone screen and swiped right. "What, Mom?"

"I'm just checking in," an uneasy motherly voice said on speakerphone.

"I'm crossing the bridge now. I told you to stop calling me so much."

"Well, how am I supposed to know? I asked you to tell me where you were."

"I don't need to tell you every time I leave home or go to the store or hang out with friends. I told you yesterday I was meeting up with friends in Santa Cruz today." Rena was about to explode. So much for the calming exercises.

The constant hovering had become too stressful since Edrea went missing. Rena had transferred to the local university near her home for the last year of college just to make her mother more comfortable. But that seemed to make her even clingier. Rena almost wished she could go back to UC Santa Cruz and live with her old roommates. Almost. They hadn't exactly provided a stress-free environment either. They were quite annoying, actually, always pestering her about turning off the lights, cleaning her dishes, and locking the front door, as if they were perfect.

Finally over the bridge and through the tunnel, the highway opened up to soft curves between the hillsides. Rena hit the gas as if escaping from something, perhaps life. Oh, that's right—vampires might be following her. That should have frightened her more than it did, but it really just pissed her off. Here she was, bloodsucking immortals in black possibly following her, and there wasn't much she could do about it. She was most likely strong enough to fight off a human, but she was nowhere near strong enough to defend herself against a vampire. She wished her life were different. She knew it was an awful thing to want, but deep down she wished one of those vampires who'd kidnapped her had succeeded in turning her too. She missed Edrea, and even though she had gone through something horrible and traumatic in her sister's world, Rena felt she was part of something bigger, something more important. Was that so horrible to want?

For a while things had been going alright. Rena and her boyfriend, Tony, had been going steady and strong for almost a year now, and he and her dog, Dingo, made life a lot more bearable. But tonight Tony had given her *the* news, bringing with it that familiar dark consuming cloud that made Rena feel heavy and miserable, a feeling she thought she'd managed to fight off for good. Tony had decided to go away for his master's degree, to New York of all places, clear across the United States. Just the thought of him living so far away sent her to that cold lonely place inside, that familiar depressing state of mind that had swallowed a few years of her past. She remembered it well. It was a horrible place to live, and she could almost taste it in her mouth. The anger. The bitterness.

Why would Tony lay this on her now? Rena thought he wanted to get more serious. She thought he wanted to be close to her. Anger surged to the surface, replacing the pain with burning in her chest. She knew blaming him for those feelings was wrong. He deserved to pursue his dreams, to follow his heart, to study psychology at NYU. But surely there were closer schools. Wasn't she just as important?

Rena's knuckles whitened over the steering wheel as tears stung her eyes and poured down her cheeks. She hated feeling weak again. She needed her sister. She needed Liron, a brother who felt more like a distant relative, seeing as he traveled so much with his band.

She sniffed in tears the moment her phone went off again.

"Speak of the devil." It was Tony. He was probably worried she left so upset. She usually spent Saturday evenings with him, but she had stormed out of his apartment when he broke the news. She didn't even say goodbye. She waited despairingly as the phone blinked on and off on the dashboard. She grabbed a tissue from the box on the passenger seat and wiped her nose before it dripped all over her. Finally, her phone stopped ringing, and she inhaled a painful breath. If she talked to him now, she'd definitely cry, and she didn't want him knowing how miserable she felt over the matter.

Forty-five minutes later, Rena turned into her court. She watched the decrepit oak tree with the twisted branches through the passenger window. It always looked so spooky in the dark, like it was hiding secrets. She looked forward to seeing Dingo, sure he was already waiting anxiously by the door in the den.

She pulled into her usual spot between the two dividers in the cul-de-sac. Nervous someone was still following her, she jumped out of her car, grabbed her duffle bag from the back seat, and sped toward the house. She glanced back at her silver sedan, which was parked sideways and taking up two spots. The two small trees on the divider swayed with the wind and whispered into the dark.

She reached the garage and wiggled the tiny garage door key into the lock on the white wall of the house. Leaves danced along the driveway and tickled her feet, which were exposed in her flip-flops. She turned the key to the right, and the two-car garage door started lifting with a jolt. Rena looked around as the metal door crept into the ceiling retractor, the metal squeaking. When the door was halfway up, she ducked underneath and made her way between her parents' cars.

As expected, Dingo was already whining in the den, the sound of his heavy tail smacking the hard floor inside the house.

When she opened the inner garage door, Dingo accosted her with erratic paws and wet kisses. She heard the TV on in the family room. She hit the garage door button on the wall outside the door before the garage door had finished opening. It jolted again when it changed direction. She dropped her duffle bag on the tiles and squatted to give Dingo a proper greeting. If he'd stop whining and crying, she could get a word in.

"Okay, okay, Dingo. I'm home. Yes, I am. I'm home."

"Rena, is that you?" her mother called from beyond the open doorway to the family room. The lights were off, but the glow of the TV flickered against the walls.

"Yeah." Rena closed the den's door securely and turned the lock. She headed through the kitchen instead of greeting her mom in the family room. She tiptoed across the tiled foyer into the hall, as if that could prevent her mother from stopping her. Dingo's nails tapped excitedly on the tiles alongside her.

"Rena, come and talk to me, honey."

Rena stopped short midway down the hallway. "Mom, I talked to you less than an hour ago."

"I know. I just want to spend time with you, that's all."

Rena felt the guilt stirring in her stomach. She'd rather not spend time with her mother when she was emotional. They would just end up arguing about things that weren't important. "I just got home. Let me settle in."

Just as Rena dropped her bag on the bed, her cellphone dinged in her hand with a text message. She looked at her phone and smiled. It was her friend, Bevie—short for Beverley and a nickname for which Rena proudly took credit. Bevie lived with her parents up north near the coast while attending university. She and Rena had met three years earlier when they worked at the Santa Rosa safari animal park. Bevie shared Rena's love for animals and wildlife conservation and was probably one of the only people on

Earth who got her. But Bevie had taken a wildlife conservation job in Oahu for two years, during which time the girls had only seen each other for one week. Rena had gone to visit her not long before Edrea had gone missing. In fact, Edrea had visited her friends in Oahu that same week and had spent some time with Bevie and Rena while she was there.

It was one of Rena's favorite memories, when she had her best friend and her sister all to herself on a tropical island. Rena still had a picture of her and Edrea in front of the ocean on her cellphone's lock screen. Bevie had taken it when they were all at a North Shore beach. Rena wished they had never returned. She and Rena hadn't fought once that week—their last happy memory before the nightmare began.

Rena looked at the message on her phone. Bevie was in town with some friends. They planned to go to their favorite dance club downtown. Perhaps that was all Rena needed to cheer her up, a girls' night out. She typed a quick response and then changed into her favorite dark skinny jeans. Dingo realized what was occurring and started whining and pacing around her legs.

"I already feel guilty, Dingo. I'll be home in a few hours. I promise."

She slipped a shimmery crimson shirt over her head and pulled the soft fabric over her stomach. She loved the way the outfit showed off her fit figure, though she wished her muscles didn't bulge so much sometimes. She was a lot more muscular than most girls, which made her stand out. Well, she didn't completely hate the attention. She was an international competitor in equestrian vaulting at the Gold Medal level, a status she worked incredibly hard to attain. She knew she should wear her muscles with pride.

Rena grabbed the fancy black pocketbook she used for outings and walked swiftly toward the front door, Dingo clinging to her heels. "Mom, I'll be back soon. Bevie's in town. I'm meeting her at that nightclub downtown."

"You just got here! Your poor dog has been dying to see you all day."

Rena stood uneasily for a moment in the foyer and smoothed her hair in front of the hall mirror. "I know," she said, unable to keep her irritation out of her voice. "It's only for an hour or two. Keep Dingo company till I get back."

"Alright," her mom said in her disappointed tone. "Please be careful, and don't go anywhere alone."

"I know, Mom."

Rena slipped out the front door, shutting it quickly as Dingo scratched the wood and yelped from inside. She knew her mom would lock it behind her and calm the helpless dog.

The moment the cool air hit her face and the trees swayed to serenade the moon in the dark sky, Rena met that feeling of freedom again. Freedom from her worries and pain. At least a temporary freedom. She appreciated the night in a different way now that she found herself amid a vampire war. It may be a dangerous world, but it was the only place she felt closer to her sister.

She stood on the deck and listened to the whispers of leaves in the breeze. Her eyes found the decrepit tree at the bottom of the street. She wondered if her so-called vampire protectors ever posted there. It was kind of exciting, really. She inhaled deeply and let out a steady breath. The stars winked through the beautiful darkness between the clouds, promising they'd always be there watching. At least for the next hundred billion years. That might as well be forever.

Rena turned into the parking lot near the club and pulled into a spot below trees that now blew more frantically in the wind.

It seemed like a storm was approaching, which made her a little nervous. A storm after a warm spring day was a bad omen as far as she was concerned. She wasn't afraid of the storm, just the uneasiness it brought, Mother Nature's inclination to change the weather without clear warning. She could take away a perfectly warm and sunny day and replace it with lightning and thunder, with darkness. Rena's heart felt like it crumbled into pieces inside her chest. Tony had felt like the sun. He had brought her warmth and hope. Now he was leaving her. He might find someone else. He might never come back. How cruel life was to sweep him away, like the storm did the calmness of the night.

On Fourth Street between its tall redwoods and historic storefronts, couples walked holding hands, groups of girls strutted buoyantly, and men stood against buildings or in lines taking it all in with grinning faces. Downtown Santa Rosa had its charm; that was for sure.

Rena arrived at the familiar brick building of Rose's restaurant and nightclub, the only downtown club that had halfway decent dance music. She stood under the little lights clinking against cherry tree branches in the chilling breeze. She was about to pull out her phone and text Bevie, but then she spotted her at the front of the line that curved around the building.

"Hey!" Bevie yelled from the club entrance while waving her hand excitedly in the air.

Rena smiled until her dimples popped when she saw Bevie's cute little chipmunk face and bouncing blond curls. Rena missed her more than she'd realized.

She'd arrived just in time to slip in front of the line. She pushed in front of a few girls on the bottom stairs who gave her dirty looks and then ran up to the top steps, where Bevie and two of her girlfriends waited to get ID'd. The closer she got to the front door and the large bouncer dressed in black, the more the night tempted her to let loose for a few hours. To forget her sorrows. Her frustrations. To dance until she sweated.

"Hey," Rena said when she reached the top. Bevie leaped toward her, wrapping her arms around Rena's neck and her legs around her waist with an explosive greeting. Rena almost fell backward, but the bouncer grabbed her arm.

The chisel-faced goon raised an eyebrow. "Did you girls want to dance tonight or check into ER?"

"I guess dancing will do for tonight," Bevie answered in her usual sarcastic tone while dropping her feet back on the ground.

The four girls stepped inside the club, which was buzzing with chattering voices and blaring pop music. They stopped in front of the little payment booth and gave a scarcely dressed girl ten dollars in exchange for club bracelets.

"So, this is Emily and Jaz!" Bevie shouted over the clamor of voices and music. She pointed to her two brunette friends, who were already consumed by the commotion. By the looks on their faces, Rena guessed they were used to smaller less lively bars.

"Hey," the girls said simultaneously with kind smiles. Rena admired their country-style attire, which was comprised of skinny jeans, brown boots, and classy loose blouses. She didn't catch which one was Emily and which was Jaz; maybe by the end of the night.

The four of them shuffled through the scattered groups of vivacious cliques toward the bar. The club hadn't filled to its capacity yet, so it didn't take long to order cocktails. Emily and Jaz went to scout out available tables with Jack Daniel's and ginger ales in hand as Bevie and Rena got caught up against the shiny mahogany bar. The handsome bartender handed them two cranberry vodkas with a wink and then sashayed to his next customer.

While Bevie updated Rena on all her recent college endeavors, Rena noticed a particularly beautiful man standing against the wall across from them. It wasn't his looks alone that caught her attention. It was the intense way he gazed at her and the seductive and inviting way he smiled. He wore loose-fitting jeans, a blue T-shirt, and a black leather jacket. She could tell he was fit, probably perfectly fit. His brown wavy hair was styled to the side, and his dark eyes had her gaping for a moment. Bevie snapped her fingers in front of Rena's face, and Rena let out a breath that she had unknowingly held in. It wasn't often she was completely mesmerized that way.

"Sorry. That guy over there is staring at me."

Bevie started to turn, but Rena grabbed her shoulder. "Don't look yet!" Rena couldn't stop from smiling. The little alcohol she'd sipped had already started to make her giddy.

"Don't forget you have a boyfriend," Bevie joked.

The comment roiled that dull burn in Rena's chest. "Yeah . . . I might not soon." She swallowed a gulp of the sweet alcoholic concoction, hoping it would chase away her pain.

Bevie's startled blue eyes widened. "You're not breaking up, are you?"

"I don't know. I don't want to talk about it right now. I just want to dance." Rena downed the rest of her cocktail and plunked the glass on the bar. She grabbed Bevie's hand and towed her toward the dance floor. A remix version of "I Gotta Feeling" by the Black Eyed Peas boomed throughout the growing number of dancers' bodies. As the liquid high buzzed through her limbs, Rena's hips and shoulders rolled and popped with each beat. Bevie took to the music just as easily, her slim body swaying gracefully, as if to more classical music. That was what Rena loved about Bevie. She was a free soul, always expressing herself in her own unique way. Rena spun around, raising her arms in the air and throwing her head back as the melody and beat resonated through her flesh.

As she completed the turn, she felt strong, cold hands gliding up her bare arms. Knowing they couldn't be Bevie's, her eyes popped open, only to be confronted by the same dark eyes she'd seen watching her a moment earlier. It was the man with the leather jacket. His body moved in synchronicity with her movements, his sweet, musky scent filling her senses, easily tempting her to reciprocate his touch. Rena smiled widely and rested her forearms on his wide shoulders. His six-foot-two-inch figure towered over Rena and Bevie.

Because it was obvious his only interest was dancing with Rena, Bevie rolled her eyes and yelled in Rena's ear. "I'm going to get another drink and find the girls."

"Okay!" Rena called back as Bevie disappeared through the spinning rays of colorful lights and bodies.

Rena's eyes met the mysterious man's penetrating gaze as he pulled her against his hard body. While their bodies moved side to side, she noticed his style, although sexy, seemed somewhat foreign. His eyes remained fixed on hers, as if searching for something behind them. She got lost in their blackness, hypnotized by them. His grinning lips moved within inches of hers when he squeezed her tighter against him. His surprisingly strong embrace startled her, making her body stiffen. Before she could pull away, his fingers pressed into her back, almost causing her pain. Their bodies ceased their movement, but he continued to stare into her eyes.

"You're starting to freak me out. What's your problem?" Rena squirmed in his rock-hard arms, her hands pushing against his defined muscular chest. Smirking, he didn't loosen his embrace. Instead, he moved his lips to her ear, and she felt the chillness of his skin against her cheek. His words seeped into her skin, accented with strong French tones. "I've been looking forward to meeting you . . . Rena."

When her name left his mouth, the chill tingled through her flesh. "Who are you?" she gasped.

"Someone who has a proposition for a very special girl."

His voice was deep and smooth and yet strangely intoxicating.

His fingers eased slightly on her back, and he lifted his head to face her again. Rena's eyes darted around the room, wondering if anyone noticed that she and the man who looked like an Abercrombie & Fitch model were standing like statues as everyone else danced. At that point, she wasn't sure if she should be scared or turned on.

Rena lifted her chin to stare into his eyes. For a moment they just stood there awkwardly without saying a word. Finally, it registered. She knew exactly who he was—what he was—even before his fangs protruded from under his lips. But she gasped and her body froze anyway when the sharp white canines popped out and then retracted before anyone noticed.

"What do you want?" Rena demanded.

He released her, and his hand slipped into his inner jacket pocket. For a split second, she wondered if he was going for a gun. Then she realized that was silly. Why would a vampire need a gun? The recent nightclub shootings happening around the United States were at the hands of disturbed humans, not vampires.

The grinning immortal withdrew a plain white business card with dark red print and slipped it into Rena's back pocket. His cool hands pressed against her back again and pulled her close until his lips were a breath away from hers. "Contact me. You might find my offer very enticing."

With that he released her and disappeared between the dancing bodies, leaving his strange offer lingering in the air along with the scent of his cologne. She was ashamed when she realized his arms, while abrasive, made her body tingle.

Rena found her way to Bevie, partly in shock, partly fascinated by her immortal acquaintance. What did he want from her? Did he know she held the genetic trait of clairvoyance in her blood, just waiting to be awoken? He must have. Dangerous thoughts consumed her, tingling through her body.

"So, what was that about?" Bevie asked as all four girls sat at a window table. Emily and Jaz stared inquisitively with raised eyebrows and excited smiles. Rena still wasn't sure who was who.

"I'm not sure. Just a really aggressive guy." Rena adjusted in her seat and looked out the window at the blowing trees.

"You think?" Bevie asked sarcastically.

Rena was already deep in thought. As the music bounced within the walls and voices blended into a clamor of chatter, reality clarified in her mind. The man wanted to make her immortal. A vampire. That was what she wanted. To be part of Edrea's world. But it came with a dangerous cost.

Her mind traveled back to Tony. She looked down at her phone. He had left her five messages. She sighed deeply as the guilt hit her like a punch to the gut. What was she thinking? Could she leave Tony for good? Leave her family? Her friends?

Rena's heavy gaze found Bevie, and she watched with love as her best friend cackled with her friends. Bevie always brought everyone joy so easily. Rena hoped Bevie felt the same way about her. Deep down she knew that she did. Rena reminded herself that she had a life in the land of the living, people who would be hurt if she disappeared like Edrea had.

Perhaps tonight was a night best forgotten.

4

Rena: Difficult Choices

Driving home from the nightclub, Rena tried to push what had happened on the dance floor out of her mind, but those mysterious black eyes lingered dangerously in her thoughts. She couldn't shake them, and she knew why. They held promises she knew would torture her. Promises of the world she dreamed to be a part of. A world where she didn't feel helpless.

She turned left onto her cul-de-sac and immediately noticed a familiar figure leaning against a parked car. It was Tony. He'd driven all the way there from Santa Cruz. Her heart clenched and then pounded in her ears.

She pulled into her usual spot in front of the house, turned off the engine, and sat frozen for a moment. Her stomach twisted into a knot as she forced down the lump forming in her throat. Tony's broad figure moved slowly through the darkness toward her window. Still, she didn't budge.

"Do you want me to stand here like some creep all night?" he asked, sounding more worried than angry.

Rena blew out a painful breath and opened the door. She got out and slouched against the car. "What more is there to talk about, Tony? You're leaving. You've made your decision." Her burning eyes found their way up to his puzzled face.

Tony shook his head, disappointed. "How can you be angry at me for getting into the school of my dreams?"

A tear beaded down Rena's hot cheek. "I'm not angry, Tony. I'm hurt. Don't you get that?"

His warm hand stroked her wet cheek, and he inched closer. "I'm not trying to hurt you. You know me, Re."

She turned her face away from his hand, trying her hardest not to cry. "I know you're not trying to hurt me. I'm just upset. I don't know what we should do. We've only been together a year, and now we'll be apart for at least four. I just—"

"It's not like we'll never see each other, Re," Tony reminded her in his usual optimistic tone. He looked down at her, compassion and playfulness in his eyes, the right side of his mouth turning up in a grin. She always thought that was the sexiest thing.

"Don't do that," she said, trying not to smile. "This is serious, Tony. You're moving away for years. How will we work that way? We might become totally different people."

"That could happen even if we lived together." Tony laughed in frustration.

"You don't understand." Rena felt her nerves flaring, and she puffed in frustration.

"I do understand, Rena." Tony grabbed her shoulders and pulled her against his chest, her arms limp at her sides. "You're afraid. That's normal. A lot of couples stay together when they're in college, Re. Long-distance relationships can work. We just have to communicate."

The snap of a twig at the bottom of the street stole her attention for a moment. She wondered if her immortal "recruiter" from the nightclub had followed her. Her cheeks reddened at the memory of his arms firmly around her. A few more twigs snapped, and dry earth rustled. It sounded like one animal chasing another. Rena squinted at the darkness down the street.

"Re? I'm right here." Tony's irritated tone intruded on her thoughts.

She looked back at him, thankful he couldn't see her blush in the dark. Her eyes dropped as she felt horribly guilty for thinking about another man—well, technically, a vampire—as Tony was standing right in front of her. Her emotions were all over the place, and she couldn't control them.

She held in a deep breath that burned in her diaphragm and then let it out slowly. She couldn't bear to look up at him yet, her eyes watching a lone leaf blow across his shoes. "Tony, I . . . I just need some time."

The silence that followed was the loudest sound she'd ever heard. It felt like her gut screamed until her ears rang and her eyes poured out tears. When she couldn't hold it in any longer, her gut finally let out a cry that she'd held back for hours. She hadn't cried like that for a long time.

Tony must have felt her pain because he drew her into his warm chest and squeezed tighter than ever before. Rena trembled as she felt his tears fall upon her forehead, causing her to sniffle even more into his clean shirt.

She breathed his scent in, as if for the last time, and then tore herself from his arms. She ran down the driveway and onto the porch, her stomach twisting so tightly into knots that she felt like vomiting.

"Re . . . I'll always love you. I won't stop waiting!" Tony's words called through the wind like sweet whispers of pain that pierced her heart.

How could words so sweet sting so badly?

Rena stopped at the door, almost hyperventilating, wanting so badly to run back to him, to run into his arms, which could always soothe her pain and take her troubles away. If she turned around now though it would be too easy. She had to be strong, at least until she knew what she wanted, until she decided her fate.

At that moment, with her back turned to the man she loved, she knew this was about more than Tony going away to school or her need to have him near. This was about her, about *choices*, difficult choices that she still had to make. Choices that could change her life and the lives of everyone she loved forever.

* * *

Rena woke up in the morning to the sound of fluttering above her head. She looked up at the green curtains flapping in front of the partly open window. It was windier than usual. An eerie wind.

She turned on her right side and squeezed a shabby teddy bear against her chest. A leftover tear rolled down her cool cheek. She had thought she'd cried them all out when she fell asleep.

She wiped the tear away and blew her bangs out of her eyes. Her left arm dropped over the bed, and her fingers searched in the back pocket of her jeans on the floor, finding the white business card. She flipped it over to the inscription. Only a number was printed on the top in red ink.

Dingo woke up from a stupor on the end of the bed, his head popping up with a curious moan when he saw Rena was awake.

"Weird, huh?" she said, flipping the card around as if the dog could read it. Dingo's head tilted to the side as his ears stiffened. "Exactly."

Her fingers inspected the surface of the white matte cardstock. The dark red ink against the bright white reminded her

49

of blood. She remembered seeing drops of red blood on the white-tiled floor at the Décret mansion during the battle. It had been a nasty fight. Deep in thought, she unknowingly brushed the little rectangular card back and forth against her lips. She sniffed a few times and realized it held the scent of the vampire's cologne. She immediately held it out in front of her at a good distance. Recalling the sensation of his hard arms around her body made her burn with guilt. She slapped the card onto her bedside table.

"Fuck, fuck, fuck . . ."

Dingo let out one of his silly Chewbacca-sounding whimpers. It made Rena smile, for a moment.

She sighed in submission. She had already made up her mind. She would call the mysterious vampire. She would meet with him—see exactly what he had to offer. When the sun set, of course. Since it was late March, that would be about 6:30 p.m. She had some planning to do and some precautions to take first, such as deciding where they would meet and what she would bring with her for self-defense—as if there *was* a defense against a vampire.

She wasn't about to bring a samurai sword to cut off his head. She was pretty sure a stake to the heart wouldn't work either. He'd just pull it out and heal. The best bet was fire, but bringing a blowtorch with her might be hazardous too.

What about hairspray and that torch lighter Dad has in the garage? she thought. She could bring her shoulder bag. The torch lighter and the hairspray would easily fit inside. If she was to meet a vampire after dark, even in public, it would be moronic not to bring some kind of protection.

Rena laughed and shook her head, then leaned over the bed to pet Dingo on his wide happy head. She was already about to do something moronic. Going to meet a vampire at night after everything she'd been through was as moronic as it could get. The problem was, she knew better than to think she and her family were truly safe. Vampires seemed to be after her no matter what protection Uri had in place. The strange vampire from last night had reached her easy enough. It was time she took matters into her own hands, once again. Something was coming. It was a feeling she had, and for some reason, meeting with the mysterious vampire felt like something she needed to do.

"I won't stop waiting." Tony's last words replayed inside her mind. Her fingers clenched at her chest, her breathing quickening. She needed to go for a run or something, or she'd go crazy. She jumped off the bed, grabbed some sweats and a T-shirt from the floor, and searched for Edrea's purple tennis shoes, which Rena had made her own.

Moments later, the cool swirling air caressed her face. The swaying trees passed her one by one, and the concrete beneath her feet blurred into a conveyer belt. She ran until all she could feel was the burn, which dulled the emotional one that was already inside her chest. But no matter how fast she ran or how bad the pain got, she could still differentiate between them, as if the emotional pain was a ball of fire that didn't relent, sustained by its own force.

At the end of the road, near a lush golf course steps away beyond the chain-link fence, Rena came to an abrupt stop. She panted there for a moment and looked up at the gray sky. When she finally caught her breath, she drew her cellphone from the pocket of her sweatpants and searched the photos of her and Tony, all the memories they'd spent together during the previous year. Her thumb swiped through them until she came to their last text conversation. It was the argument they'd had before he came to the house last night. "Please, Re, call me back," was Tony's last text. Rena's thumbs hovered over the phone. She hated ending their relationship that way. Deep down, she knew she didn't want to end it at all.

51

Rena threw down her hand with a groan. She peered around the road with frustration to see if anyone had seen her almost scream. For a Sunday, it was like a ghost town. Not even one car was in sight. She stuffed her phone back in her pocket and drew her fingers through her hair until she gathered two fistfuls of hair. She looked down at the pavement, her body shaking to stop herself from crying. One tear escaped, but she quickly wiped it away. Instead of screaming, she sprinted back toward home.

A minute of her mindless tirade passed with blurs of greenery and houses until a large white truck appeared in her tear-clouded vision. It raced toward her. For a moment she thought how easy it would be to leap in front of it and end all her pain and frustration with one blow. No more ridiculous vampires. No more choices. No more lost loves . . .

Her sprint slowed to a jog, tears rushing down her face, and then she stopped. She could never end her own life. She just wished she could stop feeling so helpless. No matter what choices she made, there seemed to be danger around every corner. Danger for her. For her family. For Tony. She had to protect them.

Only a few minutes passed before she arrived back at home. With haste, Rena searched for the right key and opened the front door. As usual, Dingo was there in the foyer shuffling over the tiles and yelping, as if he hadn't seen her in days. She couldn't imagine her life without him, couldn't imagine a world he wasn't a part of. She felt terrible that she didn't have much time for him. Well, today was a day he could come with her. She always brought him to vaulting practice on the weekends.

"Sorry, boy. I love you so much. Yes I do. Guess where we're going?" She squatted to smother him all over his face.

Rena popped up at once and hurried to her room, the dog trotting ecstatically and yelping at her side. There was no more time for tears. She had to meet Trish at the barn at eleven o'clock. Trish was one of her closest friends and her teammate. They were preparing for one of the most exciting things they may ever experience in life: the World Equestrian Games (WEG). They had four months to qualify, during which they needed to place first in three important competitions. Aside from Dingo and the people she loved, vaulting was something she lived for.

Rena grabbed some tights, a sports bra, and a tank top from the shelf in her room and ran to the bathroom to freshen up. She had half an hour, but the drive to the barn in Cotati was fifteen minutes. After sponge-bathing the parts that mattered and applying some deodorant, she swiftly changed into her workout clothes. Then she ran back to her room and grabbed her slip-on vaulting shoes and her workout bag. Dingo scratched across the tiled floor in whirls while he ran back and forth after her.

"Okay, Dingo, let's go!"

As planned, Rena and the excited dog arrived at the barn right before 11:00. Rena didn't usually arrive early, let alone on time, but she had important matters to attend to later that night. She pulled off the long dirt driveway and parked alongside the large old barn. She jumped out of the car, Dingo jumping over her seat to follow her. Trish already had her horse, Prince, tacked with the vaulting pad and surcingle when Rena and Dingo came around the front of the barn. Prince was quite the looker. He had shiny black hair and was about seventeen hands tall.

"Hey, Re," Trish greeted in her usual cheery manner as she walked toward Rena, her horse in tow.

Trish was one of those extraordinary people that Rena looked up to. Not only was she a Gold Medal equestrian vaulter, but she was also a professional acupuncturist, something she would often use to help the horses. She earned her bachelor's degree in

biology and then her Master of Science in oriental medicine. To
Rena, she was practically a goddess, and she looked like one too.
Her fair freckled skin, long wavy golden hair, and light-blue eyes
were always a sight for sore eyes.

"Hey, Tree," Rena said, already feeling more outgoing as
she neared her gleefully contagious friend. Only Rena called her
"Tree." Rena prided herself on her aptitude for great nicknames.

With Prince already handsomely tacked and ready to go,
the girls started down to the outdoor vaulting arena below the barn.
It was a large rectangular dirt arena enclosed inside a white wood
fence. Dingo ran ahead of them and darted inside. He raced clear
across the arena and back, as usual. Rena figured he did it to make
sure the ground was clear of anything that might spook Prince. The
horse had many sensitivities. He always knew if the slightest thing
was off, and that affected his performance.

"Alright, Dingo," Rena called out as she approached the
arena. "Let's tie you up."

Dingo ran to his favorite spot at the side of the arena under
the shade of an oak tree and sat in the dirt. Rena jogged over and
dropped her workout bag on a short wooden bench next to him.
Then she secured Dingo's leash around the fencepost and hooked
his collar to it. Trish met her there and tied Prince to the fence as
well. They would warm up while they waited for Trish's husband,
Fred, to come down from the house up the hill. He was also Rena's
close friend, and he usually lunged for them.

The girls started jogging around the edge of the arena.
After the first lap, Rena was already tired. She had already run a
mile earlier. She looked up at the sky and noticed the gray was
gone. The blue sky was now shining between thin white clouds. It
was perfect weather for vaulting: not too warm and not too cold.
After a few laps, Trish ran over to the Bluetooth speaker she had
already set up and prepared to start the music they used for their

routine. It was from the movie *Pitch Perfect*. Their favorite song combo of all time was "Bella's Finals: Price Tag"/"Don't You (Forget About Me)"/"Give Me Everything"/"Just the Way You Are"/"Party In the USA"/"Turn the Beat Around." They could play it a hundred times, and it never ceased to pep them up. They knew it would bring them to WEG.

Rena was stretching in the dirt when Fred made it to the arena. He was tall and slender and had a complexion that was similar to Trish except for his strikingly turquoise eyes, which almost looked inhuman.

"You guys ready?" he asked, closing the gate behind him.

"Hell yes," Trish sang from the fence where she was squatting next to the speaker. She turned her pretty freckled face toward Rena. "Re, do you want to practice anything in particular or just do the whole routine?"

"Let's do the whole routine a few times through. We really just need to smooth it out at this point." Rena tried to keep her mind from traveling from the arena back to the encounter at the club the night before.

"Sounds good," Trish said.

After Fred grabbed the horse and cantered him a few laps, Rena ran into the center of the ring to wait for the music. The moment it started, Trish ran to the side of the horse, Rena running up close behind until their strides mimicked the horse's canter. Trish was the first to mount in the routine, doing a graceful leap onto the back of the horse, landing on one bent leg while the other leg stretched down the horse's side. Then Rena did a somersault mount, curling her body up onto the neck of the horse shortly after. Their gymnastics and dance routine felt natural to them as they let the steady stride of the horse guide their movements to the music. Rena thought it was the best feeling in the world, the wind in her face while she danced with the smooth rock of the horse's canter.

The girls arrived at the point in the routine where they stood facing each other. Trish squeezed Rena's arms, ready to lift her into her jump where she did the splits in the air. Something about the way Trish squeezed her arms triggered a flashback of the vampire's embrace the night before. It threw Rena's balance off slightly. As quickly as the flashback came, Rena's legs crumbled beneath her, and she found herself underneath the horse in a heap of hooves and legs. It happened so fast that Rena wasn't sure if she was hurt or not, but she found herself sitting alone in the dirt.

Trish ran to her side, stunned. "Did he step on you?" she asked, her hands hovering hesitantly over Rena's body.

"I don't think so," Rena said, dumbfounded and a little shook up. "I think he jumped clear over me."

"Are you okay?" Fred said from the center of the ring.

Rena couldn't help but laugh. Trish joined in with her, seeing as she wasn't hurt. *If this wasn't a sign, nothing is*, Rena thought. The horse could have easily trampled her. Rena stood up and dusted the dirt off her tights and shirt.

"It looks like Prince wants to ensure you make it to Worlds," Trish said, carefully patting Rena's body for injuries.

"I guess so," Rena said, and she truly believed it. Vaulting at WEG was something that she would accomplish no matter what. She was sure of that now. Whatever choices she had to make, she would make sure WEG was one of them.

Rena moved over to Prince and hugged him tightly under his large neck while Trish patted his behind. "You're such a good guy. Thank you," Rena told him.

"That's a guy who's looking after you," Fred said with a charming smile.

"Sure is," Rena agreed, giving Prince a good pat on his side before returning to the center of the ring. "Well, let's go again," she said, as if the fall was nothing but a stumble.

Dingo wasn't worried either. He just watched patiently from the fence, like it was an everyday thing.

After practicing the routine a few more times, Rena headed home with Dingo. Upon arriving, she realized things were about to get interesting. She looked at the time on her phone as she walked down the hall to her room. Two o'clock. Only about four hours remained before the sun took its light from the sky. She peeled the vampire's white business card from the edge of her desk and studied the bright red numbers on its surface.

Staring blankly at her cellphone, she typed in the number from the card as the wind from the open window brushed locks of hair from her face. "Meet me in downtown Windsor in front of the café on the corner of McClelland and Honsa," she typed. She figured he would be there right at sundown, so she didn't bother to give him a time. Rena knew very few people who lived in Windsor, even though it was the next town over. As charming as the small town was, it wasn't a place that most of her friends frequented.

After making the first move, she felt clear-minded and confident that she was on the right track. She had a few more hours to gather her weapons and prepare for her "meeting."

She walked determinedly to the bathroom, dropped her sweaty workout clothes, and turned on the shower. Letting the hot water cleanse her past sorrows, her mind finally settled on one thing—the dangerously arousing encounter that awaited her that night.

* * *

Rena sat on the edge of her bed and stared at the pile of weaponry on the floor. It was almost 5:30 p.m., the red of the dimming sky casting her room with a pink hue. Her blue-jean shoulder bag lay on the brown carpet. Next to it was her father's black torch lighter, which was about the size of her hand, and next to the lighter was a full can of hairspray. She didn't use hairspray, so she had made a quick run down to the store after her shower. She had also driven up to Winsor and walked around the perimeter of the café where she would meet with the vampire. She wanted to make sure she would have escape routes, both from the building and also the surrounding streets, which the town would often block off for construction or street fairs. There didn't seem to be anything going on. She could park right in front of the café, and there were no road closures to impede a quick departure.

"What am I forgetting?" she asked herself and perhaps also the panting dog beside her. Her eyes surveyed the room, landing on the neatly folded blue jeans and black shirt sitting on a chair against the wall and the seemingly puny grouping of weapons on the floor.

"Liron's pocketknife!" She dropped off the bed and onto her knees and searched the floor for the pocketknife she'd borrowed from her brother. She usually didn't go anywhere without it, except places weapons weren't permitted. Her nervous hands picked through the scattered clothes and items on the floor. "Where the hell is it?"

Her gaze caught the glint of metal atop the bookshelf in front of her, interrupting her frantic search. She sighed when her eyes confirmed the shiny wooden rim covering the knife's silver blade. She snatched it off the shelf and placed it next to the torch lighter. She slumped back down in front of the pile on the floor, feeling satisfied with her complete arrangement of self-defense devices. "What do you think, Dingo?"

Dingo cocked his head to the side with a goofy expression and let out his Chewbacca groan, his big ears pointed in opposite directions. Rena smiled, feeling the burn in her cheeks that occurred when she was about to cry, and threw her arms around her favorite friend. "Don't worry about me, honey. I can take care of myself."

Dingo groaned again in disapproval. He always seemed to understand her. Rena had decided long ago he wasn't much different from a person, so that was exactly how she treated him, like a person.

She looked at the sky outside the window. Night would come in only forty-five minutes, and she wanted to leave during daylight, so Uncle Uri's vampires couldn't follow her steps. This was something she had to do in private.

She jumped off the bed and looked over at the chair where her clothes waited. Without another thought, she pulled off the long shirt she wore and dropped it on the floor. Then she unfolded the black shirt she had chosen and hung it over the rounded metal backrest of the padded brown chair. She grabbed her jeans from the seat and squeezed into them. Then she threw on her black shirt and pulled the smooth fabric over her belt buckle. She scrambled around the floor for her black booties and sat on the carpet to zip them over her ankles.

One by one, she put each self-defense item into her shoulder bag and zipped it up. Kneeling, she grabbed a red hairband from the floor and smoothed her hair into a tight ponytail.

Then, just like that, she popped up, slung the bag over her shoulder, grabbed her keys, and left to meet the mysterious vampire whose name she still didn't know.

5

Quantum Physics

When I awoke tonight in the darkness, everything that had happened the night before overwhelmed my thoughts. It would take some time to register it all. I also felt an uneasiness that came from somewhere outside my mind. I hoped it wasn't the connection to Rena that I felt when she was in trouble. It didn't feel like a frantic energy, but it was definitely heavy.

I sat up with a sigh, as if repositioning would clear my head for a moment. Under the brown velvet curtains, the glow of sunlight glimmered with a beautiful golden hue against the hardwood. I knew by the warmth and brightness of its rays that it was exactly 6:00 p.m. Strange how someone like me could tell the time that way. I reached across the bed and grabbed my cellphone from the nightstand. Sure enough, I was right on the money.

I fell back onto my puffy pillow, my eyes following the

streams of golden translucent silk flowing across the bedposts. I clapped my hands twice, and the red-shaded lamp flickered on. Its warm light brightened the room at once, making the fantastically painted mural of the cosmos on the ceiling glimmer with all its galaxies and stars. Uncle Uri had the mural painted as a gift to me. He knew some amazing people—artists, scientists, explorers. All immortal. All intriguing and brilliant. There was always something to look forward to, even when loneliness tried to seep in.

The artist who created the mural in my room was the one who had greeted Mikale and me at the doors of the Wave when we went looking for the nameless computer genius. The artist's name was Consus. The name suited him; he looked very Roman with a long nose and protruding chin and all. I couldn't stop thinking about the hidden intellectual society Mikale and I had visited. It was located in the west entrance of the Fort Mason Tunnel, only a short fleet away. We'd jumped off the China Beach cliff and traveled along the shore and under the Golden Gate Bridge until we came to Marine Drive and a little dirt trail that led to Marina Blvd. The tunnel entrance was at the corner of Marina and Laguna, somewhere I used to walk often when I was human. Of course, back then I had no idea a secret intellectual society of vampires was hidden deep within.

Once out of sight of any humans, we jumped the tunnel wall to the entrance and then the ten-foot wall that guarded the opening. It wasn't more than a footstool to an immortal. The marker my uncle told us to look for was about half a mile within the darkness of the tunnel, a blue wave painted in graffiti on the left wall. Graffiti was scattered throughout the tunnel, so we had almost missed it. We had to backtrack until we noticed a dark rectangular indent within the wall across from the image and a metal door almost completely camouflaged against the grayness of the wall. The opening in the wall was a bit jagged and looked hand-constructed. It was in a part of the tunnel where it seemed unlikely a door would be.

When Mikale and I knocked, Consus opened the door at once and asked us for the secret password, a smirk on his face. He was the one who'd given it to us in the first place.

"E equals NHV," I recited cockily. It was an equation named after the Planck postulate in quantum mechanics. Uri and Consus had tried explaining it to me as if it were a basic concept or common sense. It had gone straight over my head, but I was more intent than ever at joining this sophisticated society and learning from the best.

The Wave was everything I had imagined. Inside the walls of the large, underground, obviously vampire-constructed cavern, long blood-red drapes hung elegantly on the walls, and marble posts supported the smooth cement ceiling. A large, round maple table sat in the center of the round main room with ten velvety padded chairs surrounding it. Across the room, a large arched opening led to another round room, a library where thousands of books sat on tall bookshelves that lined the circumference. Others sat on smaller tables and cushioned chairs. In the main room, which was larger, beautiful paintings adorned the walls between the red drapes. Bookshelves and desks stood wherever they seemed to fit. Even as I lay in bed reminiscing about my time there, excitement tingled under my skin.

It hadn't been long before we'd spotted Mr. Nameless Genius. He was the first immortal my eyes locked onto after we entered. He was sitting in the library in his own makeshift study. I tried to only briefly greet the other black-cloaked immortals, but Consus stopped Mikale and me halfway through the main room with a grand introduction about my relation to Uncle Uri, who they knew was a mind reader. They also knew what that meant, that I was a mind reader. The minute they learned who I was, they stiffened in unison and blocked their thoughts, some of them not as successfully as others. It appeared Uri's genetic mind-reading theory was out of the bag since the battle at the Décret mansion. It was the only way to protect our family. If the Décret knew our secret, the Shevet needed to know it too, to know exactly what was at stake. Soon even the ISC would learn of our abilities.

It turned out the subject matter for the night's discussion was none other than mind powers. For the few minutes Mikale and I listened in, the scholars worked on their hypothesis for the quantum entanglement of consciousness. Pierre had briefed me on the concept after I was turned, which I found fascinating from the get-go. According to the quantum theories that the scholars wove together, not only could certain immortals access the quantum realm, which they referred to as "the void," they could also manipulate quantum energy with their mind for a desired effect.

As if on cue, Samuel arrived. He gave me a quick peek into his mind, so I could see Jojo was safe. I smiled with relief as he joined the discussion. He began by explaining why I was able to see the void when I looked into my own eyes in the mirror, something that had happened in the past. He also mentioned the time Uncle Uri and I entered the void together while looking into each other's eyes. Samuel said it was also behind why my energy had caused him pain when he tried restraining me during the battle at the Décret mansion. On that horrid night, he had attempted to hold me back from killing my murderer, Gustav, and some kind of powerful force expelled from my body when I tried to break free. I still couldn't wait to get Samuel alone to discuss the phenomenon further.

After Mikale and I greeted everyone appropriately, we went straight to the library. I noticed at once that the nameless vampire had blocked his mind entirely. Not a peep of a thought escaped its barriers. I found that strange because I had read his mind a year and a half earlier in the tunnels when the Décret captured him outside their mansion. Apparently, he had opened his mind to me willingly that day.

When I informed him that Uri awaited his company, Mr. Nameless sighed at the book he was studying. "Is dear Uri in need of my expertise? I expect it's nothing less than a life-threatening task," he replied with a grimace.

I nodded. "Something like that."

He was only kidding with me, of course. He was loyal to my uncle and thought of him as family. He, Mikale, and I made light of the whole "interrogation in the tunnel event," especially since Mikale had been there too, posing as a Décret guard. Then Mr. Nameless agreed to return to Uri's with us soon after. I enjoyed meeting the nameless vampire officially and sharing those few moments in the library with him and Mikale. It was another memory I'd keep safe in that place in my mind where special memories last forever.

Back at home, Uri and the computer genius sealed themselves inside my uncle's office, which unsettled me a bit. Uri didn't keep much from me, but if he did, it was usually something bad, something he needed to be sure of before letting me worry about it.

Even more unsettling, unexpected guests had arrived the previous night. I found them sitting in the astronomy sanctum when Mikale and I walked through on our way to the cottage.

Pierre and Angelique.

I had frozen the moment I saw him. I'm not sure how I made it across the room. Maybe because Mikale guided me with a hand on my lower back. Before we could step outside, I heard Pierre say my name. It was a voice that used to comfort me. Now it felt distant yet connected to another life where open wounds hadn't quite healed. Mikale shot him a glance of warning and then whispered something in my ear before heading into the garden. I was in such shock that I didn't even know what he said.

Seeing my immortal father, the man who'd betrayed my trust and hurt me deeply, triggered the self-defense mechanism we immortals have that shields our emotions. It was as if I'd shut down cold right on the spot. Too much suppressed pain was still stirring inside. I didn't care if Pierre had left the Décret or even if he'd made peace with my uncle. I couldn't face him yet. I attempted to give him only the respect of a nod before departing the room, but he stopped me with words that still lingered dauntingly in my mind.

"Edrea, I know you don't want to see me, and you have every right. I deserve your silence. But I need to apologize to you. I need you to know I'm sorry for what I've done, for how I've hurt you and Rena. When you're ready, I hope for the day you might give me another chance."

I didn't respond. I couldn't. I just stood there at the French doors with my back to him. I heard him out, and then Mikale and I walked outside into the garden. I wanted to ask him why he was at our home and if it had anything to do with my sister being followed, but I couldn't bring myself to speak to him.

Perhaps I didn't want to say anything I'd regret later. Even though I knew Pierre to be a coward, I also knew the losses he'd suffered in the process of becoming that man. I wasn't ready to forgive him for what he'd done to Rena and me, but I also didn't want to punish him more than he'd already punished himself. He could hide his thoughts from me but not his feelings. He never could hide his feelings. In the short time I had been in his presence, I felt what lived in his heart: pain, guilt, and redemption. His sorrows had become my own, just like they always had. Not even shutting off my emotions could stop them from penetrating.

Mikale was waiting at the front door of the cottage when I

arrived. I must have looked like a zombie. All I could remember was his cool fingers lifting my chin and the ocean-blue eyes that always had their way with me. He led me into the cottage, took me into his arms, and pressed his lips passionately against mine. It wasn't long before he pushed my back into the front door and explored my face with his hands as he kissed me. His kisses were so passionate, the way his sweet tongue explored my mouth. My body trembled at his touch when his hard body restrained me with just the right amount of tenderness and force.

We almost forgot where we were and then stopped before the caresses took us too far. My uncle was only feet away in the office. Sooner or later I'd have to stop that whole mess, and the thought weighed on my heart.

I sighed at the starry mural on my ceiling as I thought about that dilemma and tried to stop the tender kiss from replaying in my mind. I squinted as another memory came to mind, something strange that occurred right after Mikale's kiss. When he had finally headed out the door, that heavy external feeling poured over my body like an engulfing wave. The same feeling I had when I woke up moments earlier but with more intensity. Along with the feeling, melancholy words whispered through the air. *"I'll always love you. I won't stop waiting."*

I was pretty certain I hadn't imagined them, and I doubted they came from Mikale. Sure, we cared for each other, but we didn't profess our undying love for each other that way. It had to be Rena. Maybe something happened with her and Tony. The connection between us, our sisterly bond, seemed to intensify as time went on. I wished I could go to her, comfort her, but it was too dangerous. I had to believe distance was the only way to protect her.

The sun wouldn't set for thirty minutes, but I couldn't lie in bed any longer. I needed to ask Uri about everything that had happened last night, like whether he'd learned anything new about the vampires shadowing Rena and especially about why the hell Pierre had lounged in my favorite room in the house. It couldn't have been just to tell me he was sorry. I had an inkling he'd brought other information as well.

I jumped out of bed and ran barefoot to the door where my white robe hung. I swung it around my two-piece pajamas, which were a little too transparent to wear around the house, and ran down the cobblestone path into the garden. Inside the French doors, I saw Uri walk by the astronomy sanctum in his red plaid pajamas and black robe. He looked pensive, a white mug to his lips, and disappeared behind the wall toward his study.

I entered the house swiftly and followed him. "Uncle," I said with a hint of irritation as he sat behind his desk.

"Evening, Edrea." His tone and eyes held both sympathy and illumination. "I imagine Pierre's visit to our home has upset you—"

"*Upset* me? Uri, this man betrayed you, allowed me to be brutally attacked, so he could turn me into a vampire, and then he let the Décret kidnap and torture Rena. *Upset* is the least of my feelings for him. I don't hate my immortal father, but that doesn't mean I'm okay with him paying me a visit."

Uri bowed his head in understanding. He sat back in his leather chair with that look he had when more trying matters were at hand. "Edrea, Pierre came to me last night to divulge some very troubling intelligence. Something I feared may have transpired, which is why I had you and Mikale locate my computer-savvy friend. I need him to hack the files of the Russian scientists I've been following. If what Pierre told me is true, Rena may be in more danger than we thought. Technically speaking, not only your sister but the world."

At that moment my daddy issues with Pierre seemed like

the least important matters on Earth. I trudged toward Uri's desk and slumped into the loveseat adjacent to him. In shock, only my eyes looked up at him. "Uri, what's happened?"

"The immortals who we believe shadowed your sister two nights ago—the ones too fast to be followed—apparently, Pierre and Angelique had a run-in with a similar vampire. It seems someone sent one to attack Pierre. The attack was unsuccessful, but barely. He entered Pierre's home in the late evening when the sun was still out and attacked when Pierre was in slumber. Thankfully, Angelique had already woken and was in the next room. Only together were they able to dismember him. We're not sure who sent him, but it may have something to do with Pierre deserting the Décret."

I looked at my uncle, perplexed. "While the sun was still out? That doesn't make any sense."

Uri studied a pencil he was twirling nervously with his fingers. "I don't think these are normal vampires. I think they're something else. I think they've been *made* into something else."

I sat up stiffly on the edge of the seat. "What do you mean? What are they?"

The pencil stopped twirling, but Uri's eyes continued to study the small lifeless object, as if it held secrets. "I don't know, but I think these Russian scientists do. I think they've tampered with something. Unfortunately, Samuel wasn't able to unearth anything in Russia. That's why we need my nameless friend."

I remembered what Uri had told me about the mad scientists. They had been experimenting on themselves. They had a lab where they studied the immortal bacteria, Bacillus F, which was behind the evolution of vampires. The studies they posted online were supposedly about autoimmune health and longevity.

"Uri, are you insinuating they've created unnatural vampires with Bacillus F? How is that possible? I thought it took vampires forty thousand years to evolve into what they are."

Uri leaned forward in his chair and placed the pencil carefully on his desk. "The immortal bacteria are unlike any other organisms on Earth. They allowed human beings to evolve thousands of times more rapidly than normal in order to serve as their host. Instead of millions of years, we vampires evolved into what we are in a fraction of that time." He sat quietly for a moment and then looked up at me with genuine worry in his eyes. "I think these scientists may have succeeded with their experiments. I think they may have had mentors."

"You mean immortal mentors?" I said hesitantly.

Uri's silence answered my question. I understood then why he spent so much time in his study. A chilling fear blossomed in my core and spread throughout my body. It was a fear that I would share with my uncle from then on.

Uri's cellphone lit up and rang on the surface of his desk. Our impassive eyes watched it vibrate as it played its usual cheery tune. Finally, Uri drew it from the shiny wooden surface and put it to his ear as he attempted to loosen his limbs. "Yes," he said softly. Whoever was on the other end of the call had news that revived Uri's stiff posture. "Thank you. Make sure a guard stays posted by the house, and inform me when you locate her." Uri set the phone on his desk. He hesitated for a moment and then looked at me. "Your sister must have left the house before the sun set tonight. My guards arrived at first dark to find her car gone."

"She must have gone to meet friends or something," I said, trying not to worry. But I *was* worried. I knew Uri had kept tabs on Rena's whereabouts since the kidnapping, especially in light of recent events.

Uri leaned over the desk, resting his head on his hands. "She knows to only go out after sundown, so we can track her. They haven't found her scent yet."

I had hoped my worst fears were only that, fears. I had hoped my family would be safe. But Rena had the gift, and too many immortals knew it. There was no telling where that information had landed or into whose hands. And if the Russian scientists were involved, if they had created something even more dangerous than vampires . . .

I stood up. "Let's go find her."

6

Rena: Date With a Youngblood

A silent breeze ruffled the air as Rena arrived in the eerily calm town of Windsor. She found the perfect parking spot under the green maple trees across from the café. She had hoped there would be a curbside spot available on the same block and was relieved to find it waiting for her. It was 6:00, and the sun still shone softly from the rooftops above the park. Everything had worked out as planned; that is, until she'd spotted the vampire—in plain daylight. He appeared from behind a tree in the park like he'd known exactly when and where she'd arrive. He walked toward her car as reddish-orange beams of sunlight blazed upon his unveiled skin. That was when Rena knew something wasn't right. Once again, she was in over her head. But she wasn't afraid, and she liked the way that felt.

Minutes later the vampire sat across from her clad in fitted jeans and a dark maroon T-shirt like he was dressed for a casual date. He had let her pick the table, so she chose a bright window seat—not that it mattered. He had just walked in daylight, and vampires weren't supposed to be able to do that. Uncle Uri had told her that if a vampire was exposed to sunlight for even a few seconds, it would collapse in a painful fit. This vampire hadn't collapsed. He hadn't so much as winced in the sun. But he did appear overly amused with himself as he sat across from her, a smirk on his clean-shaved face.

"What's your name?" Rena asked after an awkward moment of staring into his dark eyes.

The vampire leaned cockily over the table and tilted his head with a grin. Rena didn't move. She was fascinated by the softness of his face, his nearly straight white teeth, even his tussled brown hair. She should have been repulsed by him, but he seemed tamer than he had been when they met at the nightclub.

"I guess it's only fair that you know mine. I already know yours," he said coyly in that familiar French accent. He leaned even closer until she could see the black outline surrounding his deep-brown irises. "It's Bassét, accent on the *e*."

"Why are you so happy with yourself? And why are you staring at me that way? Don't you get out much, Bass-ét?" Rena said with a grimace.

Bassét pressed his lips together into a smirk and fell back against the chair with crossed arms. "Actually, I do not 'get out.' And would you prefer I be displeased with myself?"

Rena wasn't amused. "I might prefer that, as opposed to your gleaming narcissism."

Bassét laughed. "Is that so?" Rena swore she saw something flicker in his eyes, something like lust and maybe a touch of vulnerability. He quickly adjusted himself and put on his serious smirk. "Now that introductions are out of the way, as they say, let's get down to business."

"Yes, let's," she said with sarcasm. She leaned back against her chair and crossed her arms, mocking him, then smiled and raised her eyebrows.

He laughed boyishly but then corrected his behavior and tried to quell his smile. He leaned forward and placed his elbows on the table. "Shouldn't you be at least a little afraid of me? Or are you as careless as they say?"

She stiffened at his comment. "You don't know who I am. And neither do they, whoever *they* are."

"I'm just saying that perhaps you should be a little more careful. Apparently, you are an important young lady, which brings me to the subject at hand. It seems your doting uncle has left you like a sitting duck in a pond of alligators. I'm here to offer you something that he and the guards that doddle around your house cannot. Actual protection—and a proposition."

Rena attempted to hide any emotional response as he studied her reaction. Her eyes narrowed. "So, you're the vampire stalking me. Where's your friend?"

A ridiculous, puzzled expression formed on Bassét's face. "I don't know what you're talking about, precious. I ride solo."

"I'm sure. Then who was the other vampire following me on Nineteenth Avenue?"

He shook his head and laughed. "You're mistaking me for someone else, obviously. Which is all the more reason to have a friend like me. I mean, if you're being stalked by vampires." He raised one eyebrow.

If what he said was true, the idea that she had more than one bloodsucking stalker made her skin crawl. "How old are you anyway? You don't talk like you're much older than me."

He grunted. "I'm *not* much older than you. My maker turned me last year. I'm but a baby vamp, still referred to as a youngblood."

"So, what are you, twenty-five?"

"I *was* twenty-five, which means I'm forever twenty-five, in this body. But I'm twenty-six, if you count my vampire year."

Rena glanced around the café.

"Don't worry about them," he said. "Human beings are mostly concerned with themselves. 'Does my hair look okay? Will he text me back? Should I cheat on my husband?' Most people are self-absorbed. I've lived long enough to have learned that at least."

Rena's eyes hardened. "Can you read minds?"

Bassét raised an eyebrow. "No, *Re,* only your uncle and your sister have that ability—and maybe you too if you were turned."

Rena stiffened. "Don't call me that."

Bassét's lips turned up at one corner. "You love this boyfriend of yours, don't you?"

"So you *have* been stalking me."

"Not for long. Your uncle's minions practically have you on a leash. They continuously run me off. They can never seem to catch me though." Bassét smirked to himself.

"How do you know of my family and our ability?" Rena asked, her shoulders hunching nervously.

Bassét's head twitched toward the window. The sun had finally set. His eyes searched the darkness outside and seemed to settle on one spot inside the park. "I know enough," he replied. "We're out of time, apparently."

Rena's eyes followed his gaze to three men in dark clothing walking through the park toward the café.

She flinched when she felt Bassét's cool hand clamp around her wrist, which rested on the table. She tried jerking her arm away, but he held fast. "What are you—"

"Listen to me, Rena," he said, looking at her with his dark

entrancing eyes, which may have concealed a hint of concern. "You are in more danger than you think, and so is your family. There's only one way to protect yourself and them." His eyes locked onto the three men who now stood across the busy street from the café. "The Décret will get their hands on you despite your uncle's efforts. Believe that. They have more power than he thinks."

Rena's breath caught. "The Décret? I knew you were with them."

"I'm not *with* anyone," he snapped. "I'm free to do as I please, but I am under their protection, and you could be too . . . if you were like me." He stood and watched the three men dodging cars as they crossed the street. They couldn't fleet on a brightly lit block full of people.

Rena peered through the window to find their dark eyes pinned on her and Bassét. Her glare fell back on the young vampire. "That's your grand scheme, to turn me into a Décret vampire?" she asked, disgust in her tone.

Bassét placed his palms on the table and leaned over Rena until his lips braised her ear. His spiced cologne drifted into her nostrils. "There's more to it than that," he whispered. His cool breath sent a chill through her body. He pulled away slightly to look her in the eyes. "Don't underestimate Nadine, Miss Rena. She tends to get what she wants."

Bassét slowly backed away as the door opened and closed behind Rena. She sat frozen in her chair and watched her new vampire acquaintance slip out the back door. The hairs on her arms stood up when the three large figures behind her shuffled back out the front door soon afterward.

Rena grabbed her shoulder bag from the floor and placed it on her lap. All her vampire repellents were in order, just in case she still needed them. Her limbs froze when her parents came to mind. If Nadine came after her again, her mother and father were in trouble too. She looked nervously out the window for anyone suspicious. Her breath caught again when her eyes fell on two figures standing in the middle of the park. Two familiar figures.

She couldn't believe it. It was Edrea and Uri. How had they found her so quickly? She jumped up from her chair and headed for the door. There was so much she wanted to tell Edrea. She wasn't sure she'd ever see her again.

The moment Rena stepped outside, they were nowhere to be seen. Nothing but leaves blowing against the grass where they had stood. Rena sighed at the lonely moon as it glowed in the sky. A cool breeze brushed through her hair. People walked by giggling behind her, oblivious to what lurked in the darkness. A world Rena and her sister were inadvertently a part of. Lately, however, she felt alone in it.

A tear beaded down Rena's cheek as she searched the darkness beyond the threshold of the park. Could it really have been Edrea and Uri? It couldn't have been a coincidence that they showed up on the night Rena decided to run off to meet a strange vampire. And those three mysterious men who came after Bassét must have been Shevet vampires. If not, Bassét would have recognized them as Décret. He was on the same team, even if he didn't see it that way.

Rena looked down at the phone buzzing in her hand. She gasped, and her chin dropped. The crazy day-walking youngblood had already texted her: "Was that as good for you as it was for me?"

"You have got to be kidding me," she said. She wasn't sure if she should text him back or not, but she couldn't deny the shock of excitement that ran through her body. She'd taken to this boy—this vampire, she reminded herself—more than she should have. She shook her head and stuffed the phone into her pocket.

She shouldn't have taken to him at all. She'd just broken up with Tony. She shouldn't already feel something for another man, let alone a vampire. She felt ashamed. Childish. Cruel. Had she loved Tony at all?

She shoved the depressing thought aside when her parents came to mind. They might be in trouble. She checked the street for oncoming cars and then ran to her silver sedan. Her curious eyes peered around the whispering park as she wondered if Bassét was still watching her from behind a tree or a bush. The thought spread like tingly warmth from her stomach to her limbs. She shook her head, scowling at herself. A vampire stalking her should do nothing but creep her out. She really needed to slap herself out of this.

What the fuck is wrong with me? she wondered. *Could he have charmed me or something, or is that just in fairytales?*

Rena jumped into her car, started the engine, and spun into a U-turn toward the main road. She'd best get the hell out of Windsor before she did something asinine, like look for Bassét or get herself kidnapped again. Maybe Bassét was right. Maybe she was as careless as he implied.

"Ugh!" Rena grunted as she sped down Highway 101 South. She needed Edrea more than ever, and yet she had been completely abandoned, left all alone with this dark family secret. Did Edrea and Uri really expect her to just move on and live a normal life after everything that had happened? And now she might have not one but three vampire stalkers. Bassét's words, "sitting duck in a pond of alligators," played through her mind over and over. Her left heel tapped nervously against the floor as her fingers tightened around the steering wheel. She couldn't help but agree. A sitting duck was exactly what she was, except she wasn't in a pond. She was a duck in a fucking ocean of alligators.

Rena felt some relief when she heard the familiar ringtone

she'd set up for when her mother called. She pulled her phone out of her pocket, stuck it in the dashboard holder, and swiped to answer. "Hey, Mom."

"Rena, where are you?" her mother asked in her usual worried tone.

"On the way home. I just met . . . a friend for tea." A harmless white lie.

"Okay, good. Dad and I are going to the casino for a little while," she said, her tone lacking enthusiasm.

Hearing this news would have pissed Rena off in the past, before Edrea went missing. But now it made her happy to know they were finally getting out of the house. It seemed like it had been a year since they'd gone anywhere.

"Okay, Mom. Stay together, and don't go anywhere there aren't people."

That was an unusual thing for Rena to say. She was turning into her worry-bee mother. At least Rena had good reason, but she guessed her mother did too. She had lost a daughter. Rena wondered if losing a sister was as traumatic as losing a daughter. She imagined it must be pretty close. Before she knew Edrea was still alive—well, partly alive, if that was what she was—she'd never felt such a heavy sadness. She never wanted to feel so horrible again. It was a shame she couldn't ease her parents' loss. Tell them the truth. But that would put them in even more danger than they already were.

The cul-de-sac was empty when Rena arrived home, except for the four small trees that coupled on the two court dividers. Rena parked in front of the house and got out of her car. She hoped Uri's guards were posted nearby. She quickly retrieved her house key as she ran down the driveway and opened the garage door. She shuffled in and pushed the button on the wall by the house door to close the garage door as quickly as possible. She waited until it closed securely with no uninvited guests slipping underneath. Dingo whined excitedly at the door, his paws taking turns pulling at the fabric of her jeans.

"Okay, okay, Dingo. I'm home." She kneeled to give him all the love he deserved. The poor dog probably hadn't been left home alone in over a year.

When Rena stood, Dingo spun in circles and then pattered over the tiles into the other room, expecting her to follow. But she remained in the den for a moment as she gathered herself. Besides Dingo's paws scratching across the tiles in the other room, the walls of the house concealed a ghostly silence. Shadows of trees outside the windows danced across the white interior and ceiling. It was unusual to be home alone, and with it came a deeper loneliness than she'd felt for a long time.

Feeling like she was in between worlds and not fully a part of either one brought the greatest desolation. It troubled her deeply that Edrea and Uri kept their distance. Knowing they watched over her from afar wasn't enough to console her. On top of everything, no longer having Tony awakened her innermost feeling of abandonment, even though leaving him was her choice.

She drew her cellphone from her pocket and stared at the text from Bassét. She studied the screen with fascination, realizing she now possessed the key to the undead. Perhaps she would maintain a connection with the young vampire. He appeared to be the most feasible tie to the vampire world, where her sister and uncle existed. If it became necessary, she would do whatever it took to protect her parents, even if that meant leaving their world entirely.

Dingo yelped from Rena's bedroom.

"I'll be right there!" she yelled, as if speaking to a person in the next room.

Rena ran down the creaky spiral staircase to Edrea's old room. She had to make sure her sister's crazy cat, Snow, was fed. She rarely saw the timid creature. Snow hid from everyone. Edrea was the only person she wasn't afraid of. Now the cat lived in total solitude. Rena wished there was a way to reunite her with her vampire mother.

Rena poured some dry food into the little feeding bowl and ran back up the stairs. She grabbed her bulging shoulder bag from the den floor and went to join Dingo in her bedroom. She dropped her bag on the floor with a clunk. It felt ten pounds heavier than when she'd left. She crawled onto the head of her bed next to where the happy dog lay and leaned against the wall. A sigh escaped her as she watched the moving shadows outside the window. Still holding her phone in her hand, she brought Bassét's obnoxious text to the screen.

"The Décret must think I'm a fool," she told Dingo. The dog lifted his head and tilted it to the side in confusion.

Rena wasn't about to be scared into joining a dark vampire coven. The last thing she would ever do was work for the evil vampire who had tortured her. Did Nadine really think she was stupid enough to be wooed into her bloodsucking mafia? Why else would the immortal witch have sent a young handsome vampire to *befriend* her, one with a sexy accent, no less?

No, Rena had a plan of her own.

She rested her hands on her bent knees, and her thumbs typed a quick message into the glowing text box: "Enough games, Bassét. You can give up on your mission. I won't be threatened into your vampire gang. I do, however, have my own 'proposal' for you."

7

The Un-death of a Fireman

The first thing that crossed my mind when I saw Rena was a deep churning guilt. I couldn't help but feel we had abandoned her, like she was a helpless creature in the wilderness left for the wolves. The worst part was, we couldn't catch the wolves that were after her blood, and if we couldn't catch them, we definitely couldn't kill them.

In reality, they weren't wolves. They were worse. Much worse. They were vampires. And if our suspicions were correct, they were super vampires. I couldn't imagine anything worse than that.

Thankfully, Rena was safe inside the corner café when Uri and I had arrived in downtown Windsor. It was only by chance that we located her. Uri's guards had connections in the neighboring towns. A friend of one of the guards had a residence on the north side of the park. He had reported seeing an unfamiliar vampire hanging around the park outside his apartment, a vampire that had an unusual scent. The alarming part of the report was that this strange vampire had been in the park thirty minutes prior to sunset.

When Uri and I arrived, the vampire in question had already fled. Three of Uri's guards believed they had seen the immortal speaking to Rena inside the café. We decided he must be one of the vampires who was shadowing her. The alternative made little sense—that Rena had gone to meet him. I couldn't imagine she would do such a thing, so I ruled out the possibility.

I wanted so badly to go to Rena when she stepped out of the café, but I was too afraid to expose her to our world more than she already was. Uri warned that unless it was a last resort, we couldn't contact her. It would give the Décret a stronger case to bring to the ISC—evidence that we broke the immortal code of secrecy. For all we knew, Rena's stalker was a Décret spy or worse: a recruiter. It was already clear how badly Nadine wanted my sister for the powers she may possess when turned.

As far as I was concerned, any vampire that got close to Rena was as good as dead. Truly dead, that is.

Uri seemed confident a few extra guards could protect Rena in the meantime, but it wasn't hard to see the doubt growing behind his normally poised demeanor.

When Uri and I arrived back home in China Beach, all the frustration over the matter manifested into a burning hunger for human blood. Because there was little I could do about Rena without making matters worse, I did what I could to escape my troubles temporarily—I fed.

The humming shore called in the distance as I fleeted through the dark streets. I didn't have any idea where I was headed. I followed the swirls of scents in the wind, arteries pulsing, people's thoughts stirring in the air. As usual, I hoped to come across someone who was up to no good. That was still the only way I could feed with a minimum of guilt.

I stopped at a corner under the darkness of a tree. A few bars and late-night restaurants were nearby, different genres of music escaping their walls. I took the scents of the night into my nostrils and closed my eyes to listen to the thoughts within reach. A man and woman kissed and fondled against a car across the street, their minds converging on a single coital image. A nicely dressed young man passed in front of me, his blood mingled with a sweet but subtle scent of cologne. He was anxious about his blind date. My gaze followed him as I breathed him in. I swallowed and sucked in my lip, almost wishing I could grab him right then and there. *No, not him.* Too innocent. Too sweet.

A blond woman in a tight purple satiny dress walking toward me grabbed my attention. Her beauty stole many gazes around the street, even mine. There was something powerful about her self-assertive posture. She knew she was a sight to see, and she loved having that hold over other people. I didn't usually thirst for a woman's blood, but something was not right with this one. Her thoughts were far from virtuous. They weren't sexual per se. They were darker than pure desire. Callous and feral.

Deep in her mind, I saw a middle-aged man and woman crying—her parents. This brought her pleasure. I saw a younger sister whom she manipulated. A boyfriend's adoration and love. She used him for his wealth. She was definitely . . . not right.

How did someone become like that? I saw no sign of abuse in her past. No pain. That was what was different about her. She lacked a certain humanity most people have. There was no compassion under her smooth, fair skin. She was the embodiment of the most sinister irony, a stunning shell on the outside, but inside was the darkest of pearls.

Would the world miss her? I thought not. But from what I

saw on the faces of her parents, her sister, and her boyfriend, a great weight may be lifted from their hearts if she, well, disappeared. It was rare that I had the intention to kill a human, but I wasn't sure I'd ever felt so tempted.

The tainted woman cut around the corner down a residential street. She didn't appear to see me. The predator within took hold of me, and I followed in her wake.

She neared a dark passage on her right between two houses. I looked for any witnesses. A man stood on the opposite corner, maybe one hundred feet from her. My gaze locked onto her through the cool breeze and rustling trees.

"Sarah!" A woman's shriek pierced the distant wind.

I stopped short and sighed. There was horror in the woman's scream, a horror I couldn't ignore, even now. Ahead of me the blond woman looked back. She raised an eyebrow and smirked when she saw me. She couldn't have been luckier.

I turned toward the scream.

"Sarah! Will! Please, someone! Please!" The woman begged, her pleas coming from about a mile away.

I fleeted at once. In a second's time, a two-story house glowing with red flames from its first-floor windows appeared in my oval of sight. I came out of fleet under the darkness of a home across the street. A woman screamed frantically, running back and forth across the lawn of the burning house. "Sarah! Will!" she screamed again and again. A child's cries came from inside the second floor of the house. Neighbors stood on their lawns and terraces embracing themselves with terror. Sirens roared nearby, and a fire engine cut the corner. "Please, someone help me! My husband and daughter!" the woman cried.

It all looked horribly helpless, and there wasn't much I could do. I was too sensitive to fire. Soon the house would be engulfed in flames, and not even I could stop what followed.

The red engine squealed to a stop in front of the home, and men in black turnouts leaped onto the asphalt. One quickly uncoiled the hose from the side of the engine. I recognized him immediately. He was the blue-eyed paramedic I'd seen a few nights earlier in the Mission District. Apparently, it was a small city. The firefighters attached the hose to a yellow fire hydrant and ran toward the house. Black smoke billowed from the front door. There was no way in. The child's cries became fainter, and I knew it was only a matter of time before the smoke and heat took her life. The father was probably dead already.

A stream of high-pressure water soared into the window where flames escaped the house. Three firemen huddled around the front door, contemplating the risks of entering. The blue-eyed paramedic was among them. The other two firefighters shook their heads and frowned. I gasped and clutched my chest when the blue-eyed man ran into the black smoke anyway, as if he had nothing to lose.

"Elias, come back out here!" one of the other men yelled. "You're going against direct orders!"

I watched like a helpless human from the darkness of the street waiting for any movement, any sign of life.

Almost a minute later, hollers of hope erupted among the crowd when a chair broke through a window farthest from the fire on the second floor. The blue-eyed paramedic hunched over the window frame with the child dangling over his arm. Firemen below scrambled to open a tarp and yelled for him to drop her. He lowered her down and dropped the seemingly lifeless body onto the tarp. "There's still a man inside!" he yelled before disappearing inside the smoke again.

Get out of there! I wanted to scream.

"She's still breathing," a fireman said on the grass below.

The mother dropped to her knees by the team and watched

85

frantically as they hovered over the small girl with an oxygen mask and medical equipment. "I'm right here, baby. I'm right here," she said and then looked toward the house with terror. "Will!"

Everyone waited in silence, a long heart-clenching silence, but no one emerged from the house. People started praying, some crying. "Please, God, please," the whimpering mother called out to the chilling night sky. "He's all we have."

The chill in the air crept into everyone's bones. They knew the father had died, as had the hero who saved the child's life.

The firefighters continued to blast the house with water, the flames finally subsiding.

"He could still be alive," I whispered to myself.

I fleeted around to the back of the home, hoping no one would see me in the glow of the dying flames. I went straight to the back door and kicked it in. Flames still crept up the walls, but they would soon be out. I had little time. I fleeted through a small recreation room, then down a hall and up the stairs on the right. The walls were blackened and peeling, melted objects on the floor. Patches of blue-and-red flames sizzled on the carpeting on the stairs. I avoided them, but as I climbed, the heat was almost unbearable. What the fuck was I doing?

At the top of the stairs, I followed the hall around to the right where there was an open door. I fleeted into the smoky room to find two men collapsed on the floor. One was the paramedic. I fleeted to the man who was most likely the father of the little girl first. When I kneeled beside him, I knew he was gone. No heartbeat, not even a murmur of one when I lowered my ear to his chest. I scooted to the paramedic's body and lifted his head to my ear. My heart leaped when I felt his weak breath and heard his faint heartbeat. But he wouldn't last even a minute. I knew that much from working in an emergency room when I was human. I flinched when firefighters entered the house below, sweeping their extinguishers. I had only moments before they made it upstairs, in which time the blue-eyed paramedic would be gone. This courageous and yet careless man they called Elias.

And just like that, I acted. My teeth sunk into my wrist and I placed my open wound over the man's mouth. I knew it would save him. Maybe he wouldn't be fully alive, but a hero like him deserved some semblance of an existence.

Men's voices and heavy footsteps came slowly up the stairs, the remaining flames simmering out in the path of their extinguishers. I looked down uneasily at the motionless man. His face was black with ash, except for the drops of red vampire blood smeared on his lips. His heart had nearly stopped, but not before my blood had entered his system. The immortal bacteria would revamp him into a creature of the night. I forced myself not to feel guilty. It was the right thing to do, wasn't it? I had given him a new life.

Then I remembered how much agony he would feel as the immortal bacteria blazed through him from the inside out. It was like fire. There was nothing I could have done to stop it. The Bacillus F paralyzed the body during the process. It was known to last from six to twelve hours. To me it had felt like days.

The firefighters finally entered the hall. I fleeted to the side window and opened it as the men approached the room through the thick smoke. I looked back at the blue-eyed man on the floor for a moment. They would declare him dead. They would notify his loved ones. They would take him to the morgue. The thought sent a chill through my limbs before I jumped out the window and into the darkness.

I stood in front of Uri's desk, hesitant to tell him what I had done. I knew the ISC had laws in place involving turning mortals; I just didn't know what they were. They hadn't concerned me until then.

"Edrea, what have you done?" he asked nimbly, one eyebrow raised.

My eyes met his and then dropped to the floor. I had never been so afraid I'd disappoint him. I crossed my arms over my stomach and clenched my elbow and waist. I searched for courage and then looked back up at him. "Well, I uh . . . I came across a horrible house fire when I went to feed tonight."

"And?" Uri pried, his eyebrows erect in the middle of his forehead.

I had to stop myself from smirking, embarrassed at my behavior. Any subtle humor that had been on Uri's face was gone. I saw only concern.

"Edrea?"

"I turned a man. He was dying."

For a moment, Uri didn't say a word. He just stared with disbelief. Finally, a sigh left his chest. "Do you have any idea what you've done, child?"

"I know. I was impulsive. I wanted to save him. He had just saved a little girl, and I thought—"

"There is an order to things," Uri said. "A process. Where is this man?" He looked more worried than I'd imagined he'd be.

"They're probably taking him to the morgue," I said nervously.

"They might autopsy him, Edrea. Do you realize that?"

My face would have paled if it were possible. "No, they would only autopsy him if he died at the hospital. I used to work in an emergency room."

"That's not what concerns me most," Uri said. "What do you think will happen when he wakes? The hunger will take him. He will feed on a human. He will threaten our existence. Do you not understand the graveness of this matter?"

"I'm sorry, Uncle, I—"

"If he leaves a mess behind, the ISC will be implicated. There will be severe consequences for you. If he does anything at all to jeopardize our kind, the responsibility lies on you."

I hadn't felt so ashamed for a long time. "I wasn't thinking, Uri. I haven't been myself after seeing Rena. I just wanted to save the firefighter."

"Firefighter?" Uri bowed his head and shook it. He was silent for a moment, and then he looked up at me with concern and sympathy. "We have to fix this, Edrea. Tonight."

I nodded. "Whatever needs to be done."

Uri picked up the TV remote and turned on the news behind me. I swiveled around.

"I am at the scene of a fire here in the heart of the Richmond District where a firefighter by the name of Elias Winter was taken to UCSF Medical Center in critical condition moments ago after saving the life of a child," a newswoman said.

My limbs went cold as the woman's voice disappeared into the background. I had thought his heart would have stopped before the firefighters reached him.

Uri picked up his phone and dialed. Mikale answered on the other end, his voice on speakerphone. "Hello."

"Mikale, there's been an incident. I'll explain later, but I need you to post at the UCSF Medical Center where a firefighter named Elias Winter has been taken. He will ultimately be in the morgue. He will be revamping."

The line was silent for a few seconds. "Understood. When do you presume he'll awaken?" Mikale asked, sounding frustrated.

"That's the problem," Uri said gravely. "It can occur anywhere between six and twelve hours."

"He was just turned?"

"That is correct. You may need assistance. When he

awakens, I'll need you to bring him here. This is imperative. Oh, and don't forget to retrieve his items and identification. I know this won't be easy, but if anyone can do this unseen and cleanly, you can."

Mikale sighed. "Okay. I'm at home. I'll call Gus and head straight there."

Uri placed the phone carefully on his desk, as if it were a fragile object. His eyes tilted up to me. "Now it begins."

I stood up. "Are we going to the hospital?" I was so anxious I was almost trembling.

Uri stood and fleeted to a file cabinet against the wall. "No. We will remain right here tonight."

"I don't understand."

"You are a maker now, Edrea. You need to be prepared for what follows." He opened a large metal drawer and sifted through folders. He returned to his desk with a manila folder filled with paperwork. He opened it and began arranging files into different piles on the desk. "Tonight we will prepare Mr. Winter's ISC paperwork."

He opened a drawer behind his desk and retrieved another thick file that was probably over one hundred pages and placed it in front of me. "Turn to page forty-five. That's the chapter on maker responsibilities. Please read it from start to finish, and do not take anything in there lightly. This is a serious matter, Edrea."

Boy, had I done it now. I slid the file toward me tentatively, the memory of my own immortal documenting coming to mind. Uri was right. More than right. I had gotten myself into a mess, and I felt foolish.

I opened the file to the appropriate chapter and stared at the text as if it were in a language I didn't understand. I had to find a way to concentrate, to make this right. Rena was still in trouble. She was the top priority. Not only had I created a vampire, I had created a vampire during a time of peril. A time that should have been spent worrying about my sister, not the revamping of a firefighter who was a total stranger.

I looked up at Uri, frightened with a sudden realization. "Uri, he'll wake before the sun rises, right?"

"We can only hope," he said grimly, not looking up from his desk.

8
He Awakens

The early morning air buzzed with disquiet. I sat in the center of my bed cross-legged as I anticipated the firefighter's arrival. I worried Mikale would not get to him in time or that something else horrible would happen. It was 6:10 a.m., and the spring sun was definitely on the rise. The stars were just barely visible when I'd checked the sky a few minutes earlier. Every inch the sun ascended over the horizon, the heavier my eyelids became. Unbearably heavy. But I would not allow myself to sleep no matter how the unrest affected my undead body, not until I knew the vampire I had created was safe.

A strange feeling hummed under my skin. A connection to someone new on a mental and physical level, and it seemed to be getting nearer.

I tried meditating under the ceiling mural of the cosmos, hoping to connect with Rena, to sense her feelings. To know if she was okay. At times like this, I wished she were there. No such luck. The morning seemed to bring too much unease, like the air had thickened with all the consequences of my actions.

I fleeted to the window and inched back one of the curtains. The stars were gone, and the light hurt my face. I fleeted to the wall where my cloak hung and wrapped it around my limbs and head. I left the cottage with haste and headed toward the back doors of Uri's house.

When I reached the pagoda, I stalled, my walk slowing under the twisted trees that hid the sun's rays. I didn't care for a moment if I felt any pain from the morning light. I was more nervous about what I'd find when I went inside. Bad news. No news. More disturbing silence and buzzing.

I opened one of the French doors and closed it silently behind me. Four restless guards in black suits sat in the astronomy sanctum. I figured Uri had asked them to stay up too. They all watched me like I'd done something wrong.

"Edrea." Uri's soft voice came from his office.

I fleeted to him and was standing in his office doorway within a blink of a second. "Uncle."

He sat calmly behind his desk and looked up at me with more ease than earlier but also with a lingering hint of disappointment. "Mikale is on his way here. They are coming in the Rolls Royce."

They? I felt some of the tension leave my body. "So, everything went smoothly?" I asked nervously.

"I wouldn't say that, but no humans were harmed—well, except the nurse Mikale was forced to put to sleep."

My eyes widened. "Oh?"

A slight smile grew on my uncle's face. "The important thing is your new immortal firefighter did not drain half the hospital, and Mikale and Gus were able to walk a dead man out of the building without being seen."

A sigh escaped my chest. "That's such a relief." I hadn't met Gus yet. All I'd heard was that he was an old immortal friend of Mikale's from Oahu, and he was here to visit for a while. He had definitely kept Mikale busy the last few days, because I'd seen very little of my Hawaiian guard.

"They still must endure the early sun when they arrive. And my guards are not happy about staying up after dawn to ensure Mr. Winters is not a danger to himself or us," Uri added.

"That's why I'm staying up too. I'll make this right, Uri." I stiffened when a car pulled into our driveway. The strange hum under my skin prickled at the surface. I scratched my forearms. Uri raised an eyebrow as if my reaction amused him. Then he stood up from his big leather chair and twitched his brow. "Well, let us welcome the new youngblood into our family."

Family? This all felt so strange. He was a total stranger; and yet so was I when I was reborn into this world of the undead.

I fleeted to the window in the hall and peeked between the blinds as Uri waited patiently at the front door. Mikale stood fully cloaked at the back passenger door of the Rolls Royce. He shielded himself from the light, wincing. He quickly opened the car door and spoke to someone inside, but no one emerged.

A tall Samoan-looking man with his hair tied into a long ponytail emerged from the adjacent door and jerked a hood over his head. It had to be Gus. Mikale leaned down and pulled a man wearing a black hoodie from the car by his arm. Most of the man's face was veiled under the hood, but he clenched a bag of blood over his mouth with both hands. Then I saw the familiar blue eyes, except they were rabid and crazed with hunger. They darted around the grounds as he shuffled toward the front door with Mikale and Gus at his sides, his fangs sunk into the bag of dark-red fluid.

I felt sick to my stomach for the first time since becoming immortal. The firefighter looked like a wild animal, and I was the one who had to tame him.

My fingers dropped from the blinds, and I fleeted back to Uri's office. I paced back and forth, fidgeting with my hands. I couldn't believe I had gotten myself into this mess.

I froze when I heard commotion at the front door, then nervous voices and jumbled thoughts before the door closed. *Should I wait here? Should I go help?* I was too nervous to move. The shuffling and voices came toward the office. I backed into Uri's desk until I was leaning against it. There was no way out of this one.

The moment they entered the room, Elias's crazed blue eyes landed on me. His face and arms had not been washed of the residue and ash from the house fire. He must have finished drinking the bag of blood, because all that was left of it was smeared over his mouth and chin, not to mention the bit that dripped down his hands. He looked like he had just eaten the entire city, and he wasn't finished yet. Gus stood sternly at the doorway, as if he wasn't sure if he was welcome yet. Mikale escorted Elias to the couch in front of me, the former firefighter now a beastly man savagely licking every last drop of blood from his fingers. I watched silently, the hum under my skin making me itch.

"How does a shower sound, buddy?" Mikale offered with a slight smirk.

I ignored the comment, too preoccupied with the mess in front of me. Plus, the unrest had caused delirium to set in.

Uri took his place beside me and faced the hungry youngblood. "Elias, I am Uri, the head of this compound. The man beside you is Mikale. He will help you with whatever you need." Uri paused to look at me directly. "This young lady is Edrea. She is the one who made you into what you are." Uri looked back to

95

Elias, who appeared utterly confused. "You can look to us as family now."

I watched as Elias took in what Uri had just told him. He stopped licking at his hands, the craze in his blue eyes landing back on me with growing fury. "*You* made me?" he asked gruffly. "What the fuck am I?" His eyes darted back and forth between Uri and me.

My lips parted, but nothing came out. I swallowed and looked to Uri for help. His cautioning eyes met Mikale's, as if demanding he remain close. Gus took a careful step forward, still unsure of his place there. I shot the large Samoan a nervous smile.

"We have what may seem like eternity to teach you about our world, my friend," Uri said, "but it is very important that Edrea answers that question." My uncle looked at me with urgency.

I couldn't have been more terrified. I inhaled and held in a breath as I addressed Elias. "I . . . I thought I was helping you," I stammered.

Elias's brow knitted, and he formed fists with his dirty hands. He looked down at the blood drying on his knuckles, and then his eyes snapped back to me.

"You're a vampire." The words spouted from my lips like I had spit something out that tasted horrible.

Mikale's eyebrows perked up in amusement. Uri remained calm and inquisitive. Gus stood immobile in the corner like a silent beast.

Elias was silent for a moment as he studied us. *These people are lunatics,* I heard him think. He looked back down at the crusting red residue on his hands as it registered that he had just downed a bag of human blood. Like a light bulb had turned on in his head, his face paled. His frantic blue eyes traveled between Uri and me, as if waiting for us to tell him this was all a hoax. "That's impossible . . . impossible," he repeated, shaking his head.

"I'm sorry," I said in a hushed voice.

"That's enough for tonight," Uri said in his soothing tone. "Why don't we show you to your room? We all need rest. You will have to stay here for a while, so we can monitor you. Do you understand, Elias?"

Elias stood rigidly and blank faced. Mikale escorted him toward the hall. Gus stepped aside, waiting for them to pass. At the doorway, the youngblood stopped. He remained there with his back to me for a moment and then looked back over his shoulder. He didn't say a thing, but his spiteful eyes glared. I swallowed as he studied my face. He searched for something, a memory. My face was familiar to him. Then an image appeared in his mind's eye. A girl in a long gray sweater stood at a street corner in the night, watching him. The girl was me. It was the night we first saw each other.

Elias stiffened, and his stare grew even colder. Then he turned away, as if it were the last time he'd ever look me in the face.

9

Rena: The Proposal

Rena sat quietly on her bed, leaning against the wall, the sunlight kissing her cheeks. Pine needles brushed against the window as a branch blew in the wind, soothing her with the memory of the night Edrea came to comfort her during a storm. It was soon after Rena had broken up with her first boyfriend. She wished Edrea were there this time too.

Her scrapbook lay open on her outstretched legs as her feet dangled restlessly over the edge of the mattress. She had sketched a pair of sad eyes. She thought at first they were Bassét's eyes; she couldn't seem to get them out of mind. Dark portals into an eternal world that lingered in her consciousness. They were always there, like a mirage, two promising dark-brown irises, forever watching her.

Her eyes narrowed as she studied the eyes looking back at her from the off-white canvas. She rolled her shoulders with unease when she realized they looked more like Tony's eyes.

She slapped the book closed and pushed it off her thighs. It slid onto the carpeted floor, landing on its spine, and popped open to the same page.

She stared at the haunting orbs, pulling her knees to her chest, as if afraid of them. The burn grew under her sternum the moment she wished Tony would text her. Call her. His voice would flow like silk over her ears. But she knew he wouldn't. He was a genuine friend. He would give her the space she had requested. She hoped he missed her as much as she missed him—if she actually let herself feel. But the pain would be too severe, and she had to concentrate on the mission.

Rena grabbed her phone from the desk and stared at the last text she'd sent Bassét. "I do, however, have my own 'proposal' for you." She wasn't sure why she had said that. It sounded clever at the time. Now she would have to think one up, and quickly. She couldn't shake the urge to prepare for something big. Something bad. Maybe her intuitions were stronger. She never understood them the way Edrea seemed to understand hers, not until the night Rena was kidnapped and tortured. After the battle at the Décret mansion, it was like every sense was on high alert. The warning that tingled under her skin had begun to itch more than ever.

Whatever it all meant, she knew one thing for sure. No matter the price, she had to do something to protect her family. Her parents. Liron.

Probably the world.

It wasn't that she didn't trust Uri and his guards. Her immortal uncle would do everything in his power to protect her and his mortal family. She knew he stayed at a distance because breaking the so-called code of secrecy could bring her family even more danger. She wanted to trust that she and her family would be safe, protected, but a strong uneasy feeling told her otherwise.

Bassét had confirmed that feeling at the café when he hinted there was something else Uri didn't know about. Like the Décret had something unimaginably dangerous up their sleeve. Rena had a feeling it may have something to do with the vampires following her, and Bassét being able to walk during daylight.

Rena's heart skipped a beat, her gaze slowly lifting as a thought came to mind. She wasn't sure how it came to her, but she knew exactly what she had to do, as if she'd known all along. Her proposal. She would ask Bassét to take her to Nadine.

A familiar chill ran down Rena's spine. It was the heavy dreariness she'd felt all along. She would sacrifice herself for her family, for her immortal uncle, for Edrea. It wouldn't be the first time.

She blinked out of her daze and sighed. This was her purpose. It had always been her purpose.

* * *

It was one of those evenings when the fog hovered low. It brushed over the stark-blue hood of Bassét's Audi coupe. Rena sat in the passenger seat, quiet as a mouse. The farther south they got on Highway 101, the thicker the fog. She tugged on her hoodie to preserve more warmth. Bassét had turned the heat on, but she couldn't get rid of the chill.

It had taken Bassét less than an hour to drive from the city to pick her up. He had arrived before sundown, like the previous time. That way it was harder for Uri's guards to follow them. Once again it appeared Bassét foresaw what she had planned. This was exactly what he had waited for. He had a mission too.

She was it.

Rena glanced over at him, wondering if she'd made the right choice. It was too late now. Bassét glanced back, but just for a second. The corner of his mouth twitched, as if to smile. He bit his cheek from the inside, and his gaze hardened with determination. Rena studied his eyes as they focused into black onyx. He would make sure they arrived at their destination.

The Décret mansion.

"How did you become this way—I mean, how did you become a vampire?" Rena asked, breaking the uncomfortable silence.

"Why the sudden interest?" he said, tilting his head.

Rena scowled at his response and looked out the window. "Did you expect me not to wonder about it?"

The car fell silent again. Up ahead, the Golden Gate materialized through the chilling fog.

"I was sick." Bassét's solemn words bit through the stillness of the black leather cabin.

Rena's curious gaze left the window, but she didn't look at his face. Instead her eyes fell on his hands, which constricted around the steering wheel. She waited. His hands loosened their grip as he let out an uneasy laugh. "I was applying to medical schools in London when it all started," he said, as if finding humor in something ironic. He glanced at Rena with an unsteady smile. "I came down with leukemia, you see . . . leukemia of all things." He laughed again.

Rena's brow knitted deeply. "I don't understand why that's funny."

Bassét shook his head with another nervous smile and then raised one eyebrow at her. "I was going to specialize in hematology." His wide smile slowly gave way as he bit his cheek again.

Rena gazed sadly out the windshield, watching the white fog roll over the red rails of the bridge. Finally, she swallowed. "I'm sorry," she said.

"Don't be. Not for me. I didn't suffer for long. If you want to feel sorry for someone, feel sorry for my parents. When they found out, let's just say I would have died a thousand times rather than see their faces that day."

"Did they take care of you, until . . ."

"No, I couldn't let them watch me die. I had planned it all out. I bought the sleeping pills for when the time came. I was going to go up into the mountains, go in peace, where they wouldn't have to . . . watch."

"Is that where it happened? Where you were turned?"

Bassét laughed, as if he found humor in his own tragedy. "No, I never got that far. *She* had been watching me. Nadine. She had eyes in my university in Paris. They'd scouted me out. Watched me. She'd figured out what I was going to do and gave me another option."

Rena frowned. "Why?"

Bassét smiled again, like he was pleased with himself. "I was selected for something, an experiment."

"And was it successful? The experiment?"

A chill ran down Rena's spine when they turned onto a familiar street, the one that led to the mansion where she'd been held captive and tortured.

Bassét grinned. "I wouldn't be here otherwise."

Rena realized when Bassét spoke of Nadine his voice seemed to soften slightly, as if he was fond of her. Rena couldn't imagine that the woman who'd imprisoned her and then had her practically burned alive could be anything but a monster. Actually, Rena was sure Nadine was a monster.

Rena froze as the car entered the tall iron gates that concealed the Décret property. The fog hung heavily over the ground below, dark vines crawling along the base of the white mansion.

"Is . . . is Nadine your—"

"Immortal mother?" Bassét finished her question as men in black closed the gate behind the car, the latch grating piercingly outside the windows. "She's not really the motherly type, but yes, her blood went into making me what I am."

Rena cringed when the car continued around the back of the mansion. She grimaced at Bassét. "What you *are*? What exactly are you?"

Bassét peered at her but gave no answer, as if it was not his secret to tell.

The car came to a stop in front of the mansion's tall rear doors. Rena swallowed hard as the passenger door opened.

"Nice to see you back," a familiar slender guard said smugly. He stood at her door, hand held out.

She ignored his hand and got out. She stepped nearer to the man, studying his pasty face and Nazi-like hairstyle. "I remember you," she said, hiding her fear. "You were in the lab when my blood was tested. Did you get any more of those Care Bear Band-Aids you were raving about?" She smiled smugly.

"I'm afraid you'll need more than a Band-Aid next time," he said, his left eyebrow curving into a sharp point.

"That's enough, Victor," Bassét said. He must have done that vampire-fleeting thing, because he now stood by Rena's side and hooked her arm with his.

Victor grinned as he led them to the door. "It was just banter. It almost feels like a family reunion."

"Doesn't it though?" Rena said. "I'm so glad to see you survived that whole battle thing, Victor," she added dryly. There she was again, provoking the wolves. She might as well have offered her neck to him. Victor raised his eyebrow in a predatory leer and slowly opened the large door to the mansion.

The moment her eyes landed on the spotless white tiles of the main lobby, fear crept back into her bones. A flashback of the last horrid night she was there intruded on her mind. The fire. Smelling her own flesh burning as she screamed. The dark red contrast of blood against the perfect white tiles on the floor. For a moment Rena stood frozen at the threshold of the awful room.

"Aren't you coming in?" Victor taunted.

Then she remembered why that night was so vivid in her mind. It wasn't only because she had been tortured. It was also the night she'd found Edrea. It was the night her sister had come for her. It may have been a terrible night, but it was also one of the best nights of her life. When she learned Edrea wasn't truly dead, just missing. That memory of seeing her for the first time since she'd disappeared helped Rena fight the fear. Nothing was more painful than losing a loved one. They could burn her alive all over again if they wished, but they couldn't break her. She was loved, and she had a family to fight for, to live for. What Bassét had told her in the car about his parents suddenly made perfect sense.

Rena looked up at Bassét and smiled, forgetting her past terrors. He smirked at first, but then his eyes softened, like they saw what was behind her smile.

"I guess I'm coming in," Rena said finally, sounding as if she remembered something she'd forgotten.

"You're a weird little thing," Bassét said.

They stepped into the oversized room. It was unnaturally quiet. The only noise was their footsteps on the tiles. There were no statue-like guards at every corner, which seemed odd. Apparently, there was no need for them.

Rena stopped and looked over her shoulder when the door thudded closed behind her. Victor must have shut it from the outside, probably to park Bassét's car.

"Nadine is upstairs in her study," Bassét said, his eyes wandering upward.

Rena's eyes followed the dark wooden railing and white-tiled steps that led up to a closed door on the eastern wall. Right below them was where the molten metal basin hid under retracting tiles. She followed Bassét toward the stairs, keeping clear of the death basin under the floor. Death was the only thing it was created for. Fire could kill humans and vampires. Even immortals could not escape mortality completely. Clearly, Nadine wanted to remind her mindless vampire drones of that truth, or anyone else she could twist to do her deeds.

Rena stopped at the base of the stairs, her eyes wavering above the floor tiles where Alexio had died after throwing her from the fire underneath. After saving her. She still felt horrible the man her sister loved had died because of her.

"Rena," the young French vampire called from above.

She started her ascent, each step careful but determined. Bassét continued to the top and waited at the door until she met him there. When she climbed the last cold step, Bassét's dark eyes found hers, silently waiting for her to be ready. He was kinder than she'd originally thought. It was getting harder to see how he fit in with this disgraceful group of creeps. Rena bobbed her head with an unsure frown and a raised brow. Then he opened the door.

Bassét stood at the entrance, and Rena stepped inside the red-lit office, uneasy but confident. It was such a large room that she almost didn't see *her*, the awful vampire witch in a vintage red velvet dress sitting at a desk near the window.

When Nadine saw her, Nadine's sadistic brown eyes gleamed, and her blood-red nails folded over her knuckles. "What a pleasure to have you, Rena," she said excitedly.

"Indeed," Rena said dryly, feigning a smile. Rena walked carefully toward the desk over a red oriental rug. On each side of the desk stood two carved wooden lamps with red shades. Dark wooden panels covered the walls, making her feel like she'd just stepped into a cabin in the middle of the woods. She wasn't surprised the long velvety drapes over the window were also blood red. "Thoughtful colors. Original. Were you behind the interior design?" Rena smirked, her head motioning around the room.

"It seems you know me well, my dear," Nadine said. "You're intuitive, like your sister." Her eyes brightened at the thought.

Nadine's fake kindness made Rena sick to her stomach. She knew the only reason she was alive was because she'd become a mind reader when turned—*their* mind reader.

"Why don't we get right to the point," Rena said, taking another step forward. "I've decided to accept your offer."

"What offer would that be, my dear?" Nadine grinned until her sharp canines popped out and glowed in the light.

Rena sighed in annoyance. "We don't need to play this game."

"There's no game to be played," Nadine said. She opened her hands in a graceful circular motion. "Go on, Rena, please enlighten me."

"You can have me, turn me into your little vampire mind reader."

Nadine stood up and clasped her hands, still smiling from ear to ear. "That wasn't so hard, was it?" she said in her thick French accent.

"I have conditions," Rena continued.

Nadine's grin faded into an aggravated smile. "Conditions?" She shifted her attention to her red nails as she pivoted her hand back and forth under the light.

Rena dropped her head and swallowed. Then she looked up and waited for Nadine to look into her eyes. "I need to know my family will be safe, both mortal and immortal."

"Of course they'll be safe," Nadine said, as if it was already done. She glided toward Rena, the wide grin reappearing on her pale face.

"There's one more thing," Rena said, stopping Nadine in mid-stride. "I want a little time first." Rena stood her ground as she studied Nadine's twisted expression. "I'm asking for one year. Just enough time to finish some things, like college. I also want to qualify for the World Equestrian Games." *And to spend quality time with my parents and Liron,* Rena thought. *Maybe a little more time to make things right with Tony. I have to make sure Dingo is okay too. Dingo, my heart.*

"You have quite a bit of nerve coming to a powerful coven of vampires to negotiate," Nadine said. "I'll give you that. But why shouldn't I just turn you right now?"

In an instant, Nadine had Rena by the hair, forcing her head to the side to expose her neck. Rena felt her cold breath upon her bare flesh. She gasped but remained calm. "Because then you might as well kill me. If you want my cooperation, you'll allow me these two simple things. I want my family safe, and I want one more human year. If you can promise me these two things, I will be at your service willingly."

Nadine released Rena's soft hair, her cold finger tracing Rena's face from her cheek to her chin. "You're a clever girl, aren't you?" She smirked and then turned toward the window. She took two fluid steps forward and then turned again to address Rena. "If I allow you this one year, I have my own condition. You will work for me in secret while you're still human, do whatever I ask of you. Do you understand?"

Rena remained still, the room shrinking around her. She swallowed hard. Then she gave Nadine a fierce look. "I understand perfectly."

On the drive home, Rena and Bassét didn't exchange one word. She watched the land soar by the window, as if she was watching her life escape her eyes. Until that night, her life in the living, all her dreams and endeavors, didn't feel like her own, like she'd watched someone else live it from the sidelines. And just like that, she dropped onto the scene, like a puppet placed on the stage, its strings clipped. Now both worlds, the living and the undead, converged in front of her eyes.

How naïvely she'd taken time for granted. How she'd underestimated its fragility. *One year*. That was no time at all. There was so much she still needed to accomplish in her human skin. She was a month away from earning her black belt in Jujitsu. Half a semester away from earning her bachelor's degree of science. And only four months away from a chance to qualify for the World Equestrian Games.

One year away from dying.

One year away from becoming a vampire.

10

Coven Dysfunction

The connection between Rena and me had taken a turn. It was weaker, like she was keeping me at a distance. I wasn't sure if she'd done it intentionally or if I was imagining it. Maybe the growing connection to my vampire progeny had caused a rift in my connection to her. I hoped that was it.

The more I thought about *him*—the firefighter I'd turned into a savage beast—the more I wondered what had been behind my actions. Had my intentions been truly selfless, or were they more selfish in nature?

I shook my head and sat up on the soft mattress. What could I possibly get out of becoming a maker? I had enough to worry about right now. Like Rena, who seemed to attract every bloodsucker on Earth. Before I concentrated on mentoring the youngblood I had revamped, I had to know she was safe.

Behind the curtains, the darkness of night had long fallen, the garden alive with crickets and the glow of moonlight. The nocturnal critters were louder than usual and the moon glow brighter, considering the way it bled under the curtains.

I grabbed my phone and glanced at the time. 11:30 p.m. I hadn't slept that late in a while. I slipped out of bed and went straight to the bedroom door. I didn't bother to grab my robe. I was already fully clothed, wearing a new pair of plaid pajamas that Uri had one of his guards pick up for me recently. I ambled down the quiet hall of my vintage cottage and opened the front door to the garden.

"Good evening, my lady." Mikale appeared in my path like a shadow of the wind. "Off to make more baby vampires?" There was humor on his handsome, glowing face, but accusation hid behind his swirling eyes.

I bit my lip and raised my right eyebrow at him. "It wasn't intentional," I said, both irritated and ashamed.

I strode around him and headed toward Uri's office. A cool breeze swept past me, and Mikale was standing before me once again. He brushed a lock of loose hair around my ear and tempted me with his blue Hawaiian eyes.

"I don't have time right now, Mikale. What is it?"

He stepped closer until I could smell the fresh garden soil smudged on his white sleeve. "I didn't mean to upset you. I was just trying to make you smile."

"I know, I'm sorry," I said. "I should be thanking you for cleaning up my mess. What you did means a lot to me, really." I smiled and let myself gaze into his blue eyes for a moment.

He inched closer, his eyes wandering down to my lips. "I miss our strolls in the city, E." His lips parted, his eyes not leaving my mouth.

My chest tingled, and I inhaled his cool island scent as I licked my lips. "I really have to talk to Uri right now."

"I know," he whispered, his breath against my lips.

It wasn't hard for my island guard to whisk me into a stupor. I missed his company and the affections we shared. But I had to fix what I had done. I owed my time to Elias now.

I took Mikale's hand and kissed the corner of his lips. He remained still, but I could feel his passions stirring under his skin. When I pulled away, the corner of his mouth twitched into a seductive smile.

"I'll see you later," I said before continuing through the Midnight Garden.

I didn't hear a response before I reached the side doors to Uri's house. I entered the moonlit astronomy sanctum and peered up at the domed ceiling as I walked through the room. I knew Uri was in his office because its light emanated its usual luster over the tiles by the front door. When I reached the foyer, I noticed guards stationed in the hall on the left where the house's living area was located. Elias hadn't left his room yet, it seemed. I walked down the adjacent hall to the office and loomed for a moment at the threshold, afraid Uri was upset with me.

"Good evening, Uncle."

"Evening, Edrea," he responded without enthusiasm.

While I watched him typing on his computer, it occurred to me that the crawling feeling under my skin had calmed. I stood up straighter and looked back at the other end of the hall. Being in the same house with Elias last night, being so close to him, had made my skin itch. That sensation was almost gone.

Instinctively, I walked toward the bedrooms, my pace slow and careful. When I reached the guards, the itch didn't return. "Show me to Elias's room please, Gus."

The large Samoan guard nodded and started down the hall, his dark ponytail bound with several elastics between his robust shoulders. I followed, not sure why I was so nervous. We continued down the hall as it bent to the right and ended with three doors, one at the end and two across from each other. A female guard with a tight blond ponytail and fitted black clothing stood in front of the door on the left. I had seen her only a few times before.

"Evening, uh . . ." I began, my eyes falling in embarrassment as I searched my scattered brain for her name.

"Taralynn," she reminded me with amusement.

"I'm sorry. I'm horrible with names. I always was." I smiled. "I need to check on Elias. Do you mind?"

She nodded and turned to knock on the door. No one responded.

"He's not in there," I said. I didn't feel even a tingle under my skin, and I definitely should have if he were in the room.

She opened the door to a vacant room and stepped inside, quickly eyeing all corners of the interior. Across from the bed, the window was open, the long, sheer tan drapes blowing in the wind.

"Shit," I said and fleeted to Uri's office. I appeared in front of his desk, no longer worried if he was upset with me. "Elias . . . he's gone."

He looked up from his computer with concern but not surprise. "I expected as much. We need to—"

"You put him in a guest room with windows?"

Subtle amusement crossed his face. "We aren't the Décret, Edrea. We don't imprison our youngbloods behind bars."

My eyes fell to the floor, and I sighed in frustration. "I'm going to look for him."

Uri closed his laptop and looked at me with expectation. "Do you know how to follow the blood bond?"

"I assume you're talking about that itchy sensation I get under my skin when he's near me," I said, unsure where to start.

Uri nodded. "Yes. Makers feel the blood bond in varying degrees. An itching sensation under the skin is one of the more blatant symptoms. In the first few months, the connection between maker and progeny is the most potent."

"But it's completely gone," I said, pacing toward the bookshelf.

"It's not gone," Uri replied. "Only less detectable. When you're within a mile or two of him, the sensation will return. Then you can follow its intensity."

My posture straightened, and I turned toward Uri. I understood exactly what he meant. "Thank you, Uncle," I said and then turned toward the hall.

"Edrea," he called. "Go alone. The sensation will be duller in the presence of other stimuli. I'll have Mikale and Gus search the city as well."

"Okay," I said, stalling at the threshold. "What about Rena?"

"My guards informed me that she arrived home not long ago." He looked down, as if holding information back. I stared imposingly at him. "Don't worry, Edrea. All I know is she arrived in an unknown vehicle. The windows were dark, so they couldn't see the driver."

I thought about that for a moment and then settled on the hopeful fact that she was safe at home. That thought was interrupted with an image of trails of bloody bodies leading to Elias, ravenous and with a dead child in his arms. It was just a fear but one that could easily become a reality.

Time to go.

I fleeted straight to my room and quickly changed into something dark. When I opened the door to leave, Mikale was standing there once again.

"Elias ran off. I'm going to look for him. Alone. Uri wants to see you and Gus in his office," I said as I closed the front door and started toward the house.

"Surprise, surprise," he said behind me.

I had already made several passes around the city with no luck. There was no trace of him. Not even a tingle beneath my skin. I started to wonder if I had what it took to be a maker. Perhaps I could pawn him off on someone else. No, that wouldn't be right. One thing I had always done, even when I was completely human, was to take responsibility for my actions.

It was a good sign there was no whiff of freshly spilled blood anywhere in the city so far. With that in mind, I fleeted to Coit Tower and found myself staring mindlessly from its top balcony over the Telegraph Hill views. Where in the world could he have gone? What was the first thing I did when I awoke as a vampire?

My body stiffened when it hit me. Surprisingly, it wasn't feeding initially. My first feed was an accident. Before I'd even thought of feeding the blood beast of my nature, I had tried to kill myself. The idea of being a murderous vampire wasn't exactly a warm feeling, and I had been set on ending my blood-sucking existence. I would have succeeded if it had been possible.

My eyes surveyed what I could see of the city. They landed on the dark foggy mist of the Golden Gate. I focused on the grand monument and traveled to the highest points of its towers. There at the top of the farthest tower was a tiny image of a man.

I took off toward the bridge and arrived at its edge within moments. I stared up at the red iron towers that reached into the cool fog, my fingers pinching my forearms. I knew the man was Elias the moment the itch returned.

Thankfully, there weren't more than ten cars driving in both directions. I focused on the center anchorage between the towers where the two main cables extend near the walkway and fleeted. Then I sprang onto one of the concrete blocks where I could access the cable that led to the second tower. I was glad I'd chosen to wear black clothing. It would make me almost invisible to the human eye when I ascended the cables. I could only hope Elias hadn't made himself visible.

I trekked up the wet, slippery cable toward the night sky while holding the railing on both sides. Gusts of chilly wind batted at my body, the ocean waves echoing into the foggy darkness. There was no way I could fleet up that thing. The slowness of human speed made me feel more helpless, and I wondered if I would be too late.

After a long while, I reached the midpoint and attempted to peer through the thick fog where the tips of the towers protruded. Even with my immortal eyes, I couldn't see the top.

Finally, I hoisted my body onto the top of the second tower. I tried to stay as low as I could to avoid the wind gusts, bracing myself in a kneeling position. After steadying my feet on the wet surface, I was surprised to find Elias standing near the edge, dripping wet.

"You can't do it, you know," I said from behind him. "How many times have you tried?"

He didn't so much as move a muscle. "I didn't try." He glared back at me. "Go away, and leave me alone, *mother dearest*," he said dryly as he turned away from me.

"Please don't call me that," I said. "It's not like you're really my son."

Elias was perfectly still and silent, as if the quiet view consoled him. The soft river of fog looked thick enough to walk on, and above, millions of stars twinkled in the blackness.

"Why are you dripping wet if you didn't try to jump?"

He was quiet for a long moment. "I slipped," he said, annoyance in his tone.

I crouched and braced myself on the cold iron below when a gust of wind threatened to unsteady me. "You slipped?" I repeated, raising my eyebrow.

"Yes, I slipped. My clumsiness followed me into immortality, okay?" He sounded ashamed.

I laughed into the cold wailing wind. Elias swiveled around as another gust almost swept him off the edge. He threw his arms out to balance himself and attempted to glare at me as the corners of his lips turned up slightly. There was sadness in his light-blue eyes, a blue that looked gray in the night. It was a beautiful sadness, a humanlike sadness.

"You look miserable. I'm sorry I brought you back, made you . . . this." My words didn't feel completely honest. His large eyes softened slightly as he studied my face but then hardened like the cold night. "What you did for that little girl in the fire . . . you saved her. I just didn't think you deserved to—"

"To what?" he snapped, his eyes glowing red when the moonlight shone into them. "Die? And what am I now, *alive*?" He turned toward the edge and squeezed the railing.

My eyes fell. "I guess it's a matter of perspective." I looked up at him with concern. "Elias, why *did* you want to die?"

He continued looking over the edge. "Who said I wanted to die?"

"As heroic as it was, you were quick to run into that burning house."

He glared at me. "I may have made a rash decision, but I wasn't committing suicide." His eyes told me he wasn't so sure. "It doesn't matter anymore, does it? You can go tell your vampire coven that I'm not trying to kill myself or drain the city or whatever."

"Listen, Elias, it's not that simple. I want to give you space, but I can't right now. You may think you have control over the bloodthirst, but it's stronger than you think."

Elias whipped his head from left to right and flipped his

palms up. "Does it look like there are any people up here? I'm not even thinking about blood right now."

"Not yet," I warned. "You fed about eight hours ago, but your hunger will return in a few hours. It's my responsibility to teach you how to tame it."

He laughed into the wind. "Oh, so you're my vampire maker *and* teacher? How grand."

"Elias, please just listen for a minute. There are laws we must abide by in the vampire world. If we don't, it draws attention to our entire immortal family."

He fleeted toward me and knocked us both into the sloped wall of the tower post, my back hitting the cold iron with a bang. The weight of his body pinned me down, his fists squeezing the sides of my black bomber jacket. "I didn't ask for this! Don't you dare put this on me!" His eyes blazed, his canines protruding from his mouth.

"Elias," I pleaded, hoping to snap him out of his rage. "What else do you want me to say? I know I took that choice away from you. I'm not blaming you for anything. If anyone's to blame, it's me. But I don't have a choice now either. Please, just let me—"

"Let you what? Make me into one of your vampire pups?" His weight became heavier against my body, his fists twisting the edges of my jacket. His sharp canines neared my neck as he thought of tearing out my jugular with his teeth.

At that moment, his enraged blue eyes gave way to pieces of his past. A wife who belittled him, cheated on him, despite the love he gave her. A controlling father he couldn't please. A childhood of bullying.

Elias's hurt stung me. I gathered strength and prepared to draw his pain into my body. "I'm not them, Elias. I'm not the people who hurt you."

The flame in his eyes died down. The rage swarming

within them gave way to agony. His fists loosened their grip as he studied my gaze. He realized I had seen inside him. His canines snapped back, his sad almond eyes widening. Before I could absorb some of his suffering, he pushed off me, stepping backward.

"Elias . . ."

He turned his back to me and fleeted, jumping off the opposite tower post toward the ocean below.

11

Rena: A Girl Against the World

The hours in senior seminar class churned slowly. It was relentless, like the turning arms of an empty ice cream maker. The classroom was unusually cold, and the project topics floating around the room were like reused ingredients. Didn't anyone want to write about anything other than veganism and closing down egg farms? This was Zoology Senior Seminar, not a PETA operation.

Rena looked around the room carefully, afraid to announce what she would write her term paper on. She didn't want to write her fifteen-page paper on meat farms or animal labs. She didn't want the other students to think she was insensitive to animal suffering, but those topics had been recycled a million times. She sighed, deciding she shouldn't care what people thought of her. She'd been through too much to be worried about such things.

"I'm doing my paper on the local mountain lion population and ecosystem conservation," she blurted out.

The instructor's strawberry eyebrows lifted, and her hazel

gaze turned toward Rena from her desk in the corner, as if the new idea was a relief. Maybe she hoped someone would come up with a new topic as well. She had probably listened to the same heated arguments more times than she could swallow. "That's a great idea, Rena," she said. "I don't think anyone has written about that topic this semester."

Rena smiled at the teacher and sat up straighter in her chair. She was glad her professor liked her idea. Some of the students agreed with the instructor in unison, but others just stared at Rena like her approach to protecting animals wasn't worldly enough. It wasn't more than a minute before they went back to discussing the elimination of all meat from their diets or the cruel treatment of chickens, cattle, and pigs. Rena cared deeply about animal suffering, but she thought it was just as important to focus on wild animals affected by human expansion.

Rena fell back against her chair, not having the mental or emotional energy to dive into the debate. Instead, her mind traveled back to the vampire situation she had gotten herself into. What had Nadine meant when she said Rena had to work for her? Rena couldn't imagine what she had planned, but she knew it couldn't be anything that would benefit humankind. She laughed to herself at the irony of her situation. Here she was in the middle of a debate about saving animals from humans when right beneath their feet they had a race of evolved immortal apes that wanted to eat humans.

Rena looked up from a doodle she was scribbling into her notebook to find the entire class staring at her, annoyed. *Did I laugh out loud?* she wondered, reddening in embarrassment. "Sorry, I was just—"

"Just what?" a thin, pasty brunette said from across the room. "Laughing at the thought of chopping chickens' beaks off?"

"No," Rena said defensively. She could tell by the looks of

the girl's skin color and the absence of muscle on her bones that she was taking the vegan thing a bit too far. "I care very much about animals. I just don't think avoiding all animal products is the only answer to ending animal suffering."

"It is though," the girl insisted self-righteously. "And besides, there are loads of studies that prove meat is unhealthy."

Oh boy, Rena thought. At that moment, she truly wished Edrea were there. Her sister would teach this girl a thing or two about how human beings had evolved to eat. Rena fought a smirk as she looked the girl in the eyes, feeling as if Edrea's boldness had somehow transferred across space right into her own core. "You know, when my sister, Edrea, was hu—" She stopped herself before that slip-up. "When my sister was alive, she had severe rheumatoid arthritis. Because of the severity of her autoimmune disease, she had a lot of severe GI problems too. She had a serious intolerance to foods like legumes, wheat, corn, dairy, and sugar. Even some nuts caused her a reaction. Legumes and nuts are a vegan's main protein source. My sister couldn't eat those things and stay healthy. She had to maintain the omnivorous diet we humans evolved to eat. Are you saying my sister should have made herself sick to satisfy your beliefs about omitting all animal products?"

The girl gaped at Rena with an appalled look on her face, but Rena didn't back down. She had no idea where the nerve had come from. She hated confrontation.

The girl ground her teeth while she appeared to think of some intelligent comeback. When her arrogant mouth opened again Rena stood up abruptly from her chair. "You know what?" she said before the girl could utter another word. "I don't want to spend my class time listening to your extreme views about how every human on Earth should live." With that Rena barged out the door, feeling as if Edrea had barged out right along with her. Rena was defending her sister's honor, after all. Besides, there was only twenty minutes left of the grueling four-hour class.

Jujitsu practice will definitely be therapeutic this evening, Rena thought as she walked toward the large blue building where she trained. It was right off Highway 12 and only a few minutes from her house. Convenience was everything at the moment, especially because she was not only working and in college but also preparing for WEG. And with the vampire world slowly creeping up beneath her feet, Jujitsu made her feel more in control—not that she could fight off a vampire with martial arts, but any sense of control helped.

Rena entered the building ready to let everything go. There was something safe and Zen about the clean white walls of the gym, which were adorned with martial arts banners and Asian tapestries. One wouldn't think Zen and self-defense went together, but they really did. Zen was all about learning to shape negativity into something controlled so that the practitioner could stare death in the face from a place of tranquility. This was Rena's place to combat the burn, to work through her troubles one grapple at a time. All the pent-up emotion inside was the steam she'd need to get her black belt the following month.

Not only was getting a black belt cool, it was also something that might be useful someday. Even though it wasn't really a defense against vampires, it would come in handy if a human attacked her. Lots of creeps out there attacked women. She learned that well after what happened to Edrea.

Rena was paired up with a big guy named Ed. He was about her age and also had his brown belt, so he would be the challenge she needed. While they practiced their sparring combinations on the mat, Rena focused all her tension into every move, as if Ed was the monster who had defiled her sister, or

Victor, the vampire she'd love to kick in the head. Maybe even the righteous girl in class who thought she had the answer to everything. She centered all those feelings into a ball of fire that she could push outside her body and shape into her defenses.

"That's great form, Rena," the instructor said in passing.

She barely heard him. She was more focused on blocking Ed's moves and finding the perfect moment to use her throwing technique to flip his large body onto the mat. That time finally came. She got his elbow in just the right position where he would have nowhere to go but up and over her back and down on the mat. Hearing his body slapping the blue mat made her giggle.

"Damn, Rena," Ed said. "Who the hell are you fighting today?"

She shrugged. "Oh, you know . . . someone pissed me off in class today."

"I'm sure that's an understatement," he said, smirking. "You've got all the moves today."

Rena smiled and walked to the benches to get some water. Ed followed and sat with her on the bench. They watched the other students spar while they rested their backs against the wall.

"You seem more and more fueled every time I see you," Ed said, leaning forward to rest his forearms on his knees. "What's been going on with you?" Ed wasn't exactly a close friend, but she always enjoyed their banter and conversation during class.

"I just have a lot going on, you know?"

"We can talk about it if you want."

Actually, they couldn't. He would think she was crazy, not to mention she would be breaking the code of secrecy.

"That's okay, Ed. Thank you though." Rena nudged Ed's shoulder and forced a smile. She knew he meant well.

She refocused on the sparring students before her and the techniques they used to disable their opponents. Learning all that she could made her feel stronger and smarter in the face of the darkness she knew existed around every corner.

Regardless of how many friends and family were there to support her, sometimes Rena still felt like a girl against the world.

12
Rena: Pet Cemetery

A month had already passed since Rena had seen her immortal sister and uncle, since she had made a deal with Nadine. Now that she had so little time to do the things she dreamed of, time itself seemed to slip between her fingers. But she had reached one goal on her list of things to accomplish before she . . . well, before she *died.* The previous night, she earned her black belt in Jujitsu. Her mother and father came to cheer her on.

Tony didn't.

She remembered the look of excitement in his eyes when she got her brown belt months earlier. He had taken her out for yogurt afterward. He was so proud. He had always been so supportive.

Her eyes burned with tears, and her stomach twisted inside as she put on some black sweats for her new job. It wasn't a *real* job. She worked for Nadine. The witch had a secluded farm on the outskirts of Bodega Bay. Beneath a rundown barn was an underground lab. An animal lab. The vampire witch tested animals with Bacillus F. Of all the things she could have Rena do, she had her tending to animals Nadine tortured. She knew Rena had a soft spot for animals.

"Evil bitch," Rena said under her breath as she sat in her car. Her fingers constricted around the steering wheel, and her chest pumped in and out with anger.

For Rena it was the worst feeling in the world watching animals suffer and having no way to stop it. It was torture, and torturing her brought Nadine pleasure. That was clear. Well, Rena wasn't going to play nice anymore. She would make the twisted woman pay. Maybe not any time soon but someday.

Rena watched the sun set during the forty-five-minute drive to Bodega Bay. The sun had never looked so beautiful and warm. Then it disappeared behind the hills, giving way to the chilly night. When she reached the fog bank, the warm residue of the sun's rays tingled slowly beneath her skin.

She turned off the curvy Bodega Highway onto Bay Hill Road. It was her and Edrea's favorite shortcut to the ocean. The road began under towers of fresh eucalyptus and then opened to a windy road through soft golden hills that seemed to stand on top of the world. At the highest point, the ocean appeared in the distance. The turnoff to the barn was under the eucalyptus, so she didn't make it to the ocean on those visits.

The tall eucalyptus stood begrudgingly through the cool fog, as if judging her. She slowly stopped her car before the rusted gate on the left. Bassét was leaning against it as he did every night she arrived. He wore his usual dark hooded sweatshirt and fitted jeans, something he wore only when he was there. It's not like he could catch a cold or that anyone from America would recognize his face, especially out there. Rena shook her head as he turned and pushed the creaky gate open. She drove forward, and he closed it behind her. Instead of stopping so he could get in her car, she continued down the long dirt road to the barn. Of course, that didn't stop him from fleeting to the passenger door of the moving sedan and getting in anyway.

"Hey," he said with a smirk as he slipped into the passenger seat and closed the door. "You don't look happy to see me."

"I'm thrilled to be in your presence, Bas-sét." She squeezed the steering wheel to avoid punching him in the face.

"You don't have to be so abrasive, Miss Rena. Would you prefer that I be an asshole?"

She raised her eyebrows in disbelief. "You are an asshole."

He laughed deviously. She fought a smile and then quickly quelled it as the car pulled up to the barn. All the poor helpless animals filled her thoughts. A tear rolled down her cheek before she realized the emotions had bubbled to the surface.

Bassét's smirk disappeared. He didn't jump out of the car the way he usually did. Instead, he turned toward her and rested his arm on the back of his seat. "What's wrong now?"

"How could you ask me such an idiotic question?"

He shook his bangs from his eye. "I can't read your mind. I don't have that power, remember?"

Rena scoffed and shook her head. In any normal situation, she might have found his thick accent sexy, but at the moment it annoyed her.

"Would it be so hard to talk to me?" Bassét asked, as if he was a friend who was there to comfort her.

Rena let out an uneasy laugh and cranked her head toward him. "Talk to you? Do you have any idea who your vampire mother is and what she's done to my family? Want to talk about that?"

His gaze shifted to the barn, as if to avoid her question.

"Nadine told me she didn't have that man defile your sister. He was only meant to—"

"Meant to what?" she snapped. "Beat her nearly to death, so she could be turned? And I guess you find it completely normal that she tried to burn me alive too?"

Rena jumped out of the car, slammed the door, and stomped toward the barn. She heard the passenger door open and shut and steps nearing.

"Rena, I'm sorry . . ."

She pried open the heavy sliding doors, their creaking drowning out his words. She didn't have enough energy to ask Bassét why he worked for such a horrible monster. She had to save her strength for the animals. For easing their pain.

Bassét closed the doors behind her as she walked across the hay-dusted dirt floor of the dimly lit interior. The tall wooden walls of a barn used to be a comfort to her, but now they reminded her only of animals crying in the night. She headed toward the right corner. Behind the last empty horse stall was the hidden stairway to the lab.

She stopped at the edge of the small tack room and bent down and flipped up a red oriental rug to reveal a wooden door. Bassét kicked the remaining carpet away and lifted the door, revealing a concrete stairway.

Rena trudged down the first barely lit stairway and then followed it down the second, which ended at the metal door to the lab. She stopped in front of the door and took a moment. Like every night she was there, she blocked out as much of her surroundings as she could. She wouldn't have noticed that Bassét had opened the door if it hadn't been for the bright lights of the lab boring into her eyes. She squinted and walked drearily into what she felt was an animal torture chamber. The door closed securely behind her.

The moment the five chimps saw her, they screeched and rattled their cages. It was as if they knew she was their only chance to escape. Their pleas scratched at her heart. She would find a way to free them, or so she hoped. Unfortunately, a vampire was always stationed there, even when the scientists were gone.

Rena peered cautiously into the three rat cages on her way to greet the chimps. She stopped in front of one of the cages when she noticed the white rat she called Flint lying immobile on the little cloth bed she'd made him. She stared for a moment, knowing he was dead.

She swallowed hard and glared up at the scientist near the back wall who was going through test tubes. His name was Arnav—the Sanskrit word for ocean. He was the kindest of Nadine's scientists, the only one who wasn't as cold as stone. He glanced over his shoulder to acknowledge her in his strange emotionless way. She remembered his dark knowing eyes from the first night she'd seen him. He was the scientist who had taken her blood at the Décret mansion.

Rena walked by the chimps' cages, running her fingers along the barred doors. A lump rolled up her throat when they cried and grasped at her fingers. She hadn't named them yet. They were too much like humans. The moment she named them, the more attached she would be. That was why Nadine tested chimps. Chimps share 96 percent of human DNA. Rena didn't know what Nadine used the animals for, but she imagined it had to do with sunlight.

"What happened to Flint?" she asked coldly.

Arnav ignored her question as he held a test tube of blue serum and carefully administered drops from a syringe of clear liquid into it.

"You killed him with your poisons, I assume," she said.

"I assume every single bottle of lotion or shampoo in your

bathroom cabinets are animal cruelty free?" Bassét smirked with raised eyebrows from a chair in the corner. His tone was accusatory, not questioning.

As much as she wanted to counter his statement, she realized she couldn't. The truth was, she wasn't sure she'd read every label of every product she used. Even in the human world, animals were tested for various reasons. Some were for medical treatments, but many were for cosmetic products, and she didn't agree with that. She hated that she hadn't done more to be part of the solution.

Rena walked over to one of the chimp cages. She unlocked the latch and opened the door. The little chimp, the smallest of the four males, jumped into her arms and wrapped his frightened limbs around her neck and waist. She squeezed him tightly as her eyes burned with tears. All her muscles constricting, she fought the wave of emotion.

She looked over at Flint's cage and put the chimp back into his. She knew what she had to do when an animal died: discard the body and prepare the cage for a new victim. It was terrible. She locked the chimp's cage and stormed over to Flint's, tears streaming down her hot cheeks. She opened the little white rat's cage and took its lifeless body into her hand, stroking its limp head with her finger. She removed his little cloth bed and folded it into her sweatshirt pocket. Then she went to the door and slammed it behind her.

Once in the barn, she sniffled on her way to the back door, the rat's body resting in her palm. She opened the creaky wooden door and took in the chilly breeze. The thick cold air felt good in her lungs. She took quiet steps toward the large oak tree that sat at the base of the moonlit hill behind the barn. The swaying tree always whispered in the wind, and she imagined it sang a lullaby to all the animals resting in peace below its gentle branches. There were already nine graves: five rabbits, three rats, and one chimp. And now Flint.

She walked to the large trunk of the tree and laid her free hand against its cold bark, as if thanking it for bringing peace to all the resting animals in her pet cemetery. She looked up at the few patches of starry sky through the fog and listened to the whispering leaves as the wind flowed through the branches. Even though this was a horribly sad place, it was the only place she could stand to be. She looked down at the hand shovel lying next to the trunk and kneeled beside it. Her sad eyes traveled over all the little graves that had stones lying on top of fresh earth.

"I'm so sorry, Flint," she said, laying his body delicately on the grass. With the little shovel, she dug a small hole about a foot down and six inches square. She took the cloth bed out of her pocket and placed it inside the darkness. Then she placed Flint's little body on his bed. She covered him with moist earth. Then she chose three stones she'd saved under the tree and placed them neatly on his grave.

"Arnav said he didn't suffer. His heart just gave out," Bassét said, standing before the graves.

Startled, she wiped her tears away, leaving smudges of dirt on her cheeks. "I don't believe a thing anyone says around here." She stood up and approached the tree, as if it could give her strength.

Bassét walked carefully toward her and leaned his shoulder against the tree, facing her. "I may be a vampire, but I'm not this evil thing you think I am. I don't want you to be hurting."

Rena gave him a skeptical look, her gaze softening when she saw what looked like pain in his eyes. "I . . . I can't . . ."

Bassét stepped closer to her shivering form, his hands lifting to her cheeks and wiping fresh tears from her face with his thumbs. He hesitantly wiped the smudges of dirt off her soft skin, his unsettled gaze falling on her lips.

Rena rolled her lips in and let them part when she noticed him staring at them. The touch of his flesh on her face, albeit cold, soothed her, and she leaned into his hand. He closed the gap between them in response, pressing his cool lips to hers, softly tasting her upper lip with his tongue. Rena had no idea what had overtaken her. Perhaps all her emotions had taken control, but she let them do with her as they wished. She moaned into the kiss, deepening it, and wrapped her arms around him. He pressed her against the tree, his thumbs wiping tears from her cheeks and chin. He pulled back, his hands dropping from her face to grip either side of her sweatshirt. His eyes found hers, and Rena gasped when she saw the look of confusion on his face. When he saw she desired him just as badly, he took her face back into his hands, kissing her deeply and caressed his tongue with hers.

Bassét's cold hands traveled down her face, his thumbs tracing down her chin and neck, then over her shoulders and the outsides of her breasts until they continued down her waist. His impassioned fingers worked their way under her sweatshirt and squeezed the soft skin of her back. Rena was so entranced by the wet, heated kiss that she didn't realize where his hands were until she felt his cool fingers. His bare touch against her flesh made her moan. She couldn't recall ever feeling such pleasure. It was almost too much to handle.

She pried her lips away, only to find herself staring into the fire of his dark eyes. Then she dove back into the kiss like it would sustain her life. He pushed into her, as if he couldn't get any closer, growling between his deep moans.

"This is reckless," she exclaimed, pushing the tips of her fingers into his pulsating chest. She wedged her forehead against his as he deliriously tried to reunite their lips again. "I don't know what's happening."

Her breaths were fast and uneven, and his matched hers, as if his lungs had reanimated to fulfill the human-like exertion. Bassét's hands squeezed her shoulders and then found the bark of the tree, his forehead rubbing gently against hers. His lips stole one last tender kiss before he pushed away.

"I don't know what came over me," he said, stepping backward.

The last patch of starry sky was still visible above, the thick fog having curved around the crescent moon. Its light glistened off their skin and turned Bassét's eyes bright red. He looked down at the misty earth and slipped his hands into the pockets of his jeans, as if he were ashamed of himself, or perhaps of what he was.

Rena's eyes found the bright moon above, her breathing finally normalizing. Then they fell reluctantly on Bassét's red eyes, which glowed like two rubies in the darkness. "I have to tend to the animals," she said. She started toward the barn, skirting around the animal graves. She stopped on the other side of the pet cemetery and looked back over her shoulder. "Are you coming?"

The corners of Bassét's mouth curved up, his body perking up slightly as he followed her inside.

13

Jule's Return

"Edrea!"

The amicable sound of my dearly missed roommate's voice drew me out of a deep meditation. I looked toward the gazebo from the garden bench on which I was sitting. Under the soft glow of the half-moon, Jule walked toward me in a long flowing blue dress.

I popped off the bench and met her at the base of the garden, throwing my arms around her neck. "I thought you were coming back next week."

"I was, but Uri called and filled me in on the possible super-vamp problem. He thought it'd be safer if I came back early." Jule didn't look as concerned as I felt. Actually, she seemed peppy about it. I raised my eyebrows and fought a smile in response to her jubilance.

Samuel emerged from the back door of Uri's house and

came down the path carrying a large flowery suitcase. "I'll leave your luggage in your room, Jule," he said in passing and then nodded to me. "Good evening, Edrea."

"Evening, Samuel," I said, smiling widely.

Jule grabbed my hand and dragged me toward the cottage. "Come on, there's so much to tell you."

"Likewise," I said. Actually, I had loads to tell her. I doubted she knew I was a maker now. A maker of a youngblood who despised me—not that I blamed him. In the month since the bridge incident, Elias and I had made little progress. The good news was, he was apparently the most self-controlled young vampire Uri had ever met. The not-so-good news was he still wouldn't talk to me, and I felt horrible about what I'd done to him.

Jule trotted ahead of me toward her room, the crescent moon casting a subtle luminescent glow through the living room window that overlooked the midnight garden. Everything in the cottage was a shade of soft gray except the light shimmer of her ocean-blue dress and the red-and-yellow long-stemmed roses in the glass vase on the kitchen table. The moment of beauty calmed my nerves as I followed her.

"Alright, ladies," Samuel said in his soothing tone as he left her room. "Do your catching up, but don't forget we leave for the Wave in an hour."

"Roger that," I said, giving him a sarcastic salute.

Samuel grinned as he headed for the front door. Uri thought it was important I learn to condition my mind abilities. He had asked Samuel to train me, starting that night. The fact that the mental connection between Rena and me had blurred concerned Uri, and he felt I should reinforce it. I hadn't thought too much of it yet, since I knew the connection between Elias and me was probably behind the disruption. Uri wasn't convinced, but I didn't mind. I wanted a reason to go back to the Wave, and my fading connection to Rena did make me uneasy.

Apparently, the guards Uri had stationed at my family's house had reported some odd behavior over the last month. Every other day, Rena would leave the house before sunset and come home between three and four in the morning. It made me wonder if it involved another man. Why else would she come home so early? That definitely wasn't normal for her, especially since she needed rest for her part-time job, vaulting practice, and college. Until I could break back into the mental connection we had, we wouldn't learn of her whereabouts.

"I'm actually excited about this Wave place," Jule said, sitting down on her puffy bed. "I've learned a lot about controlling my mind ability, and Uri thinks Samuel can teach me how to be even stronger."

I sat beside her with a bounce. "I think that's a wonderful idea. We can become scholars of the undead mind together. Do you think the Wave offers a Ph.D.?"

"Doctors of vampire mind powers. We'd be unstoppable," Jule said. We giggled for a moment before Jule grabbed my hand. "On a serious note, you have to see this. What I've learned to do is pretty f-ing cool!"

Jule bounced to her feet and unzipped her suitcase. She flipped it open and searched eagerly through her clothes and shoes. "Here it is," she said, pulling out an ancient-looking rock figurine of a voluptuous woman. She sat down next to me.

"Cool," I said. "I know what that is. It's a Venus figurine, one of the first forms of art. I learned about them when I took anthropology once upon a time."

"Yup. This one was made by early Homo sapiens in Europe about thirty-five thousand years ago." She shifted the smooth object in her hands and looked up at me excitedly. "Are you ready?"

"Ready," I said, offering her a goofy smile. I looked into her swirling bluish-gray eyes and felt her release the wall to her mind. It came down with a rush along with blurred images of her trip to England and flashes of different emotions. One involved a vivid image of a tall dark-haired man. "Wait a minute, who's he?" I asked as she tried to steady her thoughts.

"Hold on as I focus. There's time enough for that," she said with a feigned English accent and a smirk.

"No, I want to know about him now," I said, grinning.

She smiled and closed her eyes. In a flash, her thoughts were swept away, followed by gray. Her thumbs moved over the figurine's bulging belly. The gray of her mind opened to an image, like fog dissolving in the air. For a moment it felt like déjà vu because the image replayed the last few moments in reverse—Jule popping up from the bed in fast motion and walking backward to her suitcase. Then it got weird. The images flew backward like frames on a filmstrip. Some were black, which I imagined was when the figurine was inside her suitcase, but others came to life with images of all the hands the figurine had touched, with only split-second pauses.

One particular image made the zipping frames come to a halt—the moment when a peculiar blond woman first presented the figurine to Jule. It was as if the figurine was the center of the universe in Jule's mind, allowing her to see everything in its circumference, and Jule had the power to freeze the images and travel its depths. In this frame of the past, the smooth but aged grayish rock figure sat in Jule's fair hands looking up into her kind blue eyes, as if it had a mind of its own. She looked serene as she held it in her palm, fascinated by its ancient beauty, her curly blond locks falling over the fronts of the velvety green ruffles covering her shoulders and the soft white fabric enveloping her robust bosom. She seemed to like this image, and I could see why. She looked stunning.

"I'm going to go back much further now," Jule said, the left corner of her lip turning up.

I watched in her mind as the images flew by again, so quickly nothing was discernible. This occurred for quite some time, but I waited patiently in awe. Finally, the images slowed, featuring pieces of a foreign place and foreign people.

The images halted at a scene inside a cave. The figurine was unfinished; only the large protruding breasts were present. The stone didn't look like a rock. It was smoother and lighter in color, between beige and white. The middle-aged woman carving the figurine looked pre-human and dirty, her bronze leathery skin smudged with dirt and her brown hair matted. Dark animal fur clothed the bulk of her body, but her dirty feet were bare. She sat cross-legged before a fire that set the jagged cave aglow as she continuously struck the work in progress with another rock, a smaller harder-looking stone with a sharp edge.

On the other side of the fire was a man who was dressed similarly in furs. He sat on his heels, crouched over some kind of rodent he was skinning with his bare bloody hands. It was gross, actually. Both had mostly Anglo features, their bodies fit but muddy.

I gasped in awe when I realized these people were most likely some of the first modern humans from the Ahmarian culture, dating around 40,000 years ago in the Upper Paleolithic. That was the culture anthropologists believed created the Venus figurines.

"Jule, are they who I think they are? This is unreal!" I said.

As I spoke, a child covered in furs galloped on all fours behind the man who sat by the fire, pretending to be some kind of animal. I laughed when it reminded me of something Rena used to do when she was a child.

"That's my favorite part," Jule said, giggling. "Brace

yourself though. I'm about to bring you to the figurine's origin, the tusk it came from."

My eyes widened. "Tusk?"

"Yup. Mammoth."

"Shut up!"

At that, the images flew back further. They stopped after a few seconds, landing on what looked like a scene from a caveman movie. Seven men covered in furs surrounded an enormous raggedy mammoth, pointing their long spears at its belly, chest, and rear. The sky was gray with sporadic clouds, and a few ice sheets lay on patches of green, rocky earth. The ferocious men taunted the fearful bucking beast until the first spear tore through its thick chest fur. The mammoth bucked again, swinging its large white tusks and trunk back and forth, its big brown eyes pleading for its life.

"I can't watch this, Jule," I said, pulling my mind back slightly until the vision blurred.

"I know. It's horrible. Hold on." Jule let the images jump forward to the scene after the slaughter. The mammoth lay immobile and bloody on the cold ground. Two men stood before one tusk as three stood at the other. They sawed at the base of the tusks with thin sharpened rocks.

The scene saddened me, and I pulled back completely, the images lingering in my mind. "I can't watch this anymore," I protested.

"Amazing though, right?" Jule said, her blue eyes pained with emotion.

"It is, and I definitely want to do this again. I just have a hard time watching a creature suffer a slow death, animal or human."

I wasn't a vegetarian in my human life, and I was definitely a predator in this one, but I didn't relish suffering and pain. Even though I understood the cycle of life all too well and had made peace with it, I could never bring myself to watch the painful undoing of a creature.

"I feel the same way," Jule said. "This is only the second time I saw part of that scene. I always skipped over it when I was practicing." Jule tossed the figurine back into her suitcase as if it were a demonic item.

"I miss crying," I said, leaning my elbow against the pillow behind me. "Don't you? Sometimes I wish I could just have a good cry, but the tears never fall."

Jule's gaze dropped to the floor as she stroked the soft fabric of her dress. "I miss that more than anything. I was quite the crier, once upon a time." She looked up at me and smiled.

I smiled back, but the warmth quickly faded from my face. "I should probably tell you what happened while you were away. I did something awful."

Surprise filled Jule's face, but her eyebrows lifted with light skepticism. "It can't be that bad, Edrea."

"I don't know. I thought I was doing the right thing when it happened, but now I'm not sure."

Jule watched me in suspense, like she couldn't imagine what it could be. "I won't judge you. You know that."

I looked up shamefully at her sincere eyes. "I turned a man, Jule. He was dying. He had just saved a little girl in a house fire, and I couldn't just let him die."

Her eyes widened in surprise. "You turned a firefighter into a vampire?" she asked with a dry and humorous tone.

"That's not why I turned him," I said, trying not to smirk.

One of Jule's eyebrows lifted even higher. "So, where is this man?"

"He hates me, and he has every right. I'm actually not sure where he is right now, except that he must be within a few miles of here. I can still feel him."

"You can *feel* him?" Jule said, her brow still arched.

"Yeah, you know, the same way Pierre and Angelique could feel us after they turned us. It's like this strange tingling sensation that makes my skin itch," I said, pinching my arms.

"Interesting." She leaned on her side and rested her head on her palm. "I'd like to meet him."

"I'm sure you will soon," I said, sitting up and leaning straight-elbowed over the edge of the bed.

Samuel appeared from the dark hall, his shoulder resting against the wooden doorframe. "You girls ready?"

"Has it been an hour already?" I asked, smirking.

"Not quite, but I thought you wouldn't mind an early start."

Jule and I perked up and grinned, as if we shared a silent secret.

14
Lessons of the Mind

The dark, gentle bay waters flew by on our left, the lights of the city following on our right as Samuel, Jule, and I fleeted to the Wave. I felt more at ease now that Jule was back. Sharing life's ups and downs with a friend made the downs more bearable.

We stopped at the tunnel entrance, the darkness concealing our sudden materialization into real time. I always wondered how a human might react if they happened to watch at just the right moment when vampires came out of fleet. I giggled at the thought.

"Care to share what you find so humorous?" Samuel asked.

"I was just thinking about how strange it might look to humans if they saw a bunch of vampires materialize out of thin air."

"It is quite funny," he agreed. "They usually look puzzled for a moment before realizing they're most likely losing their mind." He winked at me.

Jule giggled as we approached the tall barrier to the tunnel entrance. Samuel's eyes surveyed our perimeter before he gave the signal to jump over the wall. We landed on the other side in unison. Jule and I tidied our clothes, as if we weren't about to fleet again.

"This place is a little creepy," Jule said.

"There aren't many underground tunnels in the city that aren't," I said, laughing.

We took off in fleet and stopped a few seconds later before the entrance to the Wave. Jule and I untangled our hair and smoothed out the frizz. Samuel was bald, so he just stood there waiting for us with one eyebrow raised.

"How did you guys know exactly where to stop?" Jule asked.

I pointed to the faded graffiti image of the Wave on the wall behind us and smirked.

"Okay then," she said, nodding.

"Shall we, ladies?" Samuel beckoned with a wave of his hand.

We stepped into the deep indented doorway, and Samuel knocked twice on the hidden metal door. Just like the first time I visited, Consus cracked the door from the other side. I smiled with pleasure, seeing the glimmer of his Roman nose.

"Wavelength equals H over MV," Samuel recited at the glowing space between the door and the frame.

Jule and I exchanged puzzled expressions. Consus opened the door and bade us enter, smiling warmly.

"The password has changed, I presume?" I said, smirking at Consus.

"The Broglie equation," Samuel replied as he stepped into the round room that was accented with golden hues and long red curtains. "I'll translate: the wavelength equals Planck's constant over movement times velocity. Haven't you learned all your quantum equations yet?" He winked at me.

"Oh yes, every one of them," I said sarcastically. "I can't even add basic numbers in my head," I whispered to Jule. "I'm light-years away from understanding quantum physics at a mathematical level."

Jule giggled under her breath. "Let me know if you need a tutor. I'm a quantum physics expert."

"I'm sure you are," I said, cackling. Jule looked back at me and laughed.

We followed Samuel into the room. Our faces went serious when we were met by all the straight faces that belonged to the cloaked vampire scientists. Apparently, the Wave wasn't a place to goof around.

"Girls, let's head to the library." Samuel walked gracefully around the center table and headed toward the adjoining room.

We followed him excitedly. I itched my forearms as we neared the arch of the library—not that the entire underground chamber wasn't a library. Not until I stepped into the softly glowing room did I realize my skin itched for good reason. None other than Elias was sitting at a small wooden desk with a book in one hand and a pen in the other hovering over scratch paper. I stopped short, and my chest tightened when his large blue eyes lifted from his book to glare my way.

"By the look of that man's overbearing affection for you, I'm guessing he's Mr. Fireman," Jule whispered in my ear.

I nodded slowly. "Bingo."

Jule's wide eyes studied Elias for a moment and then found my countenance, which I'm sure had a look of terror and embarrassment. Grimacing, she walked awkwardly to the bookshelf and drew out an old leather book. She opened the ancient binding and flipped through the first few pages. I remained uncomfortably still in the front of the room, my eyes wandering over the old books stacked neatly from floor to ceiling. The hairs on my arms stood up, my skin prickling as the strange familial force intensified between Elias and me. Perhaps it was because I could feel his piercing blue eyes penetrating my flesh. I avoided his gaze at all costs and walked toward the bookshelf, pretending to have spotted a text of interest.

My attention shifted to wood screeching against the cement floor where Samuel moved a black velvety armchair in front of a rose-colored loveseat with beautiful wooden trim. "Ladies," he said expectantly, his palms tilted.

Jule and I made our way to the little couch and sat on its two puffy cushions. My insides tingled with unease, and what felt like a million tiny needles pricked at my back. I turned toward the newly made vampire sitting almost directly behind me and sucked air into my tingling chest. I turned back toward Samuel and rolled my shoulders in an attempt to relax.

"This first exercise requires a lot of calm and concentration," Samuel began. I shook my head, highly aware that would be impossible with Elias sitting right behind me. "Is there a problem, Edrea?"

My eyes found Samuel's "down to business" expression. I knitted my eyebrows together and nodded over my shoulder.

"I see," Samuel said.

"Don't mind me," the familiar deep voice said behind me. A book slapped shut, causing an echo across the library. "I was just leaving."

"It wasn't my intention to run you out, Elias. I'm sure we're all sorry to have disturbed your studies," Samuel said sweetly.

My eyes dropped to the floor and searched for imperfections in the smooth cement. The itch beneath my skin calmed, indicating Elias had left the room. The farther he moved away, the weaker the sensation became, but my skin craved his presence in the absence of the thrum he left behind.

Samuel and Jule let me settle into my thoughts as they discussed some basic meditative methods to calm the mind. Their words came in and out as my thoughts circled to find a place where they could be pushed to the brink of my consciousness. The murmur of the scientists' collaborative voices didn't bother me. They actually aided and comforted me in my centering, as did the gentleness of the long red velvet curtains between the bookshelves that towered over us.

One particular thought would not cease to circle, however, and my curiosity got the best of me. "Samuel, why was Elias in the library? I mean, he must have been summoned to the Wave for a reason."

Samuel clasped his hands. "I believe Uri felt Elias should have something to occupy his mind, and he asked Consus to have Elias help with research. It turns out Elias was studying for nursing school before he died."

A horrible wave of guilt chilled my body. "Oh." There was quite a bit I hadn't gotten the chance to learn about Elias. Due to his refusal to be anywhere near me, Uri had taken over my maker responsibilities.

"If you're going to succeed in connecting to Rena mentally, all your thoughts must be focused on her," Samuel reminded me. "I want you to travel to a place in your mind that brings you comfort. It can be anywhere you've felt at peace. Perhaps that place you like in the mountains near your family home?"

I traveled to that place for a moment, to the golden strands of dancing grass, to the endless crickets' song, and the infinitely twinkling suns amidst the dark abyss. He was right. It was one of my favorite places to connect with the universe, to feel at ease.

He'd taken me up there the previous year, only months after my grandma died. But it wasn't my favorite place. No, my favorite place was a world I'd created on my own, one where no one could go but me, somewhere I was completely protected. Actually, Rena had been there too. She was the only person in the world who had met me there. That was why it was a place I could find her. It made me wonder if this special world of make-believe truly existed, like she and I had made it real.

"Have you found it?" Samuel asked.

"I have." I looked over at Jule, who was sitting quietly in her own meditative state.

"Okay, now close your eyes and see yourself there," he said. I rested my back against the sofa and did as he asked. "Push the outside world away until you can barely sense it, except for the sound of my voice." His voice had a calming gentleness that was easy to follow, a tone that seemed to travel across time and space in an ethereal way.

The grayness of my mind dissipated like the morning fog, and in its place that familiar green valley materialized. The soft grass cushioned my feet, and the old decrepit tree stood before me with its graceful twisted branches. All around me the luscious hilly valley reached into the horizon. Hidden behind the distant hills, I knew a great blue ocean waited.

"Do you hear my voice?" Samuel's soft voice wavered outside the blue-and-red sky as a white dove circled high above. I imagined it carried Samuel's essence. I let it soar at a distance.

I nodded.

"Now, imagine your sister is with you. Feel her presence around you. Hear her thoughts like they are yours."

Again, I did as he asked. I imagined her there, standing next to me on the grass, watching the pastel skies. I took her hand in mine. I breathed in the sweet air and felt it satiate my lungs, because in this world I was human again, like her. I turned to look at her, but she stared straight ahead. "Rena," I said into her ear, but my voice didn't sink in, just echoed into the distance. "Rena . . ."

The twisted tree creaked in the wind, the warm air brushing the hair off my shoulders, but it didn't seem to touch Rena because she wasn't there.

I looked up at the soaring white dove. "I can't reach her," I said, my words traveling into the sky, which turned a shade grayer. The breeze grew cooler, sending a chill down my spine. "Rena!" I called out through the wind.

"Edrea." My phantom sister's lips whispered my name, but her eyes focused on the red horizon.

The skies grayed over, and the air chilled, but the colors remained warm behind the distant hills. Perhaps that was where I could reach her, near the calm ocean water. The ocean was always somewhere we loved to go together.

Without another thought, I started walking toward the hills, toward the warm sunlight, toward the ocean I knew was there. The wind picked up with every step I took. Behind me, the old tree rocked violently. I turned and watched its branches swaying in protest. I looked ahead, grasping at my arms in the chilly wind. Something wouldn't let me go any farther. Something kept me away. The wind bit at my skin, blowing loudly until all I could hear was the freezing air screaming against my eardrums. It was too much to bear any longer.

Samuel's face materialized in front of me, along with the walls of books around us. The feeling of his hands squeezing my shoulders brought me back into the warmth of the library. I wanted to cry, but I couldn't in this world, so I just sat there silently and stared at him, my chest clenching inside.

"You will reach her, Edrea. It will take time and conditioning, but you *will* reach her. We'll try again tomorrow."

He kissed my forehead softly and walked toward the other room, as if he knew trying again would be pointless.

I blinked and swallowed my pain. The palm of Jule's hand felt warm against my arm. I turned to her and smirked. "I think she's keeping me away. She's hiding something."

Jule blinked at the floor and then looked back up at me. "What do you think it is?"

"I don't know, but it's not good."

15

Rena: The Perfect Night

The strangest sensation had unsettled Rena on the drive home from the lab. It felt like someone poking at her brain from the inside. She swore she had heard Edrea calling her name. She realized it was most likely the delirium from working late nights and getting little sleep, but something about it felt real.

She parked at the curb in front of her house, the same spot in which Edrea used to park. She turned the ignition off and embraced the silence. Soft wind blew delicate green leaves across the windshield, and the neighbor's tree in front of the car sprinkled it with little violet petals. She peered through the passenger window to see if her mother was up washing dishes in the kitchen. The kitchen light was dim, like it usually was at three in the morning, but the house appeared still, which meant her parents were likely asleep.

Her mind traveled back to the drive home, to the external

force that had poked at her brain, her sister's voice calling her name. Could it have been real? When she thought she'd heard Edrea calling to her, her body had frozen up, her mind immediately blocking the connection. The ironic thing was, only the previous month she had longed for any connection to her sister, but now all she wanted was to keep her away. Rena was ashamed to be working for a vampire as malicious as Nadine. She was ashamed she worked in a lab where vampire scientists tortured helpless animals for what could only be an evil cause. Most of all, Rena was terrified that if Uri or Edrea learned she was working for Nadine, the immortal witch might hurt her family.

Rena slung her bag into her room, watching it land with a thump and a clank on the carpet. She'd kept the torch lighter and hairspray, just in case.

Dingo whined excitedly on the bed. She slumped onto the mattress and blew her bangs out of her face. She rustled Dingo's wide wrinkled grin and smothered him with kisses on his nose when he wouldn't give up.

"I don't know what I'd do without you, honey," she said with the last breath of energy she had.

She was so tired, she didn't even have the strength to get a glass of water. She knew her body needed hydration, but she didn't feel thirsty. She felt only the incredible weight of her eyelids and the physical and mental exhaustion from working every other night at the vampire lab and every other day as a vet tech at the local pet hospital. At least there she could actually help *some* animals.

Her body fell against the warmth of the mattress, her head sinking into her pillow. The tepid breeze from outside seeped through the window above her, whispering that summer wasn't too far away. When her eyes closed in defeat, her mind replayed the moonlight kiss under the oak tree. She couldn't believe she had let Bassét catch her off guard, and in the pet cemetery of all places. It was something she'd decided not to let happen again. It had just poured more guilt into the ocean that was drowning her from the inside out. She still missed Tony and felt she had betrayed him in more ways than one.

And yet, now that a month had passed since she'd last seen him, the kiss between Bassét and her lingered at the surface of her mind. That kiss would make working at the lab all the more unbearable. It was hard enough watching the animals suffer after being injected with poison, only to bury them when their hearts gave out. She also had to avoid Bassét's constant gazes, which she swore were filled with passion and pity, though she wasn't sure which was more prominent. Sometimes she would ignore him, and somehow that would make her feel guilty too.

She had tried denying there was something between them, but that got harder as time went on. Even if she didn't want to admit it, Bassét was clearly protective of her. He'd even convinced Nadine to give her every other weekend off, so she had more time for college and vaulting—more time to pretend everything was okay. How she was able to find time for everything was beyond her. Thankfully, in only a few months she would get her bachelor of science in zoology.

Her eyes opened to the moving shadows the swaying tree cast on the walls and then closed one last time as her mind swallowed the entirety of the madness of her life. Before she fell into a deep sleep, she remembered what she'd almost forgotten.

She had made time to cram what felt like an entire life's bucket list into the twelve months Nadine had given her because that was all the time she would ever get.

* * *

The day went by in a flash of fur and barking at the pet hospital. Rena had actually gotten seven hours of sleep the night before and had woken somewhat rejuvenated. She would need to keep it up if she was going to have the energy to finish college. Her molecular ecology class was every Tuesday and Thursday, and her four-hour senior seminar class was on Mondays before Jujitsu practice. She only really had time to study on weekends and between work and vaulting workouts on Wednesday and Friday before she left for the lab at night. She should be considered a superhero.

She pulled into the parking spot in front of her bedroom window and sat in silence for five minutes after she turned the car off. It was her usual ritual to wind down before she went inside, when she could enjoy a little more daylight to herself without vampires lurking about. It was 6:00 p.m., and as it was late April the sun would set in forty-five minutes.

She jumped out of the car and hurried to her room, hoping she could get in a good run before dark. She threw on her favorite jogging leggings and a green T-shirt and then grabbed Edrea's favorite purple tennies. Dingo jumped about the room with bursts of Chewbacca groans, because he knew that meant he would accompany her on the outing.

As she finished tying her laces, her phone lit up and vibrated with a text. "Ugh." It was none other than her stalker, Bassét. Even though she wanted to hate him, his name on the screen made her stomach tingly and warm.

She rested on her hip next to the bed and opened the message. "Look outside your window," it said.

"You've got to be shitting me." She shuffled toward the window on her knees. "Fuck," she whispered.

Under the dimming sun and the reddish-blue sky, Bassét was leaning against her car with his dark fitted jeans, a black shirt, and a fashionable gray sweater. When he saw her looking at him, he quirked an eyebrow and smirked in his sexy yet annoying way.

With a puff, she popped up and stormed toward the front door, glad her parents would be at the casino until long after dark. She swung the front door open and went to confront him, intending to tell him he wasn't welcome at her home. But the moment she reached him and saw the curious determination in his dark eyes, she was tongue tied.

She stopped under the eucalyptus tree, shaking her head, her lips parting to tell him to get lost, except no words came out. Her scowl made his smirk waver, but for only a second.

"I'm taking you somewhere tonight," he said before glancing down at his shoes and then back up at her.

"Are you insane? You do realize humans need sleep, right?"

"You can sleep in the car. Besides, you'll enjoy this, I promise." He raised an eyebrow expectantly as he waited for her response.

She studied him for a moment, wondering what he meant by that. "Where exactly do you think you're taking me?"

"Just trust me, Rena. Can you do that?"

"Oh, sure. That's a great idea," she said, swiveling around and heading toward her front door.

Before going inside, she glanced back. Of course, he was still waiting there in the same position, knowing he'd already convinced her. Shaking her head in disbelief, she went inside to grab her shoulder bag, which contained her vampire-repellent weapons. She stopped in the foyer when she saw Dingo waited by the front door, eager for his walk. It made her feel terrible.

"I'm a horrible mother, honey, I know. I promise I'll make it up to you." She went to the kitchen and grabbed him one of his favorite treats—a bull dick, as she liked to call it. Technically, that was what it was. He snatched it out of her hand and ran into the living room to tear it apart on the floor.

Finally, Rena went to grab her bag, knowing Dingo would chew and swallow the entire bull dick in less than five minutes. "I'll be back soon, Dingo. Love you," she said, locking the front door behind her.

When she made it to the edge of the porch, Bassét's blue Audi was already parked in the driveway with the engine running. She sighed, feeling like a total fool, and then jumped in. She dropped her bag on her lap and rested her arms on top of it, turning to Bassét with raised eyebrows. "So, where are we going?" she asked dryly.

"You'll see. It's about a two-hour drive, so you should probably take a nap. Like you said, you're only human." He smirked and then took off down the road.

"Two hours!"

"Don't worry, princess. I'll have you back before dawn. You can sleep on the way home too."

Falling asleep in a car with a vampire shouldn't have been as easy as it was, but Rena was clearly still behind on sleep. Either that or she actually trusted the fanged immortal day-walker. She preferred to believe only the first option was true.

When she opened her eyes and looked out the window, she saw that enormous redwoods surrounded them in the dead of night. She bolted upright to find Bassét waiting patiently for her to wake up. She wasn't sure if that was creepy or not, knowing that meant he'd probably been watching her sleep. "Where are we?"

"Redwood National State Park."

Rena looked around the dark, quiet forest, realizing he'd driven clear off the road and into the middle of who knew where. "Okay . . . why?"

"If I told you, it wouldn't be a surprise, would it?"

"Like, surprise, I'm going to murder you?"

"Come on, Rena. I've had plenty of chances to murder you

already, don't you think?"

She shrugged. "So, are we just going to sit awkwardly in your car all night?"

Bassét quirked his brow with a grin and then jumped out of the car. He appeared in front of the passenger door in an instant and opened it. "Are you ready for this?" He reached in and waited for Rena to take his hand. Rena sighed loudly and grabbed her bag. "That's not a good idea," he said, making her pause. "That will definitely scare off the surprise."

Rena rolled her eyes and then looked at him, puzzled. "Okay." She placed her bag on the floor and stared at his hand in annoyance.

"It's just my hand, Rena. Nothing to be afraid of."

She took it reluctantly, and he pulled her into his hard torso, holding her firmly against him with his cool hand on her back. She raised an eyebrow as if to say, "I told you so," only to freeze when she noticed their lips were a breath apart. Her heart flipped inside her chest, and she took in a deep breath. It was hard not to be taken in by his dark eyes. They held so many feelings and stories that she wanted to learn about, even though she couldn't admit it yet. She let him embrace her for a moment, and in that instant, the only things that existed were the depths of his eyes and the crickets in the breeze.

Before she broke her promise to herself, she pried her body away and took a few steps into the moonlight that crept between the towering redwoods. She inhaled the sweet scent of the forest, letting her eyelids close when the breeze tickled her lashes.

"So, what's this big surprise, B?"

"To show you, you'll have to trust me, and you'll have to be very quiet."

She watched how the moonlight glowed against the redwoods, which reached into the sky. She remained still, even when he approached and then stopped so close to her body that his shirt brushed against her back. "Can you do that, Rena?" he whispered.

She wished she didn't crave him the way she did, but she realized it was probably too late to stop now. "I'll try."

He walked a few feet in front of her and then stood dead still, like he was listening for something. After close to a minute of silence except for the sounds of the forest, he turned to her. "I know this is going to remind you of a certain vampire movie, but it's the only way to get close enough. Hop on my back."

"Hop on your . . . are you kidding?"

"Just do it." He bent his knees and let her put her arms over his shoulders and wrap her thighs around his middle. Then he secured her legs over the folds of his arms.

"Have you really seen that movie?" she asked, poking fun at him.

"Yup." She could see his wide grin, even from behind him. "The scene in the forest was my favorite part. Hold on tight."

Before she could take another breath, the wind blew against her face, making her gasp. She squinted as a blur of shadows and dim light streamed around them. Then just as quickly, the blurs slowed, and the ground below became a ribbon of yellow before coming into focus. A bed of yellow-and-white dandelions appeared around them amid the redwoods, their soft petals accented by the gentle moonlight.

"Shhh," Bassét warned, standing as still as a deer that sensed danger. Rena listened intently but could only hear the crickets and the breeze brushing the slender redwood leaves. A minute passed before her ears attuned to the subtle snapping of a twig in the distance. Bassét shifted ever so slightly. "It's not far," he whispered. "You must stay as still as you can. Quiet your breathing too."

Fascinated, she did as he asked, clutching him so tightly that their bodies moved in unison. Her breathing slowed as he moved toward the sound of the twig snapping. His movements were so stealthy that she could barely hear his feet. He was like a predator in the night, her body twisted around him like another appendage.

About thirty feet away, she heard the faint crunching of leaves. Her eyes focused on the glow of moonlight between the trees. The shadow of a large cat-like figure moved through the dim light. Her breath hitched. It was a mountain lion. Her heartbeat thrummed louder in her chest. She swallowed hard. Bassét lightly pinched her leg in warning. He continued to take steps, so quiet that not even the crickets ceased their song.

To stop her leg from cramping, she carefully adjusted her body on top of his. She tried not to break their equilibrium, but the spasm was too painful, and the movement made the dry earth crunch beneath their feet. The mountain lion's form twitched in their direction. Rena and Bassét kept very still as the large feline moved closer to investigate. Rena felt her breath palpitate as the mountain lion drew near until it was only ten feet away. It was the most beautiful thing she'd ever seen. Mountain lions were her favorite mammal. Seeing one up close in the wild had always been a fantasy of hers. Bassét gave her legs a quick squeeze, as if to prepare her for a quick departure. She knew the cat was close enough to see and smell them, and that could make the situation dangerous.

The moment the mountain lion's gaze locked onto theirs, every muscle in its body bulged into a threatening form. It was hard to tell if it was about to attack or run. For the most beautiful moment Rena had ever experienced, she, the vampire, and the mountain lion stood perfectly still and studied one another under the moonlight. It wasn't until that moment that Rena noticed the crickets had fallen silent, and only the sound of the wind in the trees remained. She was no longer afraid. The encounter was too intense to feel fear. Instead, her rawest emotions bubbled from her core until she found herself sniffling, tears running down her face.

Surprisingly, her sobs didn't agitate the wild creature. Instead, the graceful beast slowly backed away between the trees, and disappeared into the glowing greenery. Bassét set Rena down, and she turned away to wipe the tears from her cheeks.

"How did you know I loved mountain lions?"

"I didn't," he replied quietly. "It was a lucky guess."

She turned around and found his dark eyes, which glowed red under the moonlight. "Why are you doing all of this for me?"

"I don't know. Maybe I care about you."

He watched her silently as she approached him, his eyes following her until she stood just below his gaze. She looked up at him, her arms hanging unsure at her sides. He lowered his head slightly and studied the emotions within her big brown eyes. Then, as if he yearned for her touch, he reached down and brought her hands up to his chest. When she let him do as he wished, he took both her shoulders into his hands and closed the distance between their lips, kissing her deeply. She let him because it was the most beautiful place in the world and the most magical night. It was all that mattered. All she wanted to feel.

In that perfect forest under the moonlight surrounded by all the creatures of the night, she had never felt so human.

16
An Eventful Evening

The most peculiar thing woke me tonight. It was at that moment between sleep and consciousness, when lucid dreams present as reality, or perhaps reality presents as a dream. In my case, because vampires aren't known to dream, it must have been a vision. It was the face of a man who I didn't recognize. He had smooth features, dark foreign eyes, and dark wavy hair. It was as if he floated right above me as I lay in bed, but in an instant, he disappeared.

An intense itch under my skin brought me back to reality. I knew at once that Elias was near. In fact, I could hear his thoughts outside my room. Supposedly, Consus had counseled him on mind blocking, but Elias had clearly fallen behind on his lessons.

I turned my head toward the bedroom door, my fingers scratching at my forearms. My vampire progeny's mind felt strange, uneasy, and yet curious.

I turned on my bedside lamp and swung my legs over the edge of the bed. I took slow steps across the dark hardwood, the slight glow of moonlight shimmering beneath the long curtains. At the door, I stopped and listened. Elias remained on the other side with fractured thoughts, wondering if he should knock. I decided to make it easier for him.

I inched the door open slightly. Elias's gaze met me on the other side. The anger behind his blue eyes still sizzled from their depths, but something new emerged as well, something that looked like hope—and maybe a touch of shame.

He hesitated, looking down at the floor and hiding his fingers inside the pockets of his jeans. "Can I come in?" His voice was tentative and unsure, even carrying tones of embarrassment. This was different.

I smiled warily and stepped aside, letting him open the door himself. He entered, his eyes studying the dimly lit room briefly. He went to the window, his fingers testing the softness of the velvet curtains as he pulled one open to peer outside. "I like these."

I felt my eyebrows converge. "I'm guessing you didn't come to talk about my curtains. I mean, I thought you hated me."

"I thought so too," he said matter-of-factly. The curtain fell from his hand, and he turned toward me. "I've been talking to Uri."

I walked to the end of my bed and leaned against the edge. His eyes unintentionally braised my bosom before I realized I was wearing a white nightgown that was a bit transparent.

"Sorry, let me grab my robe." I went to the door and wrapped a green robe around my body, then made my way back to the bed. "So, what have you and Uri been talking about?" I hoped he didn't think I'd tried to make a pass at him, seeing as I let him into my bedroom without being fully dressed. Of course, now he'd gotten control of his mind and blocked his thoughts.

161

His eyes fell to the floor and then wandered back up to mine. "Your uncle told me about Alexio."

My chest clenched. I was surprised they'd even talked about him. I was too taken aback to say anything. Instead, I just stared into space.

"I didn't mean to bring him up. I feel like an idiot. I'll just go." He started for the door.

"No," I said. "It's okay. It's just that I haven't talked about him for a long time."

Elias turned hesitantly toward me, like he wasn't sure why he was there. "I lost someone, my wife. I mean, she didn't die. She left me for someone else not long before I became this thi—" His head dropped, as if his words pained him. I wasn't sure if it was the thought of his wife cheating or him becoming a vampire that bothered him more.

For once I actually didn't have much to say and was more interested in listening. I wanted to know his story, his pain. I scooted back atop my soft mattress and curled my legs under my body. "You can open the curtain and let the moonlight in if you want."

His eyes flashed upward. "Actually, I'm curious to see this mural of the stars I heard Consus painted on your ceiling."

I couldn't help but smile as I clapped my hands twice to light the room. When the room was aglow, Elias's eyes widened with awe as they traveled the painted galaxies above.

"It *is* beautiful," he said. As soon as a smile crossed his face, it disappeared, like he was ashamed of showing me any glee. He turned toward the window again, pulled the curtain aside, and stood as still as night. "To be honest, I am still angry." He turned toward me, this time letting the temporarily suppressed anger surge to his eyes. "I didn't try to kill myself, like you thought, but that doesn't mean I wanted to be brought back to this world, especially as a creature that draws life from people instead of sustains it." The anger seemed tangible as it stirred again within his blue eyes.

I shrugged. "I don't know what you want me to say, Elias. I've apologized for what I did, and I still feel badly. I acted on a whim. Not that it redeems my actions, but you do realize that amongst all the people you helped save as a firefighter, there must have been a few who didn't want to come back, just like you. Did you ask all of them if they wanted to live before you saved them?" Saying that may have been insensitive, but I couldn't help being transparent with my thoughts.

His brow furrowed with intensity. "That was my job!"

"I realize that. You were a hero, which is one of the reasons I had a hard time leaving you to die. Do you not understand that just like you saved all those people, I thought I was saving you?"

He stared at me with a mixture of fury and bewilderment. He threw down his hand, turning back toward the window. He made a fist, attempting to control his emotions. With his back to me, he waited until his body calmed. "You know that feeling when you hurt so badly that you can't wait to fall asleep at night, but then you wake up in the morning to that same pain?"

I watched his back muscles draw together as he contained the same pain of which he spoke, a pain I knew well. His suffering was a sharp reminder of it, and being who I was, I could feel what he felt at that moment. It streamed like fire through my chest, burning through my limbs until I wished I could scream. But I just sat there silently and watched him.

"I thought I'd finally found happiness with a woman I loved. I was a fool. She tore me apart when she left me for someone else. I felt like I had no one. Every morning I woke up, I hoped the pain would be gone, but it never left me, not even a year later."

"Didn't you have family? Friends?" I asked as delicately as

possible.

"No close friends, the kind who stay around. I enjoyed being a hermit. I didn't want to worry my mother either. She had her own troubles. And my father . . . it's been fifteen years since we last spoke. He died a few months ago."

I wanted to take his pain away, to absorb it from him like I'd done for others, but I didn't want to take his power away, his ability to work through it himself. I'd already lost his trust by giving him immortality without his consent. "I can be your family now, Elias. I can help you find happiness again. Being undead isn't as bad as it seems. We're not exactly undead either. We're more like an evolved race."

His pupils flared. "Isn't as bad as it seems? You made me a vampire, Edrea. Haven't you read Dracula? Aren't we evil blood-drinking creatures?"

I wasn't sure if he was serious, and I couldn't help but laugh. "Please tell me you're kidding, Elias. Is that really what you believe? Do you really think we're evil? Do I look evil to you? How about my uncle? Do you *feel* evil?"

"I don't know what I believe." He let out an uneasy laugh. "What do you believe? Enlighten me. Isn't that what you're supposed to do as my maker?" He sat restlessly on a quilted jade-green bench against the wall next to the window. He dropped his elbows to his knees and tangled his fingers in his light-brown hair.

I swung my legs over the edge of the bed and sat up straighter. "I don't believe in good and evil, if that's what you mean. You know, God and the devil. I believe humans created those stories out of fear because not knowing why we exist and where we go or don't go when we die brings people more anxiety than they can handle. I don't presume to understand why anything exists or why life in the universe exists at all, let alone vampires."

"So, you don't believe in God?" he asked with a mixture of

curiosity and frustration. I couldn't help but read his unbroken thoughts, but from what I saw and felt from him, he had never believed in a personal god either.

"No. I don't believe something just because millions of other people do. I don't believe something just because it's written in a so-called holy book from thousands of years ago. There's been many, Elias. People have believed in more than two thousand gods over the course of human history. Which one should we believe in? If I had been born in India, I would have believed in Hinduism and thus many gods. If I had been born in Saudi Arabia, I'd have been a Muslim. In Italy, a Catholic. We are a product of our social construct. Who's to say one version of god is truer than another? I've always felt it was arrogant to presume one's god or beliefs are truer than someone else's, like one religion was handed to one chosen culture from a deity in the sky." I could ramble about this forever. Talking about these things was always illuminating.

He lifted his head and quirked an eyebrow, appearing interested in the subject. "Then what—or who—do you believe created the universe?"

"That's my point, Elias. I don't assume to know the answers to anything. To believe in anything absolutely isn't wise, in my opinion. Once we do that, we create walls to all other knowledge." I sighed and scooted my legs back underneath me. "But when it comes to why the universe exists, I look at it this way. If a god has always existed but didn't need to be created, why can't the quantum-mechanical fluctuations behind the Big Bang have always existed without needing to be created? Why can't existence alone be a force in itself, just like people believe a god to be? If we take into account all we've learned from science and the laws of physics, the 'god of the gaps' explanation is too simple."

Elias fell back against the wall and gave me a puzzled look. "I guess I never thought about it very deeply." As if he'd let himself get too comfortable, he sat up straight again. "Quantum mechanical fluctuations? What's the god of the gaps—never mind. Regardless of the existence of a god or gods, good and evil, how can we live this way, being vampires feeding on human blood? How does that make us good?"

I smirked. "Our choices make us good or bad, Elias, not how or what we eat. Feeding on blood is part of our nature. We can't survive without it. We can feed without harming people, and there are even ways of getting blood without feeding from the source. Basically, just like there are good and bad people, there are good and bad vampires."

"How do you know I'm the good type?" he asked. "You don't know me at all. Being a firefighter doesn't make me a good person by default. I know plenty of firefighters who aren't." He shook his head and grunted, sitting back against the wall. "It's not like I'm a firefighter anymore anyway. That life is clearly over."

"You can still help people, you know, if that's what you enjoy doing. Being a vampire doesn't have to change that. In fact, you're stronger now than you were as a human. You have the ability to help even more people than before." I looked toward the moonlight coming through the gap in the curtains, feeling drawn to the night. "Personally, nothing has ever made me feel more complete than helping people, especially people who are hurting. That didn't change when I turned, and I don't think it's changed you either."

Elias didn't respond, just got up and walked to the curtains. He pulled one back until the night sky stared down at us through the window. His anger seemed to have drifted away, but something cold remained between us. Perhaps he didn't hate me, but that didn't mean he'd forgiven me for turning him, forcing him back into a world that brought him so much suffering.

"Uri also tells me something bad is coming," he said

grimly. "That he's not sure we're entirely safe. He says I need to train to defend myself against vampires who may harm us and that it has to do with you and your human sister and your bloodline. He says you have special abilities that these vampires want to utilize. What exactly did you bring me into?" The softness in his eyes had hardened again by the time he turned to me.

Of course, he was entirely right. My lips parted as I looked up at him, but I couldn't find any words that would make our dire situation any less so. I had brought him into a war, and he was one more person I'd have to worry about. As far as he was concerned, I'd brought him from one hell into another. How different from my own maker was I really?

The sound of the bedroom door creaking broke our uncomfortable silence. I looked to the door to find Mikale stepping into the room. His ocean-blue eyes traveled from Elias to me before his eyebrows jumped. "Elias. Edrea. Hope I'm not interrupting anything important."

"Not at all," Elias said, his eyes dropping to the floor. "I was just leaving." He started toward the door, nodding to Mikale as he passed.

"Making progress, I see," Mikale taunted as he strode toward me.

I swung my legs over the edge of the bed, my head dropping in exhaustion. I puffed out a heavy sigh. In a blink, two fingers softly lifted my head back up to two beautifully familiar swirling blue eyes. "Edrea," he said sweetly, pushing himself between my knees.

Before I knew what had happened, his cool tongue slipped between my teeth and caressed mine. I wanted to stop him, but I longed for a man's touch. When I didn't reject his affections, he pulled my body into his, like I'd been his all along. Until that moment, I hadn't realized how my body had yearned for him. How easy it would be to give in to what felt like my carnal thirst, as if he were a glass of water after a week in a barren desert.

I pushed away slightly, prying my lips from his, which only seemed to intensify his cravings. "Do you think this is a good idea, Mikale?" The more I thought about it, the more I wanted him, and I couldn't widen the distance between our lips.

"Of course it's a good idea. Do you not miss me as much as I've missed you?" He drew my bottom lip into his mouth, and his tongue tenderly swept inside my mouth. The pleasure that shot threw my body and gathered between my legs was unbearable.

My skin tingled when he urgently worked my nightgown from under my buttocks and over my head, leaving my body naked. He growled as he pulled my body back into him, hoisting my legs around his back and lifting me up. Then he leaped with me clinging to him onto the middle of my bed and pressed his torso and pelvis against my bare tingling body.

As he kissed me with unabated fervor, my thoughts wandered to an unexpected place. To a night a few months earlier when we went to the nightclub under the Castro Theater. We were supposed to have spent the evening together, but instead, Mikale had joined two aggressive lady vamps at a corner table. I tried to focus as our lips and bodies entangled atop the bed, but the memory of the encounter with the two females intruded on the moment of passion. The more-than-friendly way they kissed his lips in greeting and the way their overflowing bosoms somehow became an extra growth on his body. Especially the way he had been so quick to abandon me, as if I'd suddenly become less than a priority. And just like that, my passion died, like a match blown out by the wind.

"Mikale," I pleaded, my body stiffening as I pressed my palms into his chest.

His gaze found mine, the passion in his eyes turning to

confusion as he noticed the change on my face. "What is it?"

"I can't . . . I don't feel right."

His body slid off mine, and he rested on his side, his chest against my shoulder. "Do you want to talk about it?"

I didn't look at him as I searched the words. "I'm afraid to go any further with this. I don't feel right inside. I feel more attached to you than I'm ready for."

"Attached?"

I turned to face him and found him staring at me in bewilderment. My eyes fell. "I thought I could handle this emotionally, but I guess I'm still just a girl deep down."

He brushed a lock of hair from my shoulder. "I really care about you, Edrea."

"I know you do. I really care about you too. I mean, I love you, if you get what I mean. You've been an amazing friend to me. I just can't get emotionally involved right now."

"I see."

"Do I sound ridiculous?" I laughed uneasily.

His blue eyes gleamed in his carefree way. "Not at all. You *are* still partly human, as am I, and I do get a little carried away sometimes."

"A little?" I smirked, knowing full well I was probably worse. My humor died momentarily. "I'm sorry."

Mikale sat up and swiveled to place his feet on the floor. He looked back at me warmly but seriously. "I understand, Edrea. I just feel comfortable with you. It's different with you."

I knew exactly what he meant, though I wasn't sure he knew the significance of his words. He was comfortable with me because I didn't pressure him. He was a kind and gentle man, but he wasn't the exclusive life-mate type. He was passionate and free, tied to no one, and that was the way he'd live for a long time, maybe forever. The kind of love he felt didn't seem to penetrate his core but instead resided just beneath his flesh, perhaps feeding his passions but not cultivating something deeper, something that could grow into a tangible romance.

Mikale left my bedroom with a twinkle in his eye and his impeccable charm, as if it were his immortal superpower. I scooted off the bed, shaking my head as I failed to wipe the wide grin off my face. There was something special about Mikale, something magnetic. The thing was, I knew his magnetism didn't work only on me.

I threw my nightgown back on and wandered out into the garden, taking in the moonlight and the sound of swaying trees in the breeze. I closed my eyes and inhaled the cool air to taste the night.

When my eyelids opened, my attention was drawn to the light coming from Elias's room in the east wing of Uri's house. The young vampire stood at the window, looking into the same garden. Even though it was too far to see exactly where his gaze went, I had the feeling he was watching me, studying me. It caused the tingling beneath my skin to simmer at the surface. I scratched my arms and wondered if he could feel it too. The strange metaphysical connection. When he wasn't near, something didn't feel entirely right, like his well-being affected mine.

Pierre's face flashed in my mind, making my chest tighten. Had my own immortal father experienced this? The itching? The worrying? The instinct to protect what he created, as if I was an extension of himself? I longed for him, for the relationship we once had, the parts that were good, even though it was hard for me to admit.

The night had only begun, and yet so much had already happened. Elias had opened up to me, or at least attempted to. I had finally told Mikale how I felt—after our lapse of self-control, of course. And now I yearned to reconnect with Pierre, to tell him how I felt, how he had hurt me. For the moment that would have to wait. I would never be able to mend the connection to Rena if I let every other emotion consume my conscience. I needed to find my grounding, my peace of mind.

I knew exactly what I needed. My yellow surfboard with painted blue waves came to mind. My freedom. I had a few hours to spare before Jule and I went to the Wave to practice with Samuel. Plenty of time. That familiar excitement stirred inside me. I hadn't taken to the ocean for months. I missed it terribly. Surfing the twinkling night waves had always filled me with a sense of a cosmic connection. I had stashed my board months ago in the bushes above the cliff at the edge of Uri's land. It called to me now more than ever.

17

Rena: The Last Chanukah

The first night of Chanukah came like a flash. Everything that had occurred during the last eight months was only a blur. It was December, and Rena had accomplished everything she'd hoped she would. She had completed her bachelor's degree in zoology with a 3.5 average. She'd earned her black belt in Jujitsu. She'd spent every moment she could with her family and Dingo, when she wasn't working for Nadine at the lab, of course. She even drove across the country to North Carolina in September with Trish and Prince, to compete in the World Equestrian Games, every equestrian vaulter's dream. They had placed ninth, but that was still something.

Traveling to WEG had only been possible with Bassét's help. Nadine had agreed to let Rena go under the condition that he accompany her. They'd traveled mostly in the evening, at night, or in the early morning to avoid the sunlight. Rena had convinced

Trish it was so they wouldn't overheat Prince in the Midwest and Southern heat. She'd also convinced Trish that Bassét was just a friend she'd met during a competition in Europe and that he was staying in a hostel nearby.

She had lied to all her friends, but she could no longer lie to herself. In all the months that she and Bassét had spent together, her feelings for him had gotten stronger. She had been so busy accomplishing the impossible that she hadn't realized a relationship had grown between them until it was too late, a passionate forbidden romance.

Her parents sat next to each other across the living room table on the couch, putting a little blue candle into the first branch of the golden chanukiah. Rena sat on her knees on the carpet and lit a white candle she held in her hand. Liron kneeled in front of the table on her right, sadness in his brown eyes. Dingo watched happily from his new puffy bed on the floor. As Rena held the tiny orange flame over the candlewick on the chanukiah, their voices harmonized as they sang the first prayer of Chanukah. "Baruch atah, Adonai Eloheinu, Melech haolam, asher kid'shanu b'mitvotav v'tsivanu l'hadlik ner shel Hanukkah."

No one in the family spoke Hebrew or was religious, but the Jewish holidays brought the family together to share a special tradition tied to thousands of years of history. Rena wished Edrea was there too. Without her, it wasn't complete.

She looked around the flickering room. All the lights were dim, and the two candles created a subtle golden glow around the table. The trees blew in the wind outside the window and made the night even more magical. It was the last Chanukah they'd ever spend together. In three months Rena would disappear, just like Edrea had. She looked at her parents' faces, at Liron's. They stared at the flames, still carrying the loss of a daughter and sister behind their eyes. Rena would only add to that loss. The thought grew in her throat with a heavy lump.

Her phone lit up atop the table, and she drew in a sharp breath when the name appeared on the screen. Tony. She grabbed it and pulled up the message. "Heya, Re," it said. "Happy first night of Chanukah. I'm in town on the way to the city for the holidays. I stopped at the coffee shop down the road. I was hoping you wanted to catch up. I miss you. Hope you don't mind me texting."

Rena finally let the air out of her lungs. *What was it with men just showing up without warning?* She stared at the text, the candles dancing in front of her. For a moment her family evaporated before her. She couldn't deny she missed him too. Tony was the first man who ever loved her the right way, who made her feel beautiful. Just him texting brought back a longing for a life she would never have. But she couldn't leave the world of the living without making things right with him. She let her fingers take over, typing words that almost didn't feel like her own. "I'll meet you there in 20."

She might as well bid farewell to everything at once, but first she would fully enjoy her mother's potato latkes. She popped up and headed to the kitchen to grab one from the counter. Liron followed her.

"So, was WEG everything you dreamed it'd be?" he asked as he snatched the same latke Rena had reached for.

"Hey!" she laughed and then settled for the next-best potato pancake. She placed her latke on a plate and added a spoon of sour cream and applesauce, the only way to properly eat a latke. "It was awesome. It was too bad you, Mom, and Dad couldn't fly out." She was glad, actually. They were all safer at home under Uri's watch.

She thought back to all the hard work she'd put into

qualifying for the amazing world event. She and Trish had spent nearly ten hours a week practicing for WEG between their jobs and school. After graduation, they had crammed in an additional five to ten hours to polish their routine. Rena had given it her all. She wanted to do something fantastic in the last year of her life, something she hoped would shine into her next existence, the one she'd live for an eternal night.

"I watched you compete on national television." Liron took the spoon from her hand playfully, the way he used to before Edrea disappeared. "Edrea would have been so proud of you," he said with suppressed emotion.

Rena looked up at him, feeling as if her heart stopped for a moment. It was the first time he'd mentioned their sister in a year. Rena smiled, and he smiled back. She wished she could tell him what she knew, that Edrea wasn't really gone. Not completely.

Her smile melted away the moment reality hit. What would happen to him when she disappeared?

"What's wrong, Rena?" Liron looked more than worried, even though she knew he was trying to hide it.

She forced a smile, but her insides felt like they were burning straight through her flesh. "I just miss her." She did miss Edrea. She just didn't tell him the whole truth.

"Me too."

Rena smiled and then quickly changed the subject. "Are you staying here tonight? I'm going to the café down the road to meet Tony, but I'll be back soon."

"Sounds good. I'm not leaving till morning," he said before taking a bite of his fully loaded latke.

Rena grabbed her bag from the table and picked up her keys as quietly as she could so as not to alarm Dingo. "Can you tell Mom I'll be back soon? I don't want Dingo freaking out. I'm gonna sneak out the side door."

"Sure." He didn't ask her about Tony, even though Liron always hoped they'd work things out.

As soon as Liron rejoined their parents in the living room, she slipped out the side door, closing it carefully. The moment the evening air blew against her face, she pressed her back to the door, her eyes burning. She couldn't imagine Liron having to lose another sister. It was too horrible a thought. And her parents. She wished there were another way to protect everyone she loved, but deep down, she knew there wasn't.

She was what Nadine wanted.

On the way to the café, she tried to harden her emotions. She'd done a pretty good job of it over the last five months. She had been forced to. She realized the poking in her brain she felt often was most likely Edrea trying to break through to her. It was a constant battle to keep her out. It made the guilt even worse, but at the same time, she knew it was to protect their family. She had to be strong for them. If Edrea were in the same situation, she would have done the same. In fact, staying "missing" was what Edrea had done to protect the family from vampires, to protect Rena. She realized how hard that must have been for her. How lonely.

Rena pulled into a parking spot in front of the cheerfully decorated café, two large trees with tiny Christmas lights arching over her sedan. The moon was bright and full, so bright it dimmed the stars. She looked through the windows of the café, immediately spotting Tony. He was wearing the yellow-and-gray plaid shirt she'd bought him the previous Christmas. The last time she'd met him there, he'd sat at the same table. He smiled widely the moment he glimpsed her. She couldn't help but smile too. After breaking things off with him the way she had months earlier, she was relieved he wasn't angry with her.

When she set foot inside the café and got a better look at

his handsome chiseled face and beautiful hazel eyes, her heart melted all over again. He stood when she reached the table and gave her a long warm hug. She closed her eyes and took in his minty scent.

"I've missed you so much, Re." He released her to look into her eyes. "How have you been?"

The moment she saw his honest adoring eyes looking back at her, she realized that perhaps this wasn't the greatest idea. Bassét crossed her mind, and she sucked in a sharp breath to contain her guilt. She had been so afraid she hadn't truly loved Tony, that she had taken advantage of him in some way. Why else had she moved on in only a few months? But now, remembering how wonderful it felt being near him and having him look at her with so much love, she realized she'd always loved him. She had done what she did to protect him too. A new thought hit her. What if he was in danger just by being near her?

"Tony, maybe this isn't a good idea." Seeing the joy die in his eyes killed her all over again. "I just wanted to know that you were doing well, to wish you a Merry Christmas," she added nervously.

"Come on, Re. Sit down for a bit," he pleaded.

Rena sat down hesitantly, avoiding eye contact. She rested her elbows on the table and curled her fingers under her chin.

Tony sat across from her with his back to the window. "Re, what's going on with you? You don't seem yourself. I'm worried about you. Whatever's going on, you can tell me about it. We've been close friends for years."

He grabbed one of her hands from under her chin and pulled it across the table, squeezing it in his warm hands. An unbidden tear rolled down her cheek, and she took in a deep breath, lifting her eyes to meet his. This was a big mistake. She had no idea what to tell him, and all the pain and loss from their breakup came rumbling to the surface.

"Tony . . . I . . ."

"I don't care what it is, Re, damn it!" he whispered, shaking his head. He glanced around the room before coming back to her. "We can start right where we left off. We can work through it together. I won't judge you. Don't you understand how much I love you?"

Tears flowed down her red cheeks. "I love you too, Tony, so much. I just can't focus on everything in my life right now and have a long-distant relationship at the same time."

"That's not it, Rena," he said, clearly not buying it.

"It is," she lied. She had no other answer to give him, even if she did want what he wanted deep down. Before Edrea disappeared, Tony was all she wanted.

She looked into his kind hazel eyes, seeing all the pain she'd caused him. He truly did love her, and she loved him. It made her question her choices for a moment. What if she left everything behind, tried to live a normal life? It painted such a wonderful picture in her mind of all the possibilities. Marriage. Children. A warm fun-filled life together.

A shadow of a familiar man appeared outside the window, drawing Rena's eyes to him. Bassét. Her insides froze, except for her stomach, which twisted into knots. He was standing under a tree wearing his black leather jacket, his hands inside his jean pockets. She could barely see his face, but what she could see resembled pain. Now she really felt like a monster.

Her eyes shifted back to Tony's, afraid he'd turn and see Bassét too, but all she found in his eyes were tears. How stupid she had been to believe they could make a clean break. Love wasn't clean. It was messy.

Tony wiped his tears away with his sleeves before they could fall. "I'm not going to force you into something you obviously don't want," he said heavily. "I just thought . . . I thought if I gave you time you'd—"

"Tony, this has nothing to do with our love. I've never loved anyone more than I love you. That's why I don't want you waiting around for me to be ready. I want you to live your life. You deserve that."

He got up and stood hesitantly next to the table for a moment. Then he leaned over and kissed Rena on the forehead. "I deserve *you*," he whispered before leaving her alone in her thoughts.

Rena watched through the window with tear-filled eyes as Tony disappeared from her life for probably the final time.

She left the café at once, remembering Bassét had been watching them. She was glad when she didn't find him. She couldn't bear looking into his eyes too, knowing she'd find a similar hurt that she'd caused Tony.

It was all too much. She wished she had a choice that wouldn't cause someone pain. With so much emotion to contain at that moment, she felt all the walls she'd built crumble to the ground before her. She leaned against the tree in front of her car, her body trembling. As she sobbed into the wind, she realized she didn't feel alone. It wasn't a feeling that someone was standing there next to her. It came from the inside. It felt familiar. That was when she realized what had happened.

Edrea had taken advantage of her moment of weakness. Her sister had infiltrated her mind. Rena closed her eyes, forming fists with her hands, hoping she could push Edrea out before she learned too much. She found herself on a familiar beach, the gleaming stars looking down at the turbulent waves with pity. In front of her, Edrea stood on the soft sand, and she didn't look happy. Rena froze. What had she done? It was too late.

Edrea knew everything.

18

Walls Tumble Down

I reached a grove of white-bark aspens, swaying thorny
rose bushes with white blooms concealing the spaces between each
tree. It was the only barrier between the ocean and the valley.
While I had stood at the threshold of the white forest, it was hard
to believe my physical body still existed at the Wave. I had worked
so hard over the last several months to reach Rena, and yet I had
made it only thus far. The winds were too strong in those woods,
too icy cold, and the thorns too sharp.

Then something unexpected happened.

The winds died down to a whisper, and the thorny rose
bushes stopped swaying. At that moment, that break in the storm, I
took the only chance I may have ever gotten. I ran through the
aspens toward the ocean until I reached the shore.

And then there she was, right in front of me, looking out at
the water, her brown hair blowing over her dark sweatshirt. Rena.

The waves weren't calm. They crashed turbulently before her, as if the ocean held her troubles. And it did. With each crashing wave, memories burst into the wind around us, playing out like a timeline of every memory she'd kept from me. Rena spun around at once, aware that I was there to see it all. I saw her in Nadine's office making a deal. Working in an animal lab with vampires who created some kind of serum, one that may allow immortals to walk in the sunlight. I even saw her love affair with Nadine's progeny, Bassét—a day-walker—though from what I saw in Rena's thoughts, he could only be exposed to a limited amount of evening sunlight. Everything spun around us until nothing was hidden, until her darkest secret was revealed.

Rena had promised to give her life to Nadine.

"I'm sorry," Rena said, her words echoing into the graying sky of our strange world. Everything stilled, even the ocean, the waves freezing over like glaciers. I could only stare at her in disbelief.

"Edrea." Samuel's voice brimmed the atmosphere above. A white dove hovered strangely in the still gray sky, as if from another dimension. I felt a tear roll down my cheek, a human sensation I could feel only in the make-believe world I had created. "Edrea."

The library at the Wave materialized around me. Samuel was kneeling in front of me, holding my shoulders.

"Samuel," I said with a start. "Rena. She made a deal with Nadine. She's going to let her turn her, keep her as her mind reader. We have to go for her now." I stood up, not entirely sure if what I saw was a nightmare or reality. I couldn't take the chance.

"Edrea," Jule said, standing to confront me. "Don't make any drastic decisions."

"Drastic decisions? Nadine is going to turn my sister, and Rena is going to let her. We need to kill Nadine once and for all."

Rage spilled through my veins. I realized it didn't matter anymore if we used peace or war. They would try to destroy my family either way.

Samuel stood and put his gentle hands back on my shoulders. "We don't work like them, Edrea. We never become like them."

"Are you implying we do nothing? You know, Uri was right. They're not just going to turn my sister. They're making day-walkers."

"What's going on?" Elias asked as he entered the library, seeming to have sensed my distress.

The hum under my skin from his presence no longer itched the way it used to. Knowing he was near calmed me. Everyone was silent for a moment. The silence brought me to my wits. Samuel and Jule were right. Waging an attack could make things worse.

I turned toward Elias. "Rena agreed to let Nadine turn her, to use her as a mind reader." My nervous gaze fell to the concrete floor. "Rena has been keeping me out, so she can work for Nadine in secret. The witch is making a serum that lets vampires out into the sun. One year. Nadine gave Rena a year." I walked toward the bookshelf, my fingers fisting into my hair behind my head. I spun toward Samuel. "Why didn't she come to me?"

I understood why before Samuel responded. While Uri and I had kept Rena at a distance to protect her and the family, she kept us in the dark, attempting the same.

"We'll worry about that later," Samuel said. "We must take the matter to Uri for now."

Jule stood at my side, linking my arm. "We're all in this together, as a family," she said, smiling warmly.

"Thanks, Jule." I couldn't quite form a smile.

We walked toward the library door; a newly constructed wooden door with an arch to match the opening. Elias stood before the hand-carved wood expectantly, grabbing the brass antique handle to open it. "I want to help in any way I can," he said.

I appreciated his willingness to overcome his troubles and his anger over my turning him months earlier more than he knew. The deep regard within his soft blue eyes met mine when he opened the door, and I slipped him a half-smile, all I was capable of at the moment. He closed the door softly behind us and followed protectively, as if he'd accepted us as his family at last. That realization comforted me. It even gave me hope. If a man like Elias who had been through so much sorrow could become a caring vampire, there was hope for all immortals. Even humanity.

We reconvened at Uri's house and gathered on the comfy chairs and sofas of his fire-lit office. Uri sat silently but pensively on his antique armchair, the left side of his face aglow from the fireplace. The moment we arrived, I let my walls down in my mind to let him see what I had seen without words. He didn't say a thing as we all waited patiently. Everyone figured I'd already revealed what I'd learned about Rena and her situation.

During the heavy silence, my eyes found the coppery chanukiah that sat unlit on a small round table behind Uri in the corner. It held one candle at the end and one in the middle. I had almost forgotten it was the first night of Chanukah. I had the feeling we wouldn't light it. It saddened me.

Uri finally shifted to pick up his flip phone and dial a number. As if on cue, Mikale, Gus, and Taralynn appeared at the office door. I looked over my shoulder at Mikale, glad he and the other guards were there to help. My focus shifted with surprise toward Taralynn when she accidentally let slip from her mind a brief erotic encounter between Mikale and her. She stiffened and guarded her thoughts again. My jaw dropped for a moment as I stared at them, feeling a bit of a sting. That was fast. Mikale's eyes quickly shifted from me to Uri when he realized what I had learned.

I turned back around slowly and shook the unwelcome carnal images from my thoughts. I looked at Jule, who sat to my left, wishing I could tell her what I'd just witnessed. Elias walked over from the fireplace and sat on my other side, bringing warmth from the flames.

Samuel eyed me from the bookshelf near Uri, raising one eyebrow. *Let's focus on the matter at hand,* he said in his thoughts. I looked at him strangely for a moment, wondering if he knew what had distracted me. His mind ability didn't encompass telepathy, but perhaps he'd developed a strong intuition in his 3,000 or so years.

I focused back on Uri the moment I heard him say my maker's name. Pierre. That was who he had called. "Sorry to bother you, old friend, but I was hoping you could drop by my office. We just learned some startling news." He slapped the phone closed a moment later, and I could have sworn my heart palpitated.

Muffled voices circled the den as I shut everything out for a moment. I was vaguely aware of Jule and Elias sitting at my sides the deeper I disappeared into the abyss of my mind. I had a dreadful feeling that something horrible would occur right before my eyes, and there would be little I could do to stop it. It was like watching a movie for the first time, not knowing how the story would end, except this movie was my life.

My eyes wandered over to Samuel, who was leaning against Uri's desk and mumbling indiscernibly in his ear. Couldn't my many-millennia-old vampire friend tell us what the future held? Then I remembered he didn't have much control over what elements of the future he could see. When images came to him they did so in relation to his own life. Though I was afraid he was hiding something he'd seen, something he wanted to change. He had been adamant about helping me penetrate Rena's mind over the past few months.

I sat up straight and focused on my kind African mentor. "Samuel, have you seen something?" My voice was calm, but his lengthy muscular form froze at my words. He looked at me with sympathy, as if he had a secret he could not reveal. The pearly whites of his eyes beamed with a world of worry, cradled so delicately by his silken ebony skin that shimmered with gold in the firelight. My uncle's eyes rose slowly, betraying his own worries.

"Samuel?" I pried warily.

"What I see in the future is not always clear, Edrea. You know that."

I leaned forward. "But you *have* seen something?"

Samuel's eyes hardened. "I have seen many things in my life that did not come to pass. As people's choices change, so does the future."

"Samuel, how can you withhold information at a time like this?"

"That's enough, Edrea," Uri warned softly. It always amazed me how he could get a point across and sound kind at the same time.

Samuel placed a gentle hand on Uri's shoulder. "It's okay, Uri. I understand her concern." Samuel broadened his shoulders to address me. "Edrea, some things are best not brought into the open. The images I see are for me alone. Sharing them can have dire effects that change the future for the worst, making things happen that were never meant to occur."

I understood exactly what he meant and knew he bore a heavy burden. Seeing things that may or may not transpire took great responsibility. That didn't exactly relieve my anxiety. I wasn't the only one who knew something terrible was soon to come.

My ears twitched to the sound of voices outside. Pierre and Angelique approached the front door with the external guards. My shoulders sank into the couch. One would think an immortal would become more resilient to a life like mine the more one faced dreadful circumstances that always waited somewhere around the corner. Apparently, I didn't. I was tired, weaker than I'd thought. Drained. I wasn't ready to face more. I just wanted to sink into the inner world that I had created and live there peacefully, maybe forever. Or perhaps find an abandoned island somewhere, escape the world until I was ready to face it again.

"Uri," Pierre said as he entered the room. Angelique nodded her regards at his flank, her wide green eyes overanxious, as usual.

Pierre glanced my way when he passed, his gray eyes showing concern. He never did smile much, but he always held a fondness in his eyes for me. For the split second our gazes met, a rush of memories with him loomed to the surface, as if we shared them together. They brought all sorts of feelings with them, some warm, some dark and cold. My eyes fell when his dark ones reminded me why his presence hurt me so.

My immortal father's pale face turned toward my uncle, the flames illuminating the red tones of his auburn hair. Jule's tension invaded my already apprehensive state. Since the battle at the Décret mansion, she had been on uneasy terms with her maker, Angelique, as well.

"Jule," Angelique greeted her, though in an abrasive blend of affection and authoritarianism. She wore her usual Audrey Hepburn-style dress right out of the 1950s. I remembered Angelique's style well. Her dresses were always fitted but had enough swing for fleeting.

Jule nodded, but I could feel her emotions disintegrating. She hadn't been given much of a chance to bond with her maker

186

after revamping over a year ago. Angelique had been too heavily involved with Décret authority back then, which was why I'd been assigned as Jule's junior counselor. Many Décret youngbloods had them. We served as mentors as the makers kept busy meddling in ISC legislation or whatever else they could impose themselves into to gain power for the Décret. Some had even succeeded in establishing ISC positions. I wondered what the ISC would do when they learned the San Francisco branch of the Décret had secret animal labs, so they could turn vampires into day-walkers.

"Can I assume it is as we feared, Uri?" Pierre asked grimly when he reached my uncle's shiny maple desk.

"I'm afraid it is. Edrea was able to mend the mental connection to her sister. Rena has been coerced into working in animal labs for Nadine. Your former superior succeeded in creating day-walkers, though it's not entirely clear how long these vampires with bioengineered Bacillus F can be exposed to sunlight."

"That would explain your attack, darling, how they managed to enter our apartment well before dusk," Angelique said, her hand sliding into Pierre's and squeezing with angst.

I wasn't sure if I was in shock from everything I'd learned in the last hour, but at that moment I was more curious about my immortal father's relationship to Angelique than I was anxious about the fact a new vampire race had been born, and my human sister was caught up in it. Not that I was surprised exactly. There was just something off about Pierre and Angelique, perhaps insincere, something of which Pierre was oblivious.

"Mon trésor, please do not become overwhelmed," Pierre pleaded to his mate.

My treasure? My eyebrows arched and then drew together. I stood up with a jolt. "Overwhelmed? We should be more than overwhelmed." The words spilled from my mouth, the reality of the situation hitting me like a slap to the face. "Not only has Nadine created who knows how many super vamps, but she's also probably planning to turn Rena into one of them—her own little Frankenstein baby vamp mind reader."

I almost laughed when I heard Mikale snort in the background, but this was far from funny.

Pierre dropped his companion's hand and turned toward me. "Edrea, as regretful as it is, I've come to know Nadine and her motives. If your sister is still alive after all this time, Nadine needs her. As long as Nadine feels she's in control, she will not alter her original plan. Unless she intends to revamp Rena immediately, we still have time." He watched my expression carefully, as if afraid to insult me.

"Edrea," my uncle said, leaning back thoughtfully in his oversized chair, his hands clasped over his lap. "I have to say I agree with Pierre. If what he says is true, Nadine does not plan to turn Rena for several months."

"Uri, I don't want my sister anywhere near Nadine or her crazy experiments, not for one more day."

Uri leaned forward to rest his forearms over the desk. His brow drew together until deep vertical lines wrinkled across his kind round face. His dark-brown eyes deepened with affection, reminding me of my grandmother, who was always kind. "Nor do I, my dear, but Rena has made this choice on her own, one she believes is protecting our family. I think it's important that we do not make any changes that will alarm Nadine. We will watch Rena closely until we have a plan that will not put her in immediate danger."

I sank back into the couch, feeling helpless. I knew Uri and Pierre were right. I also knew that Rena would have come to us first if it had been an option. Nadine had trapped her. To make it worse, her progeny had found a way into Rena's heart. From what

I saw in her thoughts, Bassét's intentions were not to harm her, but that was exactly what he would do, drawing her deeper into the world of the Décret.

No matter how I looked at it, I couldn't shake the feeling of dread that any choice we made would lead to a double-edged sword. That feeling was confirmed when I looked into the faces of my most respected mentors, my great uncle, who was the wisest man I'd ever met, and Samuel, a timeless warrior who was also the embodiment of kindness. Their eyes always held hope in times like this as well as a remarkable resilience. Even when they knew the road ahead could turn dark, they maintained a calm that I hoped to master one day. It was the kind of calm that only certain individuals could achieve regardless of the amount of time they lived on Earth. The ability to learn it was either part of their internal makeup, or it wasn't.

As I faced the odds that lay ahead and the darkness they could bring, I questioned who I was in every way. I hoped I could become the wisdom and strength that my mentors personified. It may be the only way to keep those I loved safe.

"Are you alright?" The concern in Elias's deep voice prompted me to find his gaze. When I saw the gentleness of his blue eyes, my mind emerged from the cocoon of thoughts and worries.

"Yeah. I just have a bad feeling."

I tried to pry my gaze away from his eyes but instead was drawn into their depths. The sincerity that lived behind the sky-blue surface warmed my core, and the fire that blazed from the center of his being seemed to pull me in like blazing ropes knotted around my ribs. There, floating in the darkness, I saw our figures embracing each other, our lips enveloped in a passionate kiss.

Heat poured over my body, followed by a wave of shame. I tore my eyes away, shifting my attention to the architecture of

Uri's desk. I was Elias's maker, for crying out loud. He must have realized I'd seen his deepest desire, because he started fidgeting violently with his cuticles.

I glanced up at Jule and then around the room, hoping no one had noticed our attraction, if that was what it was. Jule looked more startled by Angelique's presence than anything else, but she graced me with her usual empathetic smile. I relaxed when it appeared everyone was still focused on the discussion at hand. I should have been too. Before I brushed off what had happened secretly between Elias and me, I felt the urge to look over my shoulder at Mikale. Embarrassment swept over me the moment I saw his eyes, which had a look of jealousy. It felt strangely good, but it also stirred my overwhelmed emotions. I needed to pull myself together, for obvious reasons.

"We all must prepare ourselves. There may be perilous times ahead, things we've never dealt with before." The seriousness of Samuel's tone brought me back to the heaviness of our darkening situation. Our darkening world.

Jule sat up straight beside me. "Uri, if I may," she said hesitantly but with a certain pride. "I wanted to offer the support of my coven in England. They too have suspected the Décret have become a more serious threat, so they have used their mind abilities to unearth what they could. I talked to my source last night, and he said the coven is afraid the Décret has created some kind of weapon. They aren't sure what it is yet, but they're pretty certain it's a biological weapon against vampires."

I looked at her, wondering why she hadn't said anything to me earlier. Everyone gasped, and anxious voices erupted all at once.

"I didn't want to say anything until we were sure," she added, noticing the startled look I gave her.

"Everyone," Uri said, his voice calm and sovereign. The

room fell quiet again, and the air grew even heavier than it was before, if that were possible. Uri stood up slowly and leaned over the desk on his hands. "I'm afraid we must all do what we can to uncover what Nadine is up to before it's too late. We'll need all the help we can get."

19

Rena: Lonely White Flower

Bassét opened the dewy rusted gate, his form barely visible in the thick fog. The last gleams of sunlight barely shimmered across the tall eucalyptus trees that hung eerily still in the crisp air. While Rena drove through the gate, the stillness seized her as well. Something was amiss, dangerously wrong. What if Nadine had found out she'd leaked the plan to Edrea? Uri and Edrea would never do anything drastic. They were careful, lethally discreet. But still, the possibility crept deep into her bones, nestling in the marrow with frozen claws.

After she'd connected to Edrea and unintentionally shared her secrets, the link must have been severed, because she no longer felt her sister there. That made her nervous. She didn't like being kept in the dark now that Edrea knew everything. She hoped nothing horrible would come of it.

She peered around the foggy grassland and hills, rolling her shoulders and taking a cold breath. Because most things in that place felt wrong, she forced the feeling into her gut temporarily.

She stopped the car to let Bassét in. He jumped into the passenger seat and pulled his hoodie down, as if a vampire needed to stay warm. She was surprised he didn't look upset about seeing her with Tony. He just slid her his usual coy smile. The warm feeling it gave helped settle her anxiety. She smiled back, even though she tried not to, but it died like it usually did when reality hit, the realization that she was there to care for tortured chimps. They were the only ones that had survived for some reason, so Nadine stopped bringing in orders of bunnies and rats. Now there were six chimps in the lab. It was dreadful. Rena hated Nadine a little more every day and deep down hoped her sister would rip her head off. If Bassét didn't still have some creepy maker bond with the witch, she'd tear Nadine's head off herself the minute she was turned.

In truth, Rena wasn't entirely sure she had it in her to kill someone, not even an evil vampire. She didn't even kill spiders. But something told her she could kill Nadine if she had to.

Bassét stroked his fingers through the back of her hair along her neck, sending tingles down her spine and throughout her body. He watched her react to his touch, passion swirling in his brown eyes. She knew he'd grown more than fond of her, and it scared her that she returned his feelings. She wanted him in a way she hadn't experienced before. She was afraid she'd even grown to love him, though in a different way than she loved Tony. Different, but powerful. She let his fingers travel to the back of her jawbone and glide along her chin until his thumb brushed the top of her bottom lip. She couldn't help but kiss his cool flesh.

He cupped the back of her neck and pulled her toward him. Her foot hit the brakes the moment their lips collided, the car jolting to a stop. Bassét moaned as if he'd tasted the most delectable pastry in the world, his tongue stroking hers to savor every moment. She heard the car shift into park and pulled away slightly to see Bassét's hand on the shifter.

"What are you doing?" she asked. "I think our fun is over." She shook her head, smirking, and grabbed the shifter to put it back into drive.

"Come on, Rena," he said in a deep breathy tone, folding his fingers over her hand and squeezing the shifter. "I want you to enjoy at least one good thing tonight." He leaned over the armrest that separated them and kissed the flesh below her jaw, his lips kissing teasingly down her neck until her head rolled to the side in submission. There was something about the vampire that she had always had difficulty resisting. When he touched her, the world disappeared into a delightful darkness.

The moment she let her hand slip from the shifter, he reached around to grip both sides of her waist and lift her clear off her seat. He easily maneuvered her body over the divider and placed her firmly on his lap, so she straddled him. She didn't fight him as he pulled her midline against him, his forearms pressing deeply into her lower back. Her long silky bangs fell over his face when she kissed him passionately, losing any desire to stop. He took her waist into his hands again, squeezing urgently and pulling his mouth away, so he could look at her face, his lips lifting over his canines as he sucked in air with excitement.

"I want all of you. I want all of you right now," he said.

His words prompted her to grind against him, her hips swaying in a circular motion. The temptation appeared to drive him mad, because he unzipped her gray sweater and yanked it off. Then he lifted her shirt over her head with vigor, bringing her arms up and guiding them around his shoulders. Any thoughts of suffering chimps disappeared into the darkest depths of her mind as she lost herself to every brush of Bassét's tongue, every caress of his cold fingers, which felt like ice against her skin on a scalding hot day. His fingers bit into the muscles of her back and then traced the fabric of her purple bra until they brushed over her breasts. He reached around and unfastened her bra and then traced circles around her areolas, the chill of his flesh causing her nipples to harden at once. Rena moaned with pleasure and grinded more fiercely atop his lap. He growled under his breath, his eyes blackening with fervor.

"Do you have an extra pair of pants?" he whispered into her ear before he bit at her earlobes and kissed down her neck.

"Yes, why?" she asked, already out of air from her rapid breathing.

At that he ripped her sweats down the middle in one swift movement, revealing the soft flesh of her inner thighs and the lace of her leopard-print panties.

Rena gasped with excitement and surprise. "I liked those sweats!"

"I'll get you another pair," he said as he undid his zipper and withdrew his full erection.

Rena felt a ball of fire ignite within her chest, the kind that burned in a good way, in a way she could live for. She watched the pleasure solidify in his eyes when he pulled the crotch of her panties aside and entered her until he filled her completely. She yelped as the sensation consumed her like liquid pleasure soaring through her with bursts that made her throw her head back and scream his name. She moved vehemently atop him, moaning with every wave of pleasure, Bassét growling and groaning like an animal in the wild. The pleasure was so great that nothing else mattered except the energy their bodies generated; the next wave of ecstasy, the next brush of their tongues, the next thrust and throb that ignited the fire that would ultimately combust.

The final moment came with a blast, causing them to

scream out together, as if they were the only people in the middle of space, floating in their own sphere of euphoria.

Rena panted over his shoulder, so consumed with his scent and his flesh within her that it almost felt as if she had taken a part of him into herself forever. She felt a tear roll down her right cheek, and she quickly wiped it away. He had ignited every last bit of emotion that existed inside her and drawn it out, everything she was. It was the most freeing and yet terrifying feeling.

Rena and Bassét walked toward the dilapidated barn hand in hand. When they reached the large doors, any semblance of a smile on Rena's face disappeared, and she dropped his cold hand. The terrified faces of little chimps resurfaced in her mind, bringing with them a memory of a visit to a chimp sanctuary in Florida, a surprise trip Tony had taken her on for her birthday. The chimps were happy there, all having been rescued from research laboratories. She thought about how much the chimps in Nadine's lab suffered. They deserved to live happy lives too.

While Bassét opened the creaky wood door, she tried to bury any thoughts of Tony, but she couldn't help but imagine his face hovering in her thoughts, the disappointment it would hold if he knew about this place. At that moment, an idea thickened in her mind. If it were the last thing she'd ever do, she'd save her chimps; she'd save them in honor of Tony.

Rena walked into the piercingly white lab, her gaze landing on the chimp cage closest to her along the left wall. Her eyes traveled the rows of cages until she counted all six chimps. When she saw they were all still alive, she let out a sigh of relief.

Most of the chimps called out their excitement to her arrival. Two in the middle of the row looked lethargic. Rena walked over to them first, tapping on their cages to see if she could get a response. The one on the left lifted his head and whimpered.

She opened his cage and heaved him out. He wrapped his limp arms and legs around her body and rested his head against her chest. He was young, like all the rest, so he wasn't over seventy pounds. Nadine made sure to bring them in young, so they were easier to control.

Rena stepped in front of the second cage and tapped the metal bars. The female chimp sat resting against the back of the cage, her head fallen. The chimp's eyes found their way up to Rena, only to continuously roll downward, like they were too heavy to keep open. Rena's heart clenched, and she swallowed the large lump in her throat. She turned toward Arnav, who was in the far right corner working with test tubes.

"I've done everything I could to keep them comfortable," he said before she could ask. "They aren't in pain."

She scoffed. "Aren't in pain?" She walked to Arnav's side, the male chimp in her arms. "These two are near death. How is that any better?"

Arnav glanced at her in his usual way, acknowledging her efforts and concerns but not willing to help her free the chimps. She had grown fond of the vampire scientist. He was good deep down, but she could never get out of him why he continued to test chimps for Nadine. She could see he obviously did not enjoy hurting creatures, so there had to be a reason he didn't walk away. While she stood next to him holding the helpless chimp against her bosom, something occurred to her.

"Oh my God. Nadine threatened your human family, didn't she?"

Arnav didn't answer. He continued to drip a clear liquid into a vial containing a cloudy liquid. She stared at his face for the slightest flicker of emotion. She could almost see guilt swirling behind his dark eyes.

Bassét plunked down on a metal chair in the corner by the

door, the chair clanging against the wall. "Come on, Rena. Nadine is mostly talk. I doubt she'll murder anyone's family."

"How can you even say that?" she snapped, spinning toward him. She yanked up her sleeve with her free hand to expose the burn scar on her wrist. "Did you forget how I got these?"

Bassét's eyes fell to his shoes. It seemed he was in some sort of denial about what his maker was capable of. He hadn't even been in the country during the incident. He wasn't around to see any of the horrible things that Nadine did to Rena's family. She knew he didn't want to believe Nadine was a monster, and that hurt her, even if she understood his bond to the witch. She turned back toward Arnav, having no energy to argue.

"Your silence says it all, Arnav. Maybe one day we can help each other."

Rena walked back to the chimp's cage. She lifted his body onto the soft bed she'd made and petted his resting head delicately. She closed the cage and stepped in front of the second sick chimp. Rena tapped the cage again when it appeared the chimp wasn't breathing. She quickly opened the cage and touched the chimp's shoulder. Still no movement. Rena breathed in sharply and then looked away. Her teary eyes fell on Bassét. "Are you okay with all this?"

"Of course not," he said, "but I'd like to walk in the sunlight again one day. I can't bear living in darkness forever, Rena. You have to understand."

She scoffed. "Bassét, you don't really believe that's all your *mommy dearest* is up to, do you?"

He rolled his eyes, clearly refusing to believe the woman who'd saved him from the brink of death and taken him under her arm was capable of something evil.

Rena shook her head with a scowl and felt the chimp's arm for a pulse. A tear beaded down her cheek when she realized the

198

young female chimp had given up for good. She took the body, which was still warm, into her arms and walked carefully toward the door, stopping abruptly in front of Bassét.

"You disgust me." She didn't truly mean that, but she hated watching animals die and her vampire boyfriend being an accomplice to it.

Bassét looked up at her with a mixture of surprise, anger, and pain. He looked away, as if he wouldn't dare show her she'd hurt him. "Go run to your pet cemetery. As if that will bring them back to life." The minute he saw her glare, regret crossed his face. "Rena, I didn't mean it," he said, standing up.

"Stay away from me!" she screamed before running up the stairs.

Rena squeezed the lifeless chimp in her arms as she neared her favorite oak tree. She walked carefully around all the little rock graves in her pet cemetery, which seemed to grow larger every time she was there. Fog hovered above the ground like a cool haze, as if it held all the little animal souls and guided them into the atmosphere. She leaned against the comforting stump of the tree, crying to herself as her fingers stroked the chimp's forehead. She couldn't believe what her life had become. Instead of saving animals from labs like this, she was fraternizing with the enemy. She let Nadine bend her to her will, and like a fool, she had fallen for the witch's immortal son.

Rena rocked back and forth, chanting to herself, entering a state of delirium. "I promise I'll save you. I'll save you all. I'll save you all. I'll save—"

"Rena."

She looked up to find Bassét kneeling in front of her. "I'll save them all," she whispered into the black abyss of his eyes.

Bassét took Rena and the chimp into his muscled arms, kissing the heated flesh of her forehead. "I'm sorry, Rena. I'm so sorry. Let me help you bury her."

Bassét released her to wrap his arms delicately around the chimp, letting the animal's head fall back into the crease of his elbow. He took the hand shovel from the ground next to Rena and looked toward the cemetery. "Where should I put her?"

Rena's eyes weaved through the little graves until they landed on a spot next to a lonely white flower. "There," she said softly, pointing at it.

She pulled her knees to her chest and watched Bassét carry the nameless chimp to the spot near the flower. He kneeled and laid the chimp on the grass.

"No!" Rena called out, as if he'd hurt the dead animal. "Don't lay her on the cold ground." She went over and kneeled beside Bassét and carefully took the chimp from his arms.

Bassét dug determinedly until he'd created a rectangular hole in the dirt that was about three by two feet in perimeter and two feet deep.

Rena waited silently, stroking the young female's arms and head. When he was finally done, she looked around the garden of death, searching for a blanket. "I forgot her bed."

"I'll go get it," Bassét said.

"No." Rena laid the chimp's body on her thighs and pulled off her gray sweater. She held it near her torso as she placed the sweater into the dark hole in the ground.

"Don't be silly, Rena. You'll catch cold."

"I don't care. I want her to have it." She hunched over the fresh grave, holding the chimp in one arm, and fixed her sweater so that it evenly blanketed the bottom. She folded over the hood of the sweater, so it would form a pillow under the chimp's head. "There," she said. She laid the body into the grave and situated her head on the hood, as if it would bruise if she weren't careful.

Bassét used the shovel to push dirt back into the grave.

Rena used her bare hands, pushing the dirt in with her palms until it covered the body. When the grave was filled to the top with moist dirt, Rena walked toward the stump to select the rocks she would arrange instead of a gravestone. She returned with three large rocks and placed them on the dirt. She looked at the little white flower that stood next to the grave, finding beauty in its delicate form. It was like it had grown there just for this purpose.

"Do you want to say something?" Bassét asked, resting his palms on his knees.

She looked at him, her eyes having dried and her insides finally numb. "There's nothing to say. She's not suffering now. That's all that matters."

20
Trilogy of Powers

"Hi, Consus," I said to the scholar who was normally a more buoyant vampire.

"Come in, Edrea," he offered, standing behind the door to the Wave with a wary smile.

Uri had ordered me there, along with Jule and Elias. Uri was worried I'd go after Rena. He hadn't overreacted. I did want to go after her, but I knew it was safer to have a plan rather than simply act where Nadine was involved. Uri had sent spies to the Décret mansion, but nothing had been uncovered yet as far as I knew. Nadine always seemed to be one step ahead. She was insane, and her type of insanity was lethal to the world and everyone in it.

Jule, Elias, and I walked into the main room to find it quieter than usual. All the immortal scientists and scholars looked lost before paperwork and microscopes spread about the large round table. I wondered if they had their hands on super-vamp blood.

Consus appeared at my side after securing the door. He wore his usual loose pants and hanging cotton shirt, his light-brown hair pleasantly unkempt, as one would expect of an artist. "I'm afraid it's never a good sign when the scholars are speechless."

Jule, Elias, and I exchanged jittery glances. Elias still hadn't fully adjusted to our world. He held more anxiety than all of us put together. He forced his fingers inside the pockets of his jeans and studied the tension of the once-lively main room. I felt his unrest spring up under my skin. Before he had a nervous breakdown, I wrapped my fingers around his wrist. It seemed to calm him temporarily, and he let his hand fall to his side.

When his eyes found mine, the tingling picked up beneath my skin. I gave him an uneasy but warm smile and let my hand fall from his wrist, the flesh of our forearms barely touching. He had learned to guard his thoughts well, but his beautiful blue irises swirled with what looked like fear, confusion, and tenderness. The itch under my skin intensified, and I scratched my arms. That was when I realized our interacting emotions were what triggered the physical response between us, as if the bond of our immortal blood cells remembered one another. Feeling that bond made me want to protect him the same way that I protected Rena.

I turned to the Romanian artist as the anxiety recoiled inside my core. "Consus, please fill us in. What have the scholars discovered—or not discovered, should I say?" I wasn't usually so nervous, and I couldn't hide the uneasiness in my voice.

"We've known for some time that the Décret created day-walkers, or at least attempted to create day-walkers. They can tolerate only the last and weakest sun rays of dusk." The familiar masculine voice came from across the room where a man leaned over the table, bangs obscuring his face. He stood up, revealing who he was: the nameless computer genius I'd met months earlier. He nodded somberly to me before he continued. "We have studied the blood of the day-walker that attacked Pierre in his apartment. The altered bacterial DNA that allows vampires to be exposed to the sun is not what concerns us most. What we fear is that the enhancements were made not only for the purpose of withstanding daylight." He walked slowly toward us, his pensive eyes on the floor until he reached the front of the table. "We're not entirely certain yet."

Consus laid a hand on my shoulder, but it wasn't much comfort.

I looked at Jule with concern, remembering what her coven in England had suspected about bioengineered Bacillus F. Then it struck me. I focused back on the dark cryptic eyes of the nameless immortal. "They've also created an immunity to something, haven't they?"

The nameless one's brow flickered with surprise. "You *are* as intuitive as your uncle, aren't you, Edrea?" He raised his hand to the top of a leather chair and ran his fingers along the buttoned edge, his eyes tracing its form. "I was able to hack into one of the local Décret databases a few weeks ago. The information didn't make sense until Uri contacted me this evening." His gaze turned to Jule, who was standing with Elias next to a bookshelf. "It seems your English coven may be onto something. Nadine not only wants vampires who can walk in daylight. We fear now that she is attempting to create a 'superior' race that is immune to a biological weapon."

"She does seem the type that seeks ultimate power," Jule said with a touch of humor. The lightness of her tone sank quickly when the room remained silent, and all eyes landed on her. She shifted her posture and stood up straighter, not expecting to be taken seriously. All the vampires continued to focus on her, as if waiting for her to divulge what everyone was afraid to admit. "Hasn't anyone played videogames? Nadine is acquiring a *trilogy of powers* in order to be undefeated. She has Rena, who becomes a mind reader once turned and gives Nadine the power of telepathy. She has vampires who are not crippled by sunlight—albeit dying sunlight—giving her minions access to day and night. And she has a weapon that may be deadly to all her enemies, but from which she is protected."

I looked at Jule and smirked, even though her revelations were terrifyingly true. Her snark and insights never ceased to amaze me.

A book fell from the shelf behind Elias, slamming to the floor and echoing off the walls and ceiling. The noise startled everyone out of their temporary state of shock.

Elias leaned down to retrieve the book, embarrassed at his clumsiness. Everyone's attention was on him when he stood embracing the large book in his hands. He hesitated for a moment, shifting the book under his arm. "I played videogames," he said awkwardly. The nameless one's brow rose, and he rested an elbow atop the backrest of a chair, waiting for Elias to continue. Elias's gaze fell as he nervously readjusted the book in his arms. He took a slight step forward and lifted his head, his eyes traveling around the table of scientists until landing on the nameless one. "This so-called Décret superior has the mother ship. With it, she's unstoppable."

"Well, it's settled then, isn't it?" Consus said, walking around the table. "We sink this mother ship."

"Are we forgetting my sister is on that ship?" I asked, throwing my palms out.

"I'm sure your uncle is taking measures to safely get your sister off the ship," the nameless one said. He rolled his eyes and pushed off the chair. "But why are we discussing mother ships? This isn't a video game. What we need to do most urgently is find Nadine's labs and destroy this biological weapon, if that's what she's created."

"Do we look like soldiers to you?" a dark-skinned vampire with a Middle Eastern accent protested from his chair at the table. He lifted his head from his microscope. "We are but scientists and scholars."

"I doubt he's electing you or anyone else in this room, Hakim," Consus said, nervous laughter in his voice.

"I've already shown Uri telepathically where one of the labs is located," I said. All eyes turned to me. "It's under a farm on Bay Hill Road. My sister has been working for Nadine there, tending to animals they're testing. If Nadine has successfully created this weapon, I doubt she has it hidden there. She must have it at another lab or an underground facility somewhere."

"It could be anywhere," Consus said, frustrated.

"Holy shit, Jule, you might be able to find it," I said, an epiphany striking me.

"Me?" she said, a look of bemusement on her face.

"Come on, Jule. You have the ability to read the history of any inanimate object. If we can get something from the lab in your hands, there's a good probability you'll be able to trace its past movements to another site too."

Jule's eyebrow arced when she caught on to my train of thought. "Oh."

"That's not a bad idea," the nameless one said, "but it would take careful planning. We would have to infiltrate the farm undetected. You know as well as I do that Nadine has her grounds highly secured."

"Maybe we won't have to," I said. "I may be able to get a message to Rena telepathically, get her to swipe a few test tubes or instruments from the lab and leave them for us somewhere to pick up."

"When do we start?" Elias said, still holding the book under his arm.

"We may not have much time," the nameless one said, nodding to me with urgency. "However, we'll have to talk it over with Uri and call a meeting with the Shevet before anyone picks up the laboratory paraphernalia. Even if you're successful in getting the message to Rena, Décret vampires may be following her movements at all times."

I walked toward the library without further ado. "I need to contact my sister. She works in the lab tonight, I think. I can at least have her take what we need while she's there."

The library was empty, thankfully, except for the ceiling-to-floor books and vintage sofas and desks. I closed the large doors behind me the moment I stepped inside, and my back fell against the crevices of the scene carved into the wood. There was something grounding about their solid artistic form, which depicted a road winding through the countryside under the sun. I could almost sink into the mural, which would have seemed real if it weren't made from the wood of dead trees.

I didn't bother finding a place to sit and concentrate. I closed my eyes and entered a void-like place as I imagined disappearing into the mural of the doors, as if they were a portal to another world. I imagined walking along the wooden path that wound around the wooden hills, watching the grooves of their maple wood forms slowly transform into the swaying blond grasses of summer hills, curving copper dirt roads, and the deep dark blue of the sky.

It wasn't long before the scenery took the form of the familiar world Rena and I were fond of, the only place we could find each other. The blue atmosphere slowly darkened into an early evening sky. The aspen forest with dainty white roses swayed delicately in the distance. No bone-chilling winds prevented me from nearing like before, so I ran toward the beautiful white-bark trees. No sharp rosebush thorns reached like barriers between the trees, so I ran through the tall aspens until I reached the beach. I called Rena's name the moment my bare toes sank into the soft sand. She was nowhere in sight. I was alone, except for the light breeze that carried the scent of eucalyptus and the stars reflected in the still ocean water.

"Rena!" I called, my voice echoing into the distance.

A ways down the beach, a strange figure materialized faintly, someone walking along the shore. Finally, it took the shape of a woman, her flowing hair taking form as if drawn out of the gentle wind. She neared, and I saw that it was Rena.

"Edrea," she said, her voice fragile, her body still not fully materialized.

I ran to her and wrapped my arms around her neck. I felt her form solidify around me as she embraced me. "We have little time," I said, still holding her. "I need you to do something for me, and I need you to do it extremely carefully."

She pulled away and looked anxiously at me with her large brown apologizing eyes. The direness of the situation had already hardened inside of them. "Anything."

"Take as many lab instruments as you can get away with before you go home tonight. Leave them for me behind the oak tree across from the rundown gas station on Highway 12 right outside Sebastopol. Pretend you have to pee or something in case you're followed."

She started to smirk, but dreariness soon engulfed her face. "I will." She looked down at the sand as tears escaped her eyes and streamed down her rosy cheeks. "I did what I had to, Edrea. You know if Nadine doesn't have me, she'll go after Mom and Dad . . . Liron. I have to—"

"I know," I said. "You're protecting our family."

She smiled and wiped tears from her eyes.

"*Edrea*." My named echoed frantically in a masculine voice through the aspens. Rena and I both stared fretfully in that direction.

"Something's not right," I said.

"*Edrea*," the voice called again, this time more fearfully. It was Elias.

"What's happened?" I asked Rena nervously, my body starting to evaporate into the air. "Does Nadine know? Have you told Bassét anything?"

Rena grabbed for my cloudy hands, horrified. "She can't. I haven't said a word. It's imposs—"

Her trembling words died out as my mind returned to the library with a jolt. Elias stood before me, squeezing my arms. "Edrea!" he said, almost yelling. I blinked myself back to full consciousness. "Edrea, we have to go back to Uri's. Something's happened."

"What?" I said frantically.

"We don't know," Jule said, appearing by his side, "but we have to leave now."

It sounded like a storm was nearing. The air thickened, and the chill reached my bones, the chill I felt only when something dreadful awaited. I pushed the possibility out of my mind as the stream of city sights and sounds became greenery and howls of waves and wind. We arrived at the Shevet gates just as thunder boomed above.

Immortal guards with black suits and long peacoats opened the tall iron gates. The metal grated with sharp warnings in my ears. Either they had rusted over time, or I'd never noticed them shrieking before. Perhaps something just didn't feel right. The air was thick with a secret I didn't yet know. It was as if wavelengths of a darker parallel universe interposed on our own. The sensation crawled up my limbs the closer we came to the front door, gathering into something prickly and heavy in my chest.

The front door opened, and we heard nothing. Not a sound. Not even a creak.

We walked the dark hallway toward the glow of Uri's office. I knew he was in there, but something was different. Not a page turned in a book, nor did a key click on his computer. The prickly heaviness intensified, like scorching black tar.

We rounded the corner, and my nervous wide-eyed gaze found Uri behind his desk in the dim light. Immobile. His eyes black. Cold. Afraid. I'd never seen fear in them before, not like this. I turned toward Mikale. He stood tense next to the cold fireplace, his eyes wide with fear. I sucked in a breath that filled my useless lungs with anguish, every inch of my body petrifying. Uri's eyes lifted slowly and heavily, as if carrying the weight of the world with them. When they found me, they held secrets that would change the life I knew forever. I waited. His lips parted, but he didn't speak.

"Uri, what is it?" I pleaded, the anguish and terror rasping my tone.

His eyes fell, and his body stiffened. I knew whatever it was would kill me all over again. "What is it?" I screeched, my eyes jittery. "Tell me, Uncle."

Uri's black eyes met mine, revealing a hidden darkness he'd never shown me. "Edrea . . . it's your parents."

At those words the hot black tar in my chest dislodged, spilling throughout my body to the tips of my fingers and toes.

"Uri . . . what are you . . . Are they—" The words left my

lips, my thoughts unable to continue further.

His eyes, which held so many emotions—empathy, fury, fear—dropped and then met mine with fierce loyalty and love.

"They've been taken, Edrea. Before sunset. Mikale and Gus found their blood inside the house. There was a struggle of some sort. When my guards arrived, they were already gone. The dog was found dead in the kitchen. We're not sure where your parents are or if they're okay. We're not . . ."

I watched Uri's lips move, but the buzzing in my ears replaced his words. It was all I could hear. My vision clouded. My body felt like it was made of ice. I could no longer sense that anyone else was in the room as my mind fought to conceive the unfathomable.

My parents had been harmed. My parents could be dead.

21

Rena: The Storm

Hearing the distress in the unfamiliar man's voice beyond
the aspens and seeing Edrea evaporate in front of her eyes
reignited the gut feeling that something was very wrong that night.

Edrea had reached out to Rena mentally and drawn her into
their shared otherworld when Rena was in the barn above the lab
gathering chimp food. Bassét had been downstairs with Arnav. The
connection to Edrea couldn't have happened at a better time; not
only because Rena had been alone, but also because a recent
shipment of test tubes, flasks, and bandages had been on the shelf
in front of her. It made her wonder if the universe had lined up at
just the right moment. Then again, factoring in all the horrible
things that happened in the world to good people would make that
concept obsolete. Edrea would call it "wishful thinking." But Rena
liked to believe things happened for a reason anyway. She
especially wanted to believe karma would come around and bite

Nadine right in her perky ass. Rena couldn't care less if it was just wishful thinking.

She had grabbed as many different lab items as she could, focusing on things that were already out of boxes, including non-sterile flasks, glass tubes filled with serum, and plastic bags of saline. She'd stuffed them into a ragged white cloth bag that she found under one of the bottom shelves. Then she rolled the cloth with the lab items over itself as tightly as she could and stuffed them inside her shoulder bag. Her bag had been in the same area on top of a rusted metal chair. She'd left it there with the items until she came back up for another bag of chimp food.

As unsuspiciously as possible, she took the bag with her toward the large barn doors and pried one open. She didn't even bother to check her surroundings for immortal guards. She knew they were there. That would only make her actions look more peculiar. Instead, she just moved toward her car like it was the most natural thing and clicked the unlock button on her key. The car beeped once, and the lights flashed, illuminating the dark grassland around the vehicle for a split second. She wondered where the guards hid when she saw the forms of oak trees flash in the distance. She opened the front passenger door, placed her shoulder bag on the seat, and closed the door like she would any other day. Then she strode back to the barn, feeling the cryptic night following close behind.

If luck was on her side, the guards, wherever they crept from in the blackness, would just think she was preparing to leave.

She grabbed another sack she'd filled with chimp food and ran down the stairs to the lab, an eerie sense of urgency creeping through her veins. It was almost time to leave, but she wanted to get out of there sooner rather than later. Obviously, Edrea had a good reason for asking her to gather lab instruments and drop them off in a secret place. Not having any idea what that was made

Rena's skin crawl.

She opened the door to the lab a little too briskly. Arnav and Bassét looked at her, puzzled, like she'd just burst through the door with machetes in both hands. She tried to act normal, but she couldn't shake the feeling that she had to leave immediately. She carried the heavy bag of chimp food to the cages, feeling Bassét's curious eyes studying her. She unlatched the first cage where a rambunctious male chimp rattled the bars and screamed.

"Calm down now," she said sweetly before she opened the door. "Here you go." She pulled a lettuce head out of the sack. She waited for the young chimp to scurry to the back of the cage before she put it in. He was one of the newer chimps and still had some fight in him. Her heart sank knowing the serum would soon make him docile and weak. She grabbed a few pieces of fruit from the sack and then a bag of crickets, placing them in the center of his cage. Then she secured the latch and moved to the next cage. As soon as she finished feeding the chimps, she could leave for the night.

Bassét appeared next to her and took the sack out of her hand. "Why don't I feed them tonight? Go home and get some rest." His lips turned up at one side, and sexy creases feathered at the corner of his eye.

"Thanks. I'm exhausted." She looked into his dark weary eyes and wondered why he had become tenderer than usual. It was like they both had a feeling something was about to change.

She moved to the door as casually as possible. She wrapped her fingers around the cool handle and looked over her shoulder toward the quiet scientist. "See you Sunday, Arnav." Even as she said the words, she had the feeling she wouldn't work at that awful lab again. Arnav's dark gaze met hers, and he acknowledged her in his usual placid way. As strange as it was, she hoped she'd see the Indian scientist again. She hadn't gotten the chance to get to know him, to learn his story.

The dark country road reached into the distance as far as the eye could see. Up ahead the old gas station came into view and across from it the large oak tree. Rena pulled onto the grassy shoulder of the road beside the tree, hoping no one had followed her. Her brakes squeaked to a stop, making her cringe. She glanced into her rearview mirror. Not even one car was on the road. No moving shadows either. She turned the car off and stepped outside, noticing the temperature had fallen by maybe ten degrees. Dark clouds had accumulated above, barely lit by the light of the hidden moon. It felt like a storm would come. She embraced her arms and felt a chill tremble through her body. She had to get this over with as soon as possible.

She walked around the front of the sedan and opened the passenger door. She also opened the back door to make it look like she planned to squat and pee between them. Edrea had taught her that trick. She sat on the edge of the opening under the passenger seat and closed her eyes, listening for any movements. If a vampire had followed her, she'd surely hear something creeping atop the earth, like a snap of a twig or the crunch of grass. When she was sure all she heard in the night was the wind and blowing grass, she grabbed the dirty white bag that contained the lab instruments from inside her shoulder bag and made her way to the oak tree.

It was larger up close than she'd imagined. She walked around the wide trunk to place the bag behind it. The dark twisted branches above creaked in the wind, their leaves whispering warnings. The moment she laid the bag on the grass, she heard Edrea's voice shriek her name through her mind. The desperateness in her echoing voice sent an electrical shock down her spine. Rena embraced the tree with her hand, squeezing her eyes shut. When she opened them, she was back on the beach in the otherworld, Edrea shaking her shoulders. To her right, the ocean stormed violently, dark clouds nearing in the distance and lightning flashing on the horizon.

A feeling of dread filled Rena's body, making her limbs heavy. "Edrea, Edrea what's wrong?"

Tears streamed down Edrea's face, her hands dropping to her sides, trembling. Horror darkened her brown eyes. "They've taken them, Re. Mom and Dad. We don't even know if they're alive. They killed . . ." Edrea's words died, as if it was too painful to divulge the rest.

Hopelessness and paranoia spun in the blackness of Rena's mind and core as her thoughts attempted to finish the sentence. A tremor overtook her body. "Who did they kill, Edrea?" Her brother crossed her mind, tears pouring down her cheeks in sheets. "Liron?" She heard his name escape her own mouth, her head shaking back and forth.

"No, I think he's okay," Edrea said.

Rena let out a breath of relief between her apparent hyperventilation. Then her body froze when she realized the only other member of her immediate family it could be. "No, Edrea, no," she cried. "Not Dingo, please, not Dingo." She pleaded into her sister's gaze, searching for a sign of hope, but Edrea's eyes only filled with bleakness.

"I'm sorry, Rena. I'm so sorry."

Rena fell to her knees in the sand, crying out helplessly. She couldn't believe it was true. "I've done everything she asked of me. We had a deal. We had a deal," Rena cried, rocking back and forth. "Dingo . . ." she whispered desperately into the wind.

Edrea took Rena into her arms, crying with her, for Rena's pain was hers too. It had always been an unspoken truth between them. "Rena, you have to be strong." Edrea pulled back and took Rena's shoulders into her hands again. "You have to go for Liron.

You have to bring him to Uri's."

Rena sobbed into the icy wind. She wiped her tears, her eyes boring into the sand below, her body trembling with sadness and rage. Then she stiffened and sucked air through her teeth. Her gaze slowly lifted to meet her sister's. "I'm already on it." Her own voice sounded foreign.

In the otherworld, it was clearer than ever that the climate reflected their raw emotions, their dreams, even their hatred. Tonight it was their deepest despair, and it was the fire that burned within them, a pure rage they both understood.

A rage they both feared.

Rena flew down Highway 101 South toward the city, her arms trembling above the steering wheel as fury, despair, and helplessness shot through them. Thunder grumbled in the distance, dimly lighting up the sky. A storm was on its way. Somehow it felt different than all the others, like it came from a different world, a darker world, and it would carry everything she loved away with it. The shaking traveled from her arms to her chest, reaching her legs when thoughts of how Dingo must have suffered boiled to the surface like a nightmare never meant to be told. How he must have barked and fought to protect her parents. She saw her mother's trembling face in her mind, the terror it must have bore. She heard her father's screams, the way he would have struggled against his attackers as if he were in one of his night terrors, except this time it was real.

A feral scream thundered from Rena's lungs as she fought to prevent the awful images from consuming her. Edrea's words replayed in her mind. *Rena, you have to be strong.* Nadine wanted her to feel weak. Helpless. Desperate. She felt all those things, and that made her rage stronger too. The witch would go for Liron next, if she hadn't already. Rena picked up her cellphone and

dialed. She hoped, even prayed he'd pick up. She didn't believe in
a personal god, but maybe the universe listened. Maybe if she
hoped hard enough, Liron would hear her pleas. She had a mental
connection to Edrea. Why not him?

"What's up, Rena? It's almost one in the morning."

A faint cry left her chest when his voice resonated from the
phone like a whisper of hope. "Where are you?"

"Rena, what's wrong?" His voice quickly became
tremulous.

"Tell me where you are. I have to come for you. Something
. . . something horrible . . . something's happened." Her words
wavered in and out between her cries.

Liron was silent for a moment. She couldn't even hear him
breathe. "I'm at Jack's farm in Petaluma."

Her shoulders loosened a little. That was only the next exit.
She had forgotten Liron was at Jack's for his birthday party. "I'm
coming to you now. I'll be there in seven."

She ended the call to avoid any more questions. She had to
gather whatever strength she had for what followed. She glanced
nervously through the car windows as the trees and highway
divider streamed by on either side in the darkness. If no vampires
had followed her, it would be a miracle, a miracle she desperately
needed.

She laid her hand on the bag of lab instruments on the
passenger seat. She'd brought them with her instead of leaving
them to be picked up at the oak tree, now that she would go
straight to Uri's once she picked up Liron. The war had already
begun when Nadine took her parents. The vampire code of secrecy
was void as far as Rena was concerned.

The exit approached, and she pulled off the highway. She
made a quick right on Petaluma Blvd. North and sped for Stony
Point Road. She turned right and peeled down the road until she

saw the familiar country road with the missing sign and turned left. The deeper she drove into the countryside, the fewer the streetlights and the darker the streets. Instead of slowing down like she usually would, she sped up through the darkness down the narrowing bumpy street toward Jack's long driveway. It was only another mile down the road. Every hovering tree blowing in the wind and every moving shadow made her flinch and search the darkness.

As she got closer to the farm, to Liron, her nerves picked up. He could be the last family member she'd ever see alive. The thought grew in her chest like a black hole. She'd worked so hard for the vampire wench for the sole reason of protecting her family, to keep them safe. She had kept Edrea and Uri in the dark for seven months while working in the lab where they tortured animals. For what? The evil bitch took her parents anyway. What a fool she had been to trust her.

She slowed when she neared the unpaved driveway and stopped at the threshold of the property. If she had led Décret vampires right to her brother, she'd never forgive herself. She already felt it was her fault Nadine took her parents. If she had gone straight to Uri when Bassét first contacted her, maybe things would have been different. She had done what felt right at the time. Now she wasn't so sure. Tears stung her eyes the more she cried. She peered anxiously around the darkness and the swaying trees. The anticipation of telling Liron their parents might be dead, that real monsters had killed Dingo, and she had to take Liron into hiding—into a vampire den of all places—felt like an impossible task. She wasn't ready to believe it herself.

A male figure appeared out of the blackness, walking toward the car down the driveway. The night obscured his face. She just hoped he was human. Her eyes focused on the figure as he neared, the blowing trees throwing shadows over his form. She exhaled when she recognized the familiar torn khaki pants and white T-shirt with a hole by the bottom seam. Liron's face came into view, his expression empty, terrified.

Rena lowered her window. "Liron, get in. Hurry."

A black figure emerged from the darkness under some pine trees. Rena's heart jumped in her chest. Liron opened the passenger door and got in, closing it swiftly. Rena locked the doors, her eyes pinned on the figure coming out of the trees.

"Rena, what's going on?" Liron said frantically.

"Thank God, it's only Samuel," she said. She wiped the wetness off her cheeks with the sleeve of her sweater.

"What are you talking about? Who's Samuel? Rena, what's happening?"

Rena turned to Liron, hugging him tightly, both relieved and horrified that she would bring him into this world. She had felt so alone.

Liron gasped. "Rena, there's a man outside your window."

She pulled back and grabbed his shoulders. "It's okay. I'll explain everything." She unlocked the doors and let Samuel into the back seat. "Samuel is protecting us."

"Protecting us from what?" Liron pulled a pocketknife out of his sweater pocket and stared at the large dark-skinned man in Rena's back seat.

"It's wonderful seeing you again, Rena," Samuel said in the African accent that she'd missed more than she realized. She felt his cool hand squeeze her shoulder. She placed her warm hand on his, as if she wanted to test that he was truly there.

Rena turned to her brother. "Liron, this is Samuel. He's a close friend of our family, of an uncle you haven't met yet . . . and of Edrea."

Liron lowered his knife and brushed his fingers through his thinning hair, his eyes moving erratically between her and Samuel.

"Rena, tell me what's—" As if something snapped in his head, he went silent for a moment, confusion filling his face. "Rena, what do you mean a close friend of Edrea's?"

Rena swallowed, looking over her seat at Samuel for support before facing her brother. "What I'm about to tell you will come as a shock, a big shock, but we have to get on the road. Samuel will help me explain on the way. Right, Samuel?"

"Why don't you let me drive?" Samuel said. "That way you don't have to concentrate on the road."

"Okay, that works too. Liron, let's get in the back."

Liron opened his door uneasily and moved to the back seat as Rena and Samuel switched places. The moment Rena and Liron were safely inside, Samuel took off, the jolt pushing them back into the seat.

"Jesus," Liron said, grabbing his seatbelt and fastening it.

Rena was silent, pulling her seatbelt over her body with no amount of haste. She peered out her window, watching the dark countryside stream by, tears wetting her face again. She wasn't sure how she would break the news to him. She just knew she had needed him to know for a long time, perhaps so he could share the burden with her. Wasn't that what siblings did?

"Would someone tell me what the hell is going on?" Liron said. "What happened, and where are we going? Jesus Christ!"

Rena breathed in deeply and turned to her brother. He looked more anxious than she'd ever seen him, and that only made her more nervous. "Liron, I really don't know how to say this." She noticed her hands were trembling, so she hid them between her thighs. "It's Mom and Dad. They've been . . . they've been taken, Liron, and the bastards who took them killed Dingo." Tears streamed down her cheeks.

Liron's face paled, and he rubbed his palms across his thighs. Tears pooled in his eyes as he studied Rena and the strange man who drove the car. "I don't understand. What do you mean they've been taken? Are they okay?"

"We don't know," Rena said.

"Who's *we*, Rena? Are Mom and Dad okay?" When Rena didn't answer, his gaze went to Samuel, who sped down Highway 101 South at ninety miles per hour. "I don't know who you are, but I need to know what's going on right now."

Samuel's eyes found Rena's in the rearview mirror. "Rena, perhaps you should start with Edrea," he said calmly.

Liron stared at Samuel, tears falling from his eyes. He put his hand in his pocket and drew out a silky orange ribbon. He squeezed it in his hand. "She's alive, isn't she? Our sister is alive."

"You found the gift ribbon," Rena said in amazement. Seeing the ribbon brought back a world of memories, from a time when things were still okay, when everyone was safe. It was a game Edrea and Liron had played for years. It started with Liron, when he went on a camping trip in the mountains. Edrea had asked him to bring her something from the trip, so he found a little black rock and tied a ribbon around it. Edrea did the same when she went on a trip to England. She brought Liron a white stone from Pebble Beach in Brighton and tied the same ribbon around it. They passed it back and forth, tying the ribbon around little pieces of nature. That was why they called it the gift ribbon. Rena remembered how it made her feel jealous.

"I didn't find it," Liron said, as if he was still unsure. "It fell from the sky outside the hospital when grandma died." He looked at Rena with tear-filled eyes. "Rena, answer my question."

"We're going to Edrea now. She's not exactly alive, but she's not dead either."

Liron looked at Rena like she was insane, but growing inside his eyes she saw a hint of solace, as if something he'd suspected in the back of his mind had finally crystallized. "What do you mean she's not alive or dead? What is she, a vampire?" he asked sarcastically.

Samuel smirked from the driver's seat, his black eyes shining red when the moon peeked through a break in the clouds. He watched Rena closely from the mirror. "It's okay, Rena. You can tell him."

Rena looked at her brother. "You know how Edrea was always really intuitive? Almost psychic?"

"Yes," Liron said under his breath.

"Well, she has an inherited mental trait from our family that, supposedly, those of us with type O positive blood have. I have it too. Bad people—vampires—found out about it and had Edrea beaten nearly to death and turned into one of them, so it would trigger her mind powers, which only activate when we become immortals." She left out the part about Edrea's rape. She wasn't sure Edrea would want him to know. Liron didn't respond, so she continued. "Grandma's brother, Uri, who everyone thought died in a car accident, is also a clairvoyant vampire. That's where we're going to stay for a while, at his house. He's the head of a vampire coven in San Francisco called the Shevet. Edrea lives there with him."

Liron let out a sudden eruption of nervous laughter. "So, you're telling me our sister is a vampire who can read minds, and we're going to stay with her in a vampire den where our dead uncle lives, except he's also a psychic vampire who's going to protect us because bad vampires took our parents?"

"Samuel, tell him," Rena said, her thoughts going back to their parents. Imagining them hurt made her nauseous. She wrapped her arms around her stomach.

Samuel's eyes landed on Liron's in the mirror. "It's true, son. I know it's a lot to take in."

"This is ridiculous. Where's Mom and Dad, Rena?" An

uneasy look of disbelief had molded Liron's face, and it wasn't letting up any time soon.

"We don't know, Liron. Please believe me. You'll understand when you see Edrea."

Rena saw the teary idea forming inside his eyes. It was an idea he seemed to want to believe and at the same time he didn't because any normal person would think it was crazy.

Liron shook his head and then squinted at Samuel, studying him for a moment. "Don't tell me Samuel here is a vampire too?"

"Samuel is over twenty-five hundred years old," Rena said as she looked out the window. "He was part of Queen Sheba's tribe in Ethiopia."

Liron laughed again, but it didn't last. His wide-eyed stare moved between Rena and Samuel. Then he leaned abruptly against his seat, his horrified gaze traveling outside the window where lightning lit up the distant sky.

The next twenty minutes were spent in silence, except for the sound of thunder, which crept closer as they approached the city. The storm was almost there, and so was the terror of the untold future.

22

The Orange Gift Ribbon

The wind blew violently outside the hallway window, the storm nearly upon us. My fingers were glued to the blinds, my eyes not leaving the driveway. Samuel had gone for my siblings, and I couldn't feel at ease until they were safe and sound. I couldn't remember the last time I was so nervous. Just the thought of us all together again made my chest ache.

Liron thought I was dead, but I often wondered if that was what he believed deep down. Soon he would see that I was very much . . . undead. Would he be afraid of me? Would he hate me for letting him believe a lie?

Jule and Elias's soft voices traveled from the astronomy sanctum, somehow keeping me calm as I stared out the window like a child waiting for Santa, not that I knew what that felt like, even as a human child. I'd only experienced lighting the menorah during Chanukah. But the anticipation of eight days of presents may have been equally exciting. In light of the Chanukah I'd just missed with them, the memories of the holidays with my family weighed on my heart.

The mixture of emotions that circled my body made me feel more human than usual. While my body trembled just knowing my parents were likely suffering in a dark cell somewhere, my insides ached with excitement in anticipation of reuniting with my siblings. I knew that when they arrived I would feel more whole as a person, or at least closer to the person I once was.

The sun would come up in less than five hours, four and a half to be exact. The thought horrified me. I had no idea if we could locate my parents in so little time. If they were still alive, they would most likely be at the mercy of Nadine and her minions for at least another day. I couldn't even fathom the thought of what they might be going through. In a twisted way, I almost hoped they were dead. Almost.

At that moment, I understood at a deeper level why Rena had given herself to Nadine. She couldn't bear to see them hurt. Maybe I never thought something like this could happen to my parents. I never imagined Uri's guards being defeated. Maybe I was afraid to consider the possibility. To feel too deeply. As a human, I'd learned well how to activate my self-protection mode. In immortality, I'd pretty much mastered it. Now that my family was undeniably in danger, and I felt their pain more than ever, my true fears had surged to the surface.

Not even the Shevet could protect those I loved. Now that Nadine had day-walkers, no one was safe. No one.

Knowing my vampire family would do everything they could regardless of the danger involved gave me a little comfort. Mikale and Gus's mission at the moment was to search the entire Bay Area for any sign of Décret movements. I'd texted Mikale probably twenty times in the past hour, hoping for a smidgen of hope. They'd scouted out hundreds of factories and secluded or rundown buildings where Nadine may have my parents. There were still no leads. I had the dreadful feeling she was keeping them in the same place she was hiding the weapon. Nadine enjoyed big reveals and dramatic events. She had something horrible planned, most likely a war that would play out in her favor. Torturing my family was probably the most exciting thing since her revamping. The realization made me furious. We needed to get a step ahead of her somehow. So far, the lab instruments were our only possible lead, and I hoped with my entire being that Jule would have some insight with them.

A handful of tin blinds crunched under my fists the moment lights shone through the premise gates. So many heightened feelings blasted through my veins as Rena's silver car pulled into the driveway: relief, anxiety, sadness, and panic. Mostly panic.

The sedan came to a stop, and Samuel got out of the driver's seat. Two figures were barely visible in the back seat. Samuel opened the rear door nearest him, and Rena stood, her hair blowing over her face in the wind. Something was noticeably different about her. A degree of inner softness was gone. She had always seemed delicate to me, but the way she held herself as she stood so confidently beside Samuel showed a different side to her. A new side. A tougher side. That made me sad and proud.

The other door opened, and my chest tightened. Liron didn't get out right away, probably because he was terrified. For a moment I was afraid it wasn't him. Then I saw his face. He emerged from the car slowly, peering around the grounds with apprehension. He wore his same old khakis and a shirt with a hole in it. When his square handsome face turned my way, the blinds dropped out of my hands.

I fleeted to the front door and opened it, not yet showing myself. Thunder erupted from above, and droplets began to fall, wetting the ground before me. I stepped onto the doorstep, my eyes immediately finding my siblings. I wished so badly I could cry.

"Edrea!" Rena screamed. She ran toward me, throwing her arms around my neck. I had to take a step back, or the impact would have hurt her. I squeezed her in reciprocation and buried my face in her soft brown hair, which was damp from the rain. She cried as she held me, and my body trembled in response. Together again, our sisterly bond merged, like two binary solar systems finally spiraling into one.

My eyes looked up anxiously over her shoulder. Liron stood next to the car, his thin hair mussed, a wide-eyed look of disbelief and fright on his face. Our eyes met, and his unsteady feelings stung my chest and then grew heavy like an entire dimension popped into existence under my ribs. If I weren't an immortal, I would have collapsed from the avalanche of human feelings. They were too much for one person to contain. Thankfully, I wasn't exactly a person.

Rena released me and turned to our brother. "It's okay, Liron. It's really her."

A cry burst from his chest, the raindrops mixing with his tears. He quickly wiped the tears away, as if his face weren't already wet from the rain. Seeing him so fragile and feeling the depth of his raw emotions opened up a part of my core I didn't think I'd ever reach again. He edged toward me, as if he were afraid I'd disappear if he made any sudden moves.

"Hey, Liron," I said, my voice cracking with emotions that I probably couldn't explain.

He cried out again and then covered his mouth with his palm, unsure what he should do next. His thoughts were shaky with uncertainties. *Is she truly there? Are Mom and Dad okay? Am I dreaming or having a psychotic breakdown?*

"I'm really here, Liron. You're not crazy. I promise I'll do everything I can to save Mom and Dad."

228

He closed the distance between us and then hugged me tightly, the reassurance that I was really there coming out with cries on my shoulder. He was the kid brother he always had been. Feeling his embrace, which I thought I'd never experience again, brought back our entire past. Our hiking adventures in the forest. Sneaking out of our house as children and climbing the rooftop of our community temple under the stars. The gift ribbon, our favorite game. As if he'd heard my heart, he stepped back and pulled the orange ribbon from his sweater pocket. All three of us cried and laughed at once, coming together into a hug of tears, laughter, and rain.

"Why don't you come in, you three?" Uri's warm voice said from the doorway behind us. "Another minute outside, and you'll be soaked."

"Come on, Liron. I want you to meet someone," I said, gesturing with my head toward the door.

Liron walked to the door with emotion and wonderment on his face and took Uri's hand. "It's so great to meet you, Uncle Uri. Our grandmother would talk about you like you were a god." Liron smiled and looked up at his uncle. He breathed in deeply and looked back at Rena and me, who were standing behind him holding hands. Then he followed Uri into the house.

We all sat around the telescope in the astronomy sanctum. I figured it would be the most comfortable place for Liron. He had always studied the stars, and he had his own five-foot telescope at my parents' house, where the skies were darker at night.

"As soon as things are back to normal, you're welcome to the telescope whenever you want, Liron," Uri said. "Though, I suspect *normal* isn't the right word for our family, is it?" Uri leaned back against a single green chair and smiled affectionately at my brother.

Liron nodded slightly. He sat unsettled at my side, his mind spinning with so many worries that his thoughts were mostly indiscernible. I looked at Uri, who was equally worried about my parents, and then at Jule, who sat on the rug next to the donut-shaped oak table that surrounded the telescope. On the shiny wooden surface in front of her was the bag of lab items. Elias and Samuel sat across from Liron, Rena, and me on multi-colored sofas. Both of them stared curiously at the instruments, as if the items would jump out of the bag themselves. The silence in the room stirred everyone's unease, and the air held a frigid staleness I could taste on my tongue.

There was no time for family reunions that night, not when our parents were suffering somewhere. Not when the ugly fingers of human cruelty grabbed hold of our hopes and dreams.

I turned to Liron and tried to explain what we were about to do. "This is going to seem more than strange to you, but Jule is going to help us find Mom and Dad with her mind. Many of us have such an ability after we're turned. In immortality, every area of the brain can function at once, enabling vampires certain abilities. Jule is unique. She can read the entire history of an inanimate object when she touches it. I can see, hear, and feel what people do, look into their minds. I'm going to see what Jule sees with her ability."

"This is so fucking crazy. Just find them. I don't care how. We've already lost Dingo." He looked at Rena with dread on his face, realizing it was too soon. Rena started to cry. "I'm sorry." His voice cracked as tears filled his eyes.

"Jule, you ready?" I said. I could almost feel the sorrow and anxiety pour out of my eyes.

She nodded and removed the first item from the bag, a glass flask. I watched tensely, hoping that at least one of those instruments would help us see something that would lead us to

Mom and Dad.

In an instant, the images flew by, backtracking as expected through the item's history. It began with the very room we sat in to the darkness of Rena's bag and then slowed when the barn came into view. Jule's mind controlled how the images played back on rewind with sudden intermittent stops as she swept the barn's interior. Not much was visible except the old wooden beams and dirt floor and Bassét removing the flask from a cardboard box on the floor. A red oriental rug was flipped over, revealing an opening in the ground next to him.

"That's the barn where Rena worked. The lab is hidden underneath," I told Jule. "I doubt Nadine has our parents there." I looked to Rena for confirmation.

"No, they only test animals there," Rena said sadly.

Uri studied the images too, silently staring into space as he stroked his chin with his thumb.

"Keep going, Jule," I urged.

After a few more back and forward swipes of barn coverage, which moved between Bassét, the box, and an old tack room used as a lab storage area, Jule finally moved on.

For a moment there was darkness, most likely the shipment between sites. Then several things popped in and out from the image streams: various strangers removing the flask from a conveyer belt inside a factory and others boxing it.

I shook my head. "This won't show us anything. We're only going to see the factory where the flask was made. It looks like a direct shipment to the barn. Try another item, Jule."

Her mind pulled back, and she searched through more items in the bag. "What about this tube of . . . well, I'm not sure what's in it." She turned a small glass tube of clear liquid in her fingers.

Everyone focused on Rena, wondering the same thing. She

was the only one who'd been inside the lab.

"I have no idea what's in that thing," Rena said, "but I saw Arnav, one of the scientists, mixing one like it with a blue serum in the lab."

"Let's have a go," Uri said with enthusiasm.

Jule closed her eyes, and the images flowed immediately. They swept back into blackness before the hands of a familiar vampire came into view, one of the scientists I saw in the lab through Rena's mind.

"Stop there, Jule. I think that's Victor. He's one of the lab scientists, right?"

Rena laughed nervously. "That creep's no scientist. He just assists Arnav in the lab."

Jule let the images progress slowly. Victor's movements began in reverse, the tube in his hand moving away from a rectangular slot inside a Styrofoam box. A white room came into view that looked like another lab with a chemistry setup. A vampire I'd never seen before stood near the chemistry lab wearing a white lab coat. I leaned forward over my knees, hoping to see something of use.

"Go back further, Jule," I said.

The images flickered to the next black spot, when the tube was inside another box. From there we watched the images play forward slowly. Dark female hands with long fuchsia nails withdrew the glass tube from a cardboard box. The tube was empty. A storage room appeared around the tube with dirty white walls and concrete floors. A few old wooden shelves with various books and boxes sat against the walls. Light shone from a single bulb in the ceiling. The angle of the images moved to the female holding the item. I tensed in surprise. It was Devika, one of Alexio's past lovers. I hadn't seen her since the battle at the Décret mansion over a year earlier.

"What's *perfect curls* up to now?" Jule asked sarcastically.

I couldn't help but grunt a laugh through my nostrils. "I can only imagine."

Devika walked out of the room into a darker hall. An office behind a half-open door flashed at one far end of the hall before she entered the same bright lab we'd just seen moments earlier. It was right across from the storage room. She handed the empty tube to the man in the white lab coat. He poured a clear liquid into it, topped it, and handed it to Victor. The images blackened when Victor placed it into the slot in the Styrofoam box.

"Damn it, there's got to be something else," I said.

Jule pulled back, carefully placing the tube onto the table. "There's still a few more," she said, her voice lacking her usual optimism.

"What's going on?" Liron asked nervously. He twirled the silky orange ribbon through his fingers as if it gave him comfort.

"We haven't seen anything helpful yet," I said, sounding just as anxious.

Jule grabbed the next item, and we watched its history too, to no avail. Then the next one and the next one. Every uneventful item placed onto the table was like a piece of our hope lost. When we came down to the last item, the room fell to a deadly silence.

I looked around at everyone's dire expressions, feeling little solace in the shared hopelessness. I was glad I didn't have to face this alone though—face the possibility my parents had been tortured and murdered.

Jule picked up the last item, a pair of metal tongs. We watched her from the edge of our seats, hoping this wasn't all for nothing, that we hadn't just wasted an hour staring at lab instruments as my parents suffered.

Jule's mind delved into the object's past, streaming mostly through darkness. This one showed us nothing more than the first flask. It was useless.

Rena cried as she watched Jule place the last item onto the table. "I'm sorry, Edrea. I took what I could. There was always someone watching."

"It's not your fault, Rena. Nothing is your fault," I said. I could see that she blamed herself for everything.

"What do we do now?" Liron asked. His face reddened, and his eyes pooled with tears. He was on the verge of breaking down.

Uri looked up, finally breaking his concentration. "We wait. Mikale and Gus won't stop searching until they find their trail. Pierre is on the way with Angelique to help too."

I couldn't accept that. There had to be something else we could do. "Samuel, isn't there anything you see? Anything that can give us some clue?"

Samuel looked up with a heavy face. "I'm sorry, Edrea. All we can do is wait."

No one said another word. Rena continued to cry. Liron joined her. We didn't move from our seats.

We waited.

As if for the world to end.

23

Rena: The Prada Purse

Rena watched the stormy night outside the window from the couch. She wished she had the power to delay the rise of the sun, which would occur in only three and a half hours. That was all the time they had left to save her parents. Waiting until the following night was a horrible option but one they might have to face.

She looked to her vampire sister on her left and then to her brother and realized a piece had been added to her inner being. The three of them being together again made her feel a little stronger. She no longer had to face this nightmare alone. She looked back at Edrea as a heavy realization filled her heart. Edrea had gone through so much worse than her. Her life had been torn away from her in the most horrible way. She had been turned into a predator and forced to leave her family behind. She must have felt so lonely and afraid. Rena looked at Uncle Uri with his sweet, round face and then at Samuel and his warm dark eyes. She was so glad Edrea had a family there, a family with whom she could embark into eternity.

Rena reached over to squeeze her siblings' hands. "We're going to save Mom and Dad no matter what. We're going to do it together." They squeezed her hands back, nodding warily.

Edrea picked up her phone when it buzzed on the couch. She read the text, which made her expression even heavier than before. She typed a quick message.

"Is that Mikale? Are there any leads?" Rena asked fearfully.

"No. Nothing yet." Edrea smacked the phone down on the table in front of her, scooting to the edge of the couch. She stared at the lab instruments, as if they hid something she had overlooked.

"What is it?" Liron asked, moving to the edge of the cushion to join her.

Samuel stood up and started toward the foyer, like someone had just arrived. Uri followed. Edrea and Jule looked in that direction as well, as if they had also heard someone coming.

"Pierre," Edrea whispered. She turned her ear toward the foyer as Samuel and Uri greeted Pierre and Angelique at the front door. Then, as if no hopeful news had come, she turned back toward the instruments. "Jule, I want to look at something again. Can you show me the test tube's past, the part in the hallway between the storage room and the lab?"

Jule perked up from her spot on the carpet and scooted her knees toward the table. "Sure."

Rena moved closer to the table as well, hoping that by some miracle their mind abilities would rub off on her, and she could see what they saw. Jule picked up the test tube and held it in her hands. Edrea closed her eyes and squinted determinedly.

"Stop there, Jule," Edrea said. "Go back to the first moment she steps into the hall, and focus on the lighted room at the end of the hall on the left."

Jule's eyes moved beneath her eyelids, her brow knitting together.

"There," Edrea said. "Can you focus on the room?"

Rena and Liron waited on edge. For a moment, Rena could almost see what they saw. She imagined a dark hallway and a bright lab. Then she imagined an office at the end of that hall. She wondered what they saw inside it. The suspense had her leaning over her seat.

"Who's that woman sitting behind the door? All I can see are her legs and hand," Edrea said, leaning forward.

"I know that purse," Jule whispered. "That black quilted Prada purse under her hand. Can you see it?"

Rena moved even closer to the edge of her seat, almost slipping off.

"I see it. What is it, Jule?" Edrea sat up straighter.

Jule and Edrea's eyes popped open when Uri and Samuel returned to the astronomy sanctum with Pierre and Angelique. Jule's eyes were particularly large as she stared at Angelique, who stood at the front of the room. Edrea pivoted carefully to study her as well. Rena watched her sister's eyes move over the vampire and land on the item the woman held in her hand.

A black quilted Prada purse.

Rena sucked in a cold breath. Uri was suddenly quiet as well. He looked intently at Angelique, as if waiting for her to explain herself. Pierre had a look of confusion on his face.

"What is it?" Angelique asked, a tone of feigned innocence in her voice. Her eyes moved nervously between all the staring eyes.

Jule stood up confidently with the test tube in hand, and addressed her immortal maker. "Since I've known you, Angelique, you've never once parted from that handbag. Not once. You never put it down."

Rena and Liron flinched when Edrea leaped off the couch, disappearing from between them. She appeared directly in front of Angelique. Elias jumped up from the couch in front of the window, not sure what to do. Everyone watched in shock as Edrea's body hardened like a predator about to strike—everyone but Uri. Rena had the feeling Edrea had shown him mentally what they had unearthed.

"Jule, dear, what are you saying? What exactly is going on?" Angelique's anxious green eyes flared beneath her vintage brunette curls. She clasped the little black purse close to her bosom.

"What is the meaning of this?" Pierre asked, moving his body to shield his mate. His pained eyes didn't leave Edrea, as if he believed this was all to hurt him for their past.

Uri and Samuel moved to either side of Angelique. Uri wrapped his hand firmly around Angelique's upper arm, making her flinch. "I'm sorry, Pierre, but we will need to question Angelique. My human family is in danger, and I will do whatever it takes to save them."

"This is ridiculous, Uri. Please unhand my mate." Pierre's body stiffened defensively, his shoulders broadening under his iron-gray suit.

Edrea ignored his response. Seeing the hurt in his gray eyes made Rena feel sorry for him. But that only lasted a moment. She remembered how he'd allowed her to be tortured at the Décret, how he allowed Edrea to be tortured and murdered, and how he was now shielding a woman who could lead them to her parents.

Some people never change, she thought.

Samuel stayed at Pierre's side, placing a gentle hand on his shoulder to show understanding and injunction. Pierre stood frozen in place as Uri directed Angelique to an armchair in the far corner of the room. Edrea followed them, snatching her phone from the table as she passed the telescope. She typed a message into her phone, which Rena imagined was to inform Mikale.

"Please don't make this difficult," Uri warned, standing over Angelique. "We have very little time to help Edrea's parents."

Jule walked toward the corner of the room, skirting near the window. She hid the test tube within her fist. "Angelique, please. I know you have goodness in you. Help us."

Angelique's defensive eyes followed her progeny. "I don't know what you *think* I know, but—"

"That's enough," Edrea spat, stepping closer to the woman. "I saw you in the office down the hall from the lab. I saw your precious Prada purse. I saw your bronze nail polish. Your purple pointed flats. I even saw the beauty mark on the bend of your thumb."

Angelique stared, at a loss for words, her dark eyebrows knitting with bewilderment. Edrea had said Jule's maker wasn't aware of Jule's abilities, and they would keep it a secret for Jule's safety. Angelique probably suspected Edrea had somehow penetrated her mind instead.

"Trésor, what are they talking about?" Pierre asked, uncertainty growing in his voice. He took a careful step closer.

Angelique's gaze met his with guilt, but Rena wasn't sure if she showed any regret. Angelique's eyes moved from Pierre to Edrea and then settled on Uri. "You have no idea what you're up against. I'd rather not be on the side that doesn't stand a chance."

Pierre looked shocked but not surprised, for he had aligned with Nadine out of fear for a long time as well. Rena wondered if they had to worry about him changing sides again. At that thought, Bassét entered her mind. He was already on the wrong side, turned by the very woman who took Rena's parents.

Did he know Nadine would kidnap her parents? Is that why he let her go home early tonight? Out of a guilty conscience? She picked up her phone and texted Bassét. Just the thought that he might have something to do with this made her nauseous. "Please don't let them hurt my mom and dad," she wrote.

"Tell me where my parents are," Edrea demanded, taking another threatening step toward Angelique.

Liron dropped his head into his hands, anxiously brushing his fingers through his hair. Rena imagined this was a nightmare for him to be thrown so abruptly into this world. She took his hand into hers and held it on her lap.

"Don't you understand?" Angelique continued. "I may as well be dead if I tell you anything."

"The Prada purse," Liron said, as if having a sudden epiphany.

Everyone's gaze fell on Liron, like he were a mute child who'd spoken for the first time.

Angelique clutched her purse tighter, her eyes moving around the room with confusion.

Jule appeared in front of her maker in a flash of color. She ripped the little black purse from her arms before Angelique knew what had happened.

"What the hell are you doing?" Angelique protested.

Jule started out of the room with the purse but stopped at the threshold. She turned around slowly to face her maker. "You have your secrets, Angelique. I have mine." With that, she left toward Uri's office.

Uri stood to address the remaining vampires. "Samuel, Elias, please attend to our guests until Mikale and Gus return. Everyone else, kindly follow me."

Rena and her siblings followed promptly behind Uri. Edrea stayed close to Liron, appearing not to trust Pierre and Angelique.

Rena kept at Liron's side too. She felt protective, even as the baby sister. When they arrived at the office, Jule was already waiting on the couch with the purse on her lap. Edrea sat quickly beside her. Uri remained watchful by the hall, probably in case Pierre and Angelique tried anything.

"Let's hope this damn Prada purse shows us something, Jule," Edrea said. She folded a knee beneath her and pivoted her body to face Jule.

Rena and Liron embraced by the fireplace as the girls closed their eyes to search the purse's past. The crackling fire warmed them from behind and illuminated the room like a beacon of hope. Something told Rena they might be in luck.

A minute passed, but to Rena, it felt like an hour. She and Liron watched as quietly as possible, making sure not to break Edrea and Jule's concentration.

"Holy shit, I can't believe it," Edrea said excitedly. "She's actually putting the purse on the dashboard."

"She must be in a car with some sort of shipment—" Jule's words were cut off as her body stiffened.

Edrea went silent as well. She turned abruptly to sit forward, dropping her feet on the floor and squeezing the edge of the couch. "I'm gonna kill her," she hissed.

"What's going on?" Liron asked, stepping toward the girls. "What do you see?"

Edrea's eyes remained closed, her brow tense. "It's Mom and Dad . . . they're in the back seat. Their heads are covered. Victor is driving."

"Can you see where they are?" Rena cried from the fireplace. She tried to hold herself together, afraid she would go into shock. She had to stay present to help save them.

"Not yet," Edrea said, her eyes moving rapidly under her eyelids.

"That's Highway 37," Jule said. They're driving toward the East Bay."

"Keep the focus on the road in front of the car, Jule," Edrea said. "Speed the images until they turn off on an exit."

The girls were silent for a little while. Then they jumped.

"There," Edrea said. "They're exiting onto Walnut Ave. toward Mare Island."

Rena and Liron let out the breaths they had been holding.

"Left on G Street," Jule said, sounding hopeful.

Rena quickly typed everything they said into her phone.

"Right on Nimitz Ave.," Edrea continued, on edge.

"They're stopping at that large brick building with the broken windows," Jule said. "It looks like some sort of abandoned factory."

"What's happening?" Rena asked after a nerve-wracking pause. She moved toward the girls to stand by Liron again.

Edrea had a pained look on her face. She hesitated before answering. "They're taking Mom and Dad into the building. They have their hands tied behind their backs."

Rena covered her mouth with her palm to cry under her breath, tears wetting her cheeks and hand. Liron wrapped his arms around her.

"We know where they are now," Uri said calmly by the hall. "Let's gather as much information as we can."

"Angelique is escorting them in. How could she?" Jule said with disgust. "How could she do this?"

"Follow them closely. We need to see where they've left them," Edrea said.

Jule maintained her concentration, her body still. "They're going down those concrete stairs. They're taking them into a concrete room down the hall to the left. There are two metal chairs."

"They locked them in," Edrea said, her tone grating. "They left them alone in the dark. There's a guard outside the door."

Rena typed everything into her phone, tears dropping onto the screen.

"What are we waiting for?" Liron said, raising his jittery voice.

"We have to know the building, know where everything is, how many vampires there are," Edrea said. "We need to be prepared."

"Angelique went back upstairs," Jule said. "We've been here before. She's going toward the office."

"Nadine," Edrea hissed. "I figured she was in the office."

"It looks like that's all we're going to get," Uri said. "Let's get ready. Rena and Liron, stay here with Jule and Elias."

"I'm going," Rena said. "I'm done feeling helpless."

"Our parents are there," Liron agreed. "I'm coming too."

Uri edged into the room, arching his brow. "It's dangerous. You won't be able to protect yourselves against vampires."

"Nadine wants me alive," Rena said, unafraid. "Probably Liron too. He has O positive blood like Edrea and me. Besides, I brought my vampire-repellent weapons." She smirked for a moment at Uri.

Uri studied them, deep in thought. "We can't be sure we can protect you."

"I know," Rena said brazenly. "But it's more dangerous if we don't go. It's what Nadine wants. She'll hurt my parents if she doesn't have me. Even if it all ends tragically tonight, even if you lose, she'll come after me anyway. I'm going to fight. I'm going to fight for the ones I love."

"Do stakes work?" Liron asked, broadening his shoulders and tugging the front of his sweatshirt with both hands.

Rena gave him a funny look. "You have to cut their heads

off or burn them to ashes."

"A samurai sword then," he said, looking around. "Does anyone have one of those?" Rena had never seen him so fearless, or maybe foolish.

"We'll find you something," Uri said.

Everyone's attention shifted toward the front door as it opened and closed.

"Mikale and Gus just arrived," Uri said. "As soon as we've filled them in, we'll head to Mare Island on foot. Edrea, you will go with your siblings by car. Take Jule and Elias with you for extra protection."

"Alright," Edrea said, standing up swiftly with Jule.

Uri started out but then stopped at the edge of the room, his face falling. "I'm afraid it's not only our family we must protect tonight. The entire world will be in danger if we don't stop them."

Rena remained in the den alone for a moment, swallowing any rising fear and hopelessness. Her eyes found the flickering flames and watched how they danced in the darkness. She picked up her phone and looked for a response from Bassét. Her heart dropped into her stomach.

No messages.

24
Dove of Death

I didn't dare tell Liron and Rena all I had seen in Jule's mind. I didn't dare tell them that I had seen blood on my father's white shirt, that he was hunched over his knees, crying. That my mother struggled in her seat, thrashing around in the back of the car, trying desperately to break free from her bindings. That Victor laughed behind the steering wheel, as if their pain amused him. It was the most awful thing I'd ever seen.

They were my parents, but I didn't know if I could save them.

Uri had locked Angelique in a cell in the basement with a bag of blood. Only he and Samuel had the key. I wasn't sure if it was for our safety or hers. He knew very well that I wanted to tear her head off. Pierre was distraught over it, but he said he wanted to help us however he could. He told me he wanted to prove himself to me. I wanted to trust him, but something pricked inside my sternum, warning me that he hurt me once, and he could hurt me again.

I waited in the den with Jule and Elias as Uncle Uri prepared my siblings for war, a vampire war they had no chance of winning in their human form. Jule and Elias had changed into battle clothes. Jule wore black leggings and a tight black tank top. She had tied her long blond hair into a tight ponytail. Elias wore fitted dark-blue jeans and a navy-blue T-shirt.

He watched me strangely with his soft blue eyes. It was a look of devotion and respect. There was no more anger for me behind his gaze. He looked afraid but not for himself. I smiled warmly at him when I felt our bond tingle under my skin. I wanted to tell everyone that everything would be okay, that we would all be okay, but I wasn't sure.

"Uri actually had a samurai sword," Liron said, entering the room with a decorated black-and-red leather scabbard strapped to his side by a maroon cloth belt. Rena walked in behind him wearing a strange brown leather belt where she secured her torch lighter and a hairspray can.

I smirked at them, shaking my head. "You guys look ridiculous."

"Samuel let me borrow the belt." Rena shook the hairspray can at her side. "This is a full can. I can do some damage with this thing if I have to."

Jule, Elias, and I stared at them for a moment. Their lives were in our hands regardless of what weapons they possessed.

"No matter what happens tonight, you two have to stay together," I said. "Promise me."

They nodded and gripped their weapons tighter, as if it were a natural reflex. We had all agreed that as dangerous as it was, they would be safer if they came to Mare Island.

I turned my head back and forth between Jule and Elias at

my sides. "You'll stay with them, right?" Something felt wrong about asking them to risk their lives for my family. I'd never seen either of them fight before.

"You would do the same for me," Jule said.

Elias looked down at the floor and back up at Jule and me. "We're a family. We protect each other. But as Uri said, this is bigger than just us."

"Are you both prepared?" I asked.

"When I was in England, I studied more than my coven's aptitude for clairvoyance. They too have been preparing for war," Jule said. She didn't look happy about it.

I turned to our newest family member. "What about you, Elias?"

"I've learned a thing or two these past few months. And don't forget I was a firefighter as a human."

"Interesting," Rena said.

Uri came into the room and tossed me some keys. "I want you to take my Mercedes, Edrea. It will get you there quickly."

Gus and Mikale stood behind my uncle, ready to defend. Mikale's fearless eyes met mine with a private promise. I nodded in response, finding it difficult to tear my gaze from his.

"Consus is waiting outside with Samuel," Uri said. His kind brown eyes circled those of us in the room with care and warning. "Edrea, the plan is for you to get to your parents without being seen. We still have the element of surprise. Nadine won't be aware we've located their Mare Island headquarters. Jule and Elias will protect your siblings. Mikale and Gus will be your defenses. The rest of us will worry about Nadine and the Décret. We have guards around the perimeter of the site if needed."

Uri moved toward the window and looked between the blinds. Then he turned around with a look of concern, his forehead sinking into three creases. "Now listen closely, everyone.

Angelique was right. We have no idea how advanced Nadine's weapons are. Once you have the parents, get out. Take them straight to Mikale's place in Twin Peaks. The keys are there," he said, pointing to the keys in my hand.

A foreboding feeling circled the room as we all nodded. We were aware there might be losses, but we were ready to fight for those we loved.

Uri gave us a quick hopeful smile and then headed outside with Gus and Mikale. The rest of us hesitated for a moment, looking each other in the eye, like it might be the last time. I finally had my brother and sister close to me again. I also had a coven that put kin before all else. It wasn't the first battle some of us would see, nor was it the first time we had faced danger. But we had a family we couldn't bear to lose, a bond that grew stronger every day. At that moment, as we looked into each other's eyes, there were no humans and no immortals. There was only . . . us.

* * *

The rain pattered on and off against the car roof and windows. The sky thundered with dark clouds that lit up intermittently as we neared Mare Island. The storm followed us like an omen. I sat in the back seat of the Mercedes with Liron to my left and Rena to my right. Elias was in the driver's seat, his knuckles tight around the steering wheel. Jule watched the road apprehensively from the passenger seat. I got flashes of her thoughts, which felt like déjà vu times three. We had just traveled this road in the Prada purse's past, and now we were retracing the same path as we drove down Highway 37.

My uncle, Consus, and Samuel followed alongside the car, fleeting in and out of sight in the distant fields on either side of the highway. They wore dark clothing, so they would be less conspicuous. Liron and Rena watched them appear out of thin air as they fleeted around the marshes flooded with rainwater. I turned to look outside the rear window, searching for Mikale and Gus. They popped in and out of sight in our wake. I caught glimpses of Taralynn, who followed as well, her thin figure clad in black, her blond ponytail whipping in the wind. I couldn't help but feel we were all traveling to our doom.

I sat back and took my siblings' hands at my sides, my eyes refocusing on the road ahead. We didn't truly have a plan. We had no time for a plan. Only hours remained before sunrise. I couldn't imagine how we would pull this off. I just knew we had to try.

When we turned off the highway onto Walnut Ave., our fate was sealed like the dark overcast above. Only a fraction of the storm clouds were lit under the moon, which seemed to be hiding from the storm. The rain eased as we turned onto G Street, then Nimitz Ave., and drove past numerous abandoned buildings. It was like a ghost town. Then the car stopped. The second building ahead on the left was the one I'd seen my parents go into. It was a large two-story brick building, many of its windows broken, the red bricks faded with age. I wouldn't have been surprised if Freddy Krueger himself had walked out to greet us.

The car crept a block from the building, its headlights off. There was only one gated door on the street side of the building, and the building stretched the entire block. It looked like it went on forever. We stopped about a hundred feet away and backed the car behind stacks of rusted metal beams in a rundown construction site on the other side of the street.

"Who's that?" Liron asked, jumping in his seat.

My eyes moved to the front of the car as a vampire faced us outside. It was the nameless one, dressed in black, ready to fight like the rest of us. His long bangs hung down his soft cheekbones, wet with rain. I smiled. He always seemed to turn up when we needed him most.

A beautiful brunette vampire woman with light-brown almond-shaped eyes joined him at his side and took his hand, her long brown ponytail soaked from the rain. She was the same woman I had seen in his mind when the Décret detained him for questioning in the tunnels. Her tight black jeans and black leather jacket told me she meant business. She clearly didn't let him hide her away any longer. She would defend her mate. I saw a hint of fear in his eyes that was more prominent than before. He wasn't there to fight for us only. No one was.

The nameless one and his mate walked into the darkness under the metal beams. Uri, Consus, and Samuel met them there. I couldn't see the rest of the team yet.

"Stay here for a minute," I said to my siblings. I reached over Liron and opened his door.

I walked to the corner of the tall metal beams, my eyes studying the brick building down the road. There was no movement. My gaze traveled to the second floor, where dim light came from a few windows at the southern end. I saw movement between numerous plastic-covered pods across from the north side of the building. Mikale, Gus, and Taralynn came into view. They appeared to be doing a reconnaissance of the premises. The three of them fleeted past me and stopped in front of Uri. When I turned to join them, I saw Pierre had arrived too.

"There are only four doors, one on each side of the building," Mikale said. "We took down two guards on the northern side. If there are any more, they're most likely inside. Like Uri said, it doesn't appear they expect to be found."

I motioned to Elias and Jule in the car and joined Uri and the gang. "We should enter the side door on the north side of the building," I said. "It's closest to the stairs where I saw them take my parents."

My siblings approached, Jule and Elias flanking them.

Liron held the hilt of the sword like his life depended on it, his eyes jolting around the street. Rena stood fierce and calm, like she knew exactly what to expect. I watched her in awe for a moment before turning my gaze upon Liron. I felt fear pouring from his trembling form.

"Liron, how are you holding up?" I asked, my brow drawing together with worry.

He broadened his shoulders. "I'll be okay. Let's get Mom and Dad before it's too late."

I looked at my uncle. "What do you plan to do, Uri?"

"The rest of us will try the front door," he said. "We'll knock the good 'ol fashioned way. I hope to reason with Nadine. At least it will draw attention away from the side of the building you will be entering."

"There's no reasoning with Nadine," Pierre said. "She doesn't have a reasonable bone in her body."

As I watched my immortal father interact with the group, my inner being yearned for his support. I hoped this time he'd be true to his words. Even if I was afraid to believe it, I needed him back in my life.

"I don't suspect she will, Pierre, but perhaps we can buy a little time as we extract Edrea's parents," Uri said.

At those words, we all faced the building, which stood cold and wet like a nightmare in the dark. The sky thundered above, the clouds flashing with light into the distance. Cool raindrops trickled down our faces and danced upon the asphalt. The storm hadn't finished with us yet.

I walked toward the seemingly desolate building, looking back to ensure my siblings and soldiers were following close behind. Mikale and Gus appeared at my sides, Jule and Elias behind Liron and Rena. Taralynn fleeted ahead, zipping in and out between pods. My uncle and his team disappeared into the night.

251

We reached the first pod across from the side door. The large pod's plastic cover protested in the wind under the spatter of rain. I wondered what was protected underneath and if it was human-made or vampire. On the eastern side of the building, the Napa River splashed against the concrete where the land cut off.

Taralynn appeared next to us again. "The site is clear."

Mikale and Gus went ahead, fleeting directly to the side door. They tried at its handle carefully. It was locked. They both stiffened as if they'd heard something inside. Mikale put a finger to his lips as their bodies flattened against the bricks on either side of the door. I ushered everyone to stay out of sight behind the pod as I peeked around the corner. The door to the building opened, and a large immortal stepped into the rainy night. At that moment, I was glad it was raining. The raindrops slapping against the ground would distract from other sounds.

Before the immortal was aware of the intruders, Gus fleeted to him and twisted his head off with one violent movement, followed by a crunch. The immortal's body fell to the wet ground, his head landing with a thud before it rolled toward us. When it stopped, the head's dark eyes stared straight at me. Even as a vampire, the sight made me cringe.

I turned to Jule and Elias and my siblings, who all stood with their backs against the wet plastic covering the pod. "Stay here until I motion to you."

Taralynn stayed at my side, and we fleeted to the front of the pod. Mikale peered inside the building, watching for any witnesses as Gus threw the large body over his shoulder and fetched the detached head. Then Mikale carefully closed the door a crack as Gus fleeted toward the waterfront and dumped the body into the river. The Samoan vampire returned in a flash, and Mikale motioned to me with a nod.

I turned around and met Elias's watchful eye, which peered

from behind the pod. I gestured for him to follow. His head disappeared behind the wet plastic. Jule came first. Then my siblings followed, walking carefully toward the building. Elias stayed close behind them, his hands on their backs, nudging them to move quicker through the darkness and rain. When we reached the building, I heard my siblings' hearts thumping over the rain. I knew mine would have too, if it could.

Mikale kept his ear to the crack in the doorway, listening for any movement, his eyes wide and intense. The rest of us remained frozen. I could barely hear my siblings breathing, just the beating of their hearts and the rain slapping against the building in the waves of the wind.

My chest constricted when Mikale inched the door open. Liron's body began to tremble again. That made me more nervous. Jule put a gentle hand on his shoulder, attempting to calm him. I met Elias's worried gaze, his eyes resembling the gray storm clouds in the dark sky. They drew me straight into his thoughts. He sheltered me there for a moment, and we floated in the darkness of his consciousness. His palm rose to my cheek, the coolness of his thumb tracing down my face and chin. In his mind, his eyes captured the color of the purest blue sky.

I don't want anything to happen to you, he said. *I care about you, and I'm sorry for how I've acted recently.*

Don't worry about that, Elias. I'm sorry too. Like you said, we're a fam—

Before I could finish my thought, he took my face between his hands and laid his lips upon mine. It took a second to register what had just occurred, but it felt strangely real. Warmth hummed through my body. I could even feel the tingle between the flesh of our lips. I pulled out of his mind, my wide eyes finding his. They were the color of the storm again, and they fixed on me with intense emotion. Worry. Fear. Courage. Maybe even love. My lips tingled with the memory of his kiss.

"Okay, carefully, everyone. Be ready for anything," Mikale whispered, taking a step through the open doorway.

I eyed my brother and sister. Liron's muscles tensed, his eyes blackening with fear as his fingers adjusted again and again on the hilt of his sword. Rena's eyes fixed beyond the doorway, one arm hooked protectively around Liron's as the other hand gripped her torch lighter. I admired their courage. I was proud. I wouldn't let anything happen to them.

I shifted my stance to battle mode and stepped into the building after Mikale and Gus, finding myself in what looked like a huge empty factory. Dust and dirty paper swept across the gray concrete floor, sucked in with a rush of wind. Long lights hung above in rows. Only the ones on the left side of the room were lit, and they buzzed and flickered, casting dull light against the cracked concrete walls. Against the wall ahead of us were two doors. To our right was a hallway and the top of the dark stairway that led underground, where my parents were—where I hoped they still were.

I listened for voices. That was when I heard the knocking on the door at the other side of the building. My uncle's team had made their first move. Shuffling sounded in the distance, then a man and a woman's voices. The woman's voice sounded commanding. I recognized it immediately. Nadine. I looked back at Rena. She stiffened with the same realization. Jule gave me a knowing glance of warning. My eyes did a rapid survey of the room as Mikale and Gus fleeted to each door before listening intently for any noise behind them.

"We need to get them out now," I whispered, my anxiety spiking to the next level.

Taralynn stepped ahead of me and fleeted to the dark hallway on the right. She edged her head around the corner and then motioned for us to follow. I crept toward her, waving for my siblings to keep close.

Taralynn floated down the cold concrete stairway and stopped at the bottom, where it was dark. She threw up a hand before I took a step down. Then she held up three fingers. There were guards—three of them—which was both good and bad news. The good news was they were still guarding something, which meant my parents most likely hadn't been moved. The bad news was we would have to fight and kill three more vampires.

At that moment I realized something that hadn't occurred to me amidst all the panic and distress. My parents were probably still not aware I was alive. Unless, of course, Nadine had filled them in after their detainment, along with the fact that we were all vampires. I wasn't sure what to expect, except that my arrival would come as a complete shock.

Taralynn motioned violently with her finger toward the way we had come, mouthing Mikale's name. I turned to Elias and Jule and motioned for them to fetch our Hawaiian guards. The boys appeared at the top of the stairs with a gust of wind. I threw up three fingers and then pointed downward, mouthing, "Three guards." They took to the stairs at once, stopping in the darkness at the bottom.

"Someone please tell me why you're doing this. Why are we being held here?" a frantic woman cried in the distance. I felt my heart rip down the middle. I knew my mother's voice. I would still know it even if I had lived a thousand years. I had to stop myself from fleeting toward the horrifying sound.

Rena and Liron appeared at the top of the stairs, a look of terror upon their faces. Rena held her hand over her mouth, tears streaming down her face. Liron's eyes welled with tears, but then the fear disappeared from within them. In its place was the same rage Rena and I knew. I placed my hand on his shoulder until he focused on me. "Wait," I mouthed. He looked toward the bottom of the stairs, his body trembling not with fear but with hatred.

My mother cried in the background, tearing us all apart. Then I heard my father's weak voice. He was crying with her. I couldn't stand it. At that moment I knew I'd rather die than ever hear the sound of my parents terrified and crying again.

"If you don't stop your wailing, I'll suck the life out of you myself," a man's apathetic voice said.

My parents' cries died down to a whimper. It was clear that Nadine and her minions had made it known they were vampires.

"That's Victor," Rena said, her words barely audible. She wiped the wetness from her cheeks and broadened her shoulders.

Mikale looked up at me, his eyes vigilant. He waited for my signal that we were ready. I nodded. He winked sweetly at me, as if to say not to worry, but in his eyes I saw so much more, all our adventures and time together sweeping through my mind. I smiled back at him. Then he turned to Gus. The moment Gus nodded, they fleeted toward the guards. In a fraction of a second, we heard muffled yelps, the tearing of vampire flesh, and the smashing of concrete.

We rushed down the stairs and stopped at the base of the hall, which was lit by a single bulb dangling above a metal chair that was tipped over. Gus had disappeared around the corner of a long hall, the sound of shattering glass and banging in his wake. Mikale wrestled with the immortal I recognized as Victor. They fleeted around each other like two tornados, destroying anything in their path. Dust clouds filled the air around them. Not far from them, I recognized the door my parents were behind. In front of it was the metal chair with its legs in the air.

Mikale and Victor's bodies bashed into the wall across from the door and halted, Victor's arms firmly locked around Mikale's head. I stepped forward, ready to defend him, but

Taralynn beat me to it, fleeting to his rescue. She leaped onto Victor's back and attempted to lock her arms around his head, but she wasn't quick enough. He pulled out from beneath her, freeing Mikale, who made a strange gasping and coughing sound on the floor. In a flash, Victor had Taralynn pinned to the farthest wall, where the hall bent to the left, the blast causing another metal chair to ricochet off the walls. Mikale fleeted after them.

I was about to fleet to my parents' cell, but Elias wrapped his large hand around my forearm. "Someone is coming."

I tuned in to movement above us as Mikale and Taralynn fought Victor in the distance, pieces of concrete and furniture flying from behind the corner. "We have to get them out now," I said.

I fleeted to my parents' cell, my siblings sprinting behind me. Elias and Jule ran behind them at human speeds.

When I reached the door, I yelled to my parents. "Get away from the door!" I heard gasps and shuffling, then complete silence from within. I kicked the door in. It slammed open with a bang. My mother and father screamed, but when they saw me, their eyes went wide. A thousand thoughts spun through their minds at the sight of me standing there like a ghost. They didn't know if they should scream or cry. My father wondered if this was another one of his night terrors. They were always so real.

"Edrea? Edrea, is that really you?" my mother cried. My father stood frozen against the back corner, his frightened eyes glued to me.

"It's really me, Mom. We need to get you out of here now."

Liron and Rena moved behind me, so that they could see them too, so my parents would know I wasn't a hallucination.

Rena rushed into the room, which reeked of urine, and took Mom's arm. Liron lifted Dad from against the wall. "We have to go now," he said frantically. "They're coming for us."

I backed away from the door, letting my parents and siblings run out. My parents' confused eyes didn't leave me for one second. Elias and Jule guarded the hallway as my family ran toward the stairs.

Before we could reach them, my sister was ripped from my mother, disappearing. My mother screamed, falling to the ground. I searched the hall for Rena frantically. There against the far wall, Victor held her against him, her head locked under his arm. Rena struggled, attempting to pull his arm from her throat. Mikale and Taralynn stood only feet away, careful not to make another move as Victor could kill Rena with one squeeze. I inched forward. The memory of the battle at the Décret came to mind, when I almost lost her. I wouldn't lose her this time either.

"Son of a bitch," my mother hissed, standing with her fist in her mouth. "If you harm my daughter, I will fucking kill you."

Victor laughed. He knew my mother was no match for him, but I swore I saw a tinge of fear in his eyes. My mother could be particularly scary.

"Everyone stay right where you are," he said, "or I swear I'll tear her pretty little head right off."

At those words, several footsteps pattered down the stairs. Elias and Jule spun toward the sound and took a step back to ready themselves. They stepped back again and raised their fists when two immortals appeared at the bottom of the stairs. I gathered my parents and brother and hurried them to the center of the hall. My mother and father gripped my arms, a look of amazement and fright in their eyes. Where was Gus? Where were my uncle and everyone else?

"Now everyone walk upstairs very slowly," Victor said, giving Rena's throat a squeeze until she squeaked in pain. "You two go ahead of me," he said, motioning with his chin to Mikale and Taralynn.

They did as he asked. Everyone did. We didn't have a choice. My human family was too fragile. We all walked slowly up the stairs. The smell of mold wafted down, tainting the air. Every step felt like walking closer to our tragedy, but I would figure something out. I'd come up with a way to save them. Uri wouldn't let anything happen to them. He would save us . . . like last time.

A shiver ran down my spine as I wondered if Uri was alive. It didn't make sense why they hadn't come to help us. Surely they'd heard the fighting. The screaming. Nadine's mysterious weapon came to mind as we followed her guards.

When we reached the top of the stairs, I saw they holstered guns at their hips. Why would vampires need guns?

We followed the guards to the left and walked along a damp chilly hall, bursts of wind and rain whistling through several broken windows. It was so strange how I could feel the chill at times like this—feel afraid. Human. My parents shuffled along the cold concrete below our feet. They kept close behind me and terrifyingly quiet, Liron flanking by the window. I looked back at him. The nightmare had already solidified in the darkness of his eyes. Behind him, Rena walked stiffly under Victor's hold, his hand clamped around her throat, ready to puncture her jugular. I caught the look of helplessness in Elias and Jule's gazes every time they glanced back. They watched my eyes closely, waiting for some sort of signal to fight back, to do something. Anything. We couldn't though while Victor had Rena like that. While my parents or Liron could be murdered in an instant.

My focus shifted back to the guns. That was when I put it all together. The bullets were laced with something that could weaken vampires, maybe even kill them.

The next time Jule and Elias looked my way, I formed a gun shape with my fingers and motioned to the guards ahead of us. They looked forward again, their bodies tense. They lent me their thoughts in unison. They had suspected the guns were meant for vampires. I had been too concerned for my human family to notice the guns earlier. If Nadine could take us out with one shot, my family didn't stand a chance.

We neared an open door on the street side. The wind had picked up, but the rain had stopped. I peered through the long stream of windows to find several dark forms standing outside the building. I spotted Uri and clenched my chest with my hand, feeling some relief. Then I saw Samuel, Consus, Pierre, and the nameless one and his mate. Several other guards I recognized as Shevet stood behind them. Then I saw Nadine, Devika at her side. And Bassét. He stood to her left. Rena gasped in pain, and I knew it wasn't because Victor had hurt her. She had seen her vampire lover too. He'd betrayed her. He had been with them all along.

We followed the two guards out the door. When I stepped outside, Nadine turned to me, as if she knew my scent. "Such a long time, Edrea." Her bright red lips turned into a wide smile, revealing her sharp canines.

My eyes fell to the strange long gun she held in her hand. I realized it had a silencer on its barrel. I found Uri's eyes. *Don't make any sudden moves*, he warned. My eyes traveled to the ground behind him where a vampire lay immobile. His skin was the color of ash.

My furious gaze moved to Nadine. "You'll never stop, will you? It's not enough for you to be a Décret superior. Your hunger for unlimited power just itches under your skin, doesn't it?"

Nadine took a few steps toward Rena and me. "Perhaps," she said, eyeing us like we were her only tickets to success. She pointed her gun at Liron. "Handsome brother. He'd make a spicy immortal. He's O positive too, you know? The three of you would make quite the power trio of immortal mind readers."

"Leave my family alone," Rena said. Victor clenched

Rena's throat tighter, making her choke for air. Bassét stepped forward, an armed guard at his side immediately throwing his arm in front of him.

Nadine eyed a guard and motioned toward my father. The guard fleeted to his side and knocked him to his knees. My father cried out, trembling on the ground. "No, no, please." The guard took his head between his hands, ready to snap his neck. My father screamed and cried.

My mother ran to pry the vampire off, but he was like a statue made of steel. He elbowed her, and she fell back to the wet ground. "Leave him alone. Take me. Please, take me," she begged, tears streaming down her freckled face.

I clenched my fists, trembling, not sure what to do. No matter what I did, someone I loved would die. Jule and Elias stood behind Liron with looks of terror. Mikale and Taralynn were being held at the door with guns to their backs. I turned back to Uri, pleading for him to make one of his miraculous moves, but he looked just as stuck, just as rattled. We had no defenses against a biological weapon. Nadine had planned her perfect comeback.

"Nadine, when will you have enough? Is this how you want to live out eternity, hurting people? Making people suffer?" Uri asked, his voice calm and steady but more fragile than ever before.

"Your attempts to poke at my conscience are useless, Uri. It died long ago, when I was a human. Honestly, I couldn't care less if you and your little family suffer. I just want you to share a little bit of your precious powers. Is that so much to ask?"

"We don't use them to hurt people, Nadine. You seek power, using fear and pain to bend people to your will. We will never live that way. We use our abilities only for the goodness of humankind."

"We're getting nowhere here. Kill him, Darnel," Nadine ordered the vampire holding my father's head. The vampire's muscles flexed, one elbow rising as his fingers clenched my father's chin.

"Please, please!" my father screamed. My mother fought and screamed viciously in a vampire's embrace behind him, Liron and Rena screaming and crying behind them. This was it. Someone was about to die. I had to do something. I watched my father struggle helplessly, the most horrifying vision. Before I fleeted toward him, my eyes found Rena. Nadine needed her. She played on our fears. She wouldn't kill her if she could help it. Not after all this effort and planning to have her. To have me. To have all of us. I looked straight ahead, ready to risk my immortal life for the father who raised me. To risk everything.

I closed my eyes for a second as I entered slow time. When I opened them, Samuel was at my father's side. With a thin metal wire, he sliced through the vampire's neck. I fleeted toward the vampire holding my mother, at the same time hearing a strange popping sound. I ignored it, set on tearing the bastard's head right off. In slow time, I saw my mother fighting her captor at the end of my window of sight. I heard the clicking of triggers around me. I vaguely realized the popping sounds were shots and hoped we were fast enough to evade the bullets.

I was barely conscious of Jule and Elias fleeting in and out of the walls of my vision, appearing to fight off vampires near Liron, who stood against the building. I reached my mother's captor, a large dark man with black eyes. A gun slid under my feet. I didn't care how it got there. I picked it up and pulled the trigger, aiming at his head. He was too fast, and he disappeared, my mother falling to the ground before me.

She crawled to my father and wrapped her arms around him. They dragged themselves along the ground to the side of the building where Liron stood with his sword in the air. I fleeted to their side and shielded the three of them with my body. Then my eyes locked onto Rena and Victor. Her big brown eyes returned my gaze. They focused on me, and I saw a decision form within them.

Rena withdrew the hairspray can and torch lighter from her belt and pointed them at Victor's leg. She sprayed the fuel and ignited the mist, creating a spout of fire that raced up his pants. Taken by surprise, he dropped his arms from her throat to slap the fire away. Rena didn't hesitate. She raised the can to his head and sprayed him with more fire. His hair ignited like a match. Liron ran toward Rena and Victor. He lifted his sword and swung the blade at his neck. Victor's flaming head dropped with a thud to the concrete, his mouth wide open, his eyes rolled back and bloody.

I swiveled around in response to a choking sound behind me. Devika had Elias's throat in her hand, throwing him repeatedly against the brick wall. I couldn't see Jule anywhere. I fleeted toward them as Elias grabbed a handful of Devika's hair. I could read in Devika's unsettled mind that she wanted to punish me for Alexio's death. She blamed me for it, because he had died saving Rena. The truth was, she was jealous he chose me over her. I wrapped my fingers around her wrist and pried her hand from Elias's throat while lifting the gun to her pretty head. "Elias, protect my family. I'll take care of this one. Then I need to find Jule."

He nodded, covering his throat with his hand.

I threw Devika against the wall. She overpowered me, flipping me to the ground and clamping her hands over my throat. When my back hit the concrete, the gun flew out of my hand, sliding across the ground. I took her curls into my hand and grabbed her throat with my other hand, both of us growling. "You don't like to mess up your perfect curls, do you?" I taunted.

"You killed him, you bitch!" There was unbidden rage in her eyes, pure hatred for me.

I kicked the ground, trying to free myself. Devika grabbed

something and wrapped it around my throat. It felt cold and sharp, and it cut into my tough skin. I pried my fingers under her hand, turning my head to the right to find the gun. Instead, I saw a body. Another one of our soldiers. Devika smiled crazily, tightening the wire over my throat. I struggled against her, but it cut deep. My parents' screams came in and out in echoes.

"Edrea!" Rena screamed. I heard a pop. Devika's smile disappeared, her eyes going wide and darkening. She fell off me. I sat up, peeling the wire from my throat. Elias stood above me with the gun, his hand reaching for me. I took it, and he pulled me up, his eyes bleak. Then he fleeted back to my family's side.

My eyes searched the battle scene for Jule. I couldn't see her anywhere. I couldn't find Mikale or Gus either. Through the thickening fog on the street, Consus, Uri, and Samuel fought a whirlwind of vampires. They all fought for my family and me. The urge to fleet into the storm of fists and bullets consumed me, but I had to get my family out of there.

Pierre appeared at my side. "It's time, Edrea. Get your family to the car with Elias. I'll find Jule."

I hesitated, afraid to leave without Jule. Afraid to fully trust Pierre so soon. My worried eyes found my family. They embraced each other against the building with tears in their eyes. Rena's gaze bore into me, ready to follow my lead.

"Trust me, Edrea," Pierre said.

The fighting seemed to ease into an eerie silence. I stared blankly into the hazy morning fog, its dewy mist bringing warning. The sunlight would illuminate the sky soon enough. I focused on Elias. "Get my family to the car."

He wrapped his arms around them at once, lifting them cautiously from the ground. I turned my eyes to the new stillness. Uri, Samuel, and Consus stood on the street facing the building. In front of the building, Nadine remained with a gun in hand, staring my uncle in the eye. Through waves of transparent mist several vampires lay dismembered on the ground. I searched the scene of death for Mikale and Gus. I wondered where they were, if they were okay. Jule was nowhere to be seen. I hoped Pierre would find her. The fear that they'd been killed seeped into my bones.

My parents walked rigidly toward the car behind me, Liron and Rena embracing them ahead of Elias, who walked stiffly behind them, ready to take a bullet if need be. They all flinched as gunshots sounded overhead. Consus fleeted into the distance, presumably going after those who shot at us.

Nadine's furious gaze shifted to the movement behind me. It seemed she'd exhausted the majority of whatever soldiers were on guard there, which meant she was even more dangerous. She was desperate.

"Edrea," she said with hatred in her tone. "Your sister has made a deal she cannot get out of. She will stay put, or your uncle will die right before your eyes."

My eyes landed on Uri. Behind him stood an immortal who had come out of nowhere. He held a gun to Uri's head.

"Don't listen to her, girls," Uri said calmly. "Get everyone out now."

Samuel stood at Uri's side, his fingers outstretched at his sides. He looked at me strangely, like there was a secret between us. Then he fleeted toward Nadine before I could blink. My undead heart jumped at the sound of a pop. My eyes watched his slender body fall to the ground. I screamed as his head hit the concrete. Without another thought, I fleeted toward Nadine, hoping I was faster than her bullets.

In slow time, I heard Rena scream my name. When I was a split second away, Bassét came into view, his hand on Nadine's gun. He struggled against her, attempting to pry it from her hand. I heard another pop behind me. I feared it was my uncle, but I kept my focus on Nadine. Bassét was able to wrestle the gun away the moment I reached her. She spun around and swung her arm to bat me off. The blow sent me to the ground, and I slid several feet into a parked truck.

I shook it off and stood against the cold metal door. My eyes found Samuel. He was still immobile on the concrete. I searched for Uri, but he had disappeared. Furious and concerned for those wounded and possibly dead, I looked for Nadine. I spotted her kneeling next to a headless Décret soldier with her back to me. I wondered for a moment who he was. I got ready to attack her because she looked vulnerable, but Rena ran to me with her hairspray can and torch lighter in hand.

"Rena, what are you doing? Go back to the car. I need to finish this."

Bassét stood a few feet away, still pointing the gun at his immortal maker, a paranoid look in his dark eyes. It made me wonder if he would really kill her.

"I'm part of the reason we're in this mess," Rena said.

As Rena spoke Nadine spun around with another gun. I heard two pops. My body flinched, but I didn't feel the bullets pierce me. That was when I realized Rena was standing unusually still right in front of me.

"No!" Bassét screamed.

"Rena?" I said anxiously, my mind not grasping why I wasn't hit.

A pool of blood seeped through the front of her shirt. She fell to the ground, gasping, Samuel's body not far from hers. I sank to my knees, not understanding what had happened.

Rena lay on the ground, crying and coughing up blood. "I'm sorry, Edrea. I'm sorry."

Her blood poured out onto the concrete, and my body entered a sort of shock. "Rena, you're hit," I said faintly. My body shook, my mind blackening. I didn't know what to do.

I lay Rena's head upon my lap, and in a flash, Bassét was at her other side. I looked up, afraid Nadine would shoot again. To my right she stumbled into the building, holding her side with a bloody hand. Bassét had shot her. I yelled for my uncle and Consus, but no one came. Rena continued to gasp and cry, and her heart palpitated unevenly. Panic poured through my veins, my insides twisting with helplessness. I couldn't give her my blood. It would do no good against the bullets laced with whatever antibiotic was meant to kill Bacillus F.

I looked up to see Liron running toward us.

"I can save her," Bassét said frantically, his hands moving erratically over her body. "The poison won't affect me. I can turn her into a day-walker. It has to work."

I felt a warm sensation on my back. I noticed the sky was no longer black but a dark shade of blue. My body trembled. The sun was close to the horizon. We had little time. My baby sister would die in my arms. I nodded to Bassét. His teeth sank into his wrist, and he drizzled blood over Rena's mouth. She was barely conscious, but she swallowed. Her body went into convulsions. Helplessness seeped like dry ice from my chest to my limbs as I watched her suffer, as I watched her possibly take her last breath. Liron slid to a stop in front of us, his sword dragging across the ground, the pain and fright in his eyes slicing through my heart.

"We need to get her to Mikale's," I said harshly.

Bassét picked up her limp body. "Let me take her, please."

I studied his fearful expression, afraid to trust him but more worried about Rena. Then I remembered he had shot his own maker in an attempt to save us. I nodded, and he and Liron ran toward the car. "I'll be right there," I cried, watching Rena's limbs dangling like death in Bassét's arms.

I was so consumed with fear that I had trouble registering

the situation before me. My eyes finally set on my humble African mentor at my knees. His hands still moved at his sides. I shuffled closer to him, sorrow and pain gathering in my chest. I knew there was no hope. I took his hand and squeezed, looking into his partially open eyes, which were always so kind and knowledgeable. They stared up at the sky, which was a lighter shade of blue. I knew the sun would burn me, even if it wasn't direct sunlight, but I didn't care. I couldn't leave my dear friend who had saved my life more than once.

I touched the smooth ebony skin of his head. "I love you, Samuel. I will stay with you," I said, wishing I could cry, but no tears came.

"I know, Edrea," he whispered between raspy coughs. "I love you too, child." His eyes were fixated on something above. "Well, look at that," he said, the side of his mouth turning up.

I trembled with sadness as his eyes glazed over. I barely heard a car screech to a stop to my left. I studied the way his eyes traveled to a far-off place, no longer anything behind them. His glossy irises stared up into the sky, and the sky stared back at him, reflecting a clear morning blue. I realized the storm had finally passed, the clouds dispersing. I looked up too, ignoring the burning on the back of my arms from the morning light.

Right there above us, fluttering in a circle was the most beautiful sight, a familiar sight. A white dove.

Samuel's white dove.

25

Rena: The Road to Tomorrow

My eyes opened to pitch blackness. My body felt like it
was floating above the soft mattress beneath me. My fingers dug
into the silk sheets that covered my chest. I didn't remember
owning silk sheets or a mattress that soft. That should have made
me anxious, but it didn't. Was this a strange dream, the kind where
I woke up within a dream? My shoulders tensed as screams
shrieked in the back of my mind. Something told me they were the
screams of people I knew, people close to me. They were distant
screams, like they belonged to someone else's thoughts, not mine.

I sat up in bed with a jolt. A foreign room slowly came into
focus. Long dark drapes. Elaborate crown molding. Elegantly
carved corners of an armoire and similar bedroom furniture. My
body and limbs felt lighter. A lot lighter. That was when I noticed
the wetness beneath me. It didn't smell of urine, but the mattress

269

was soaked. Whatever it was, it was disgusting. I peeled out of bed and tore off my wet clothes. I tossed them onto the mattress and wrapped the wet sheets into a ball around them. Then I placed them between the bed and the window.

I went to the chair at the corner of the room where I found neatly folded clothes. I recognized them as Edrea's. A green T-shirt and gray cotton slacks. I threw them on. I turned toward the opening between the drapes when something about the moonlight stole my attention. It was the way it glimmered, as if with tiny silver dust. I reached out and touched the light, my skin appearing firmer and more shimmery than normal. I swore I could almost feel the light. Wait, no, I *could* feel it, but just barely. It tingled against my skin with a subtle tickle.

I leaned against the windowsill and stared out into a neighborhood I'd never seen before, finding it hard to tear my gaze from the bright moon and the way it turned the clouds a silvery white. I had never remembered the clouds looking that color at night. At that moment, I realized something was poking at the back of my mind, something I should know or maybe remember. I was afraid it might be something terrible, but I couldn't remember a thing. The distant screams echoed in my mind again, and I took in a sharp breath. I frowned when I realized the air felt different in my lungs, not satiating. I blew the air out and breathed in again. The once-natural process didn't feel natural or even necessary anymore.

I squeezed the curtain between my fingers when the dream I had before I woke sliced through my mind—the burning agony that had torn through my body for what felt like eternity. I remembered I couldn't move. I was petrified in a bed of fire. Something was not right.

Footsteps neared outside the bedroom. The wood floor creaked. I shook my head and pressed my fingers against my ears.

The bedroom door opened. I turned slowly to face whoever was there. Her form glowed in the moonlight. I focused on her face. It was my sister, Edrea. For the life of me, I couldn't remember what had happened or why I was in that strange place.

"Re?" she said, taking a soft step forward.

"What's going on, Edrea?"

She didn't answer. She appeared in front of me, taking me into her arms and squeezing. My arms hung at my sides as I stood there in confusion.

"I don't remember anything. Why am I in this place? Why do I feel so strange?"

Edrea pulled back and stared curiously into my eyes. Her eyes shone red in the moonlight. "Oh, Re. I'll explain everything. But first you need to feed. I'll be right back. Stay here." She disappeared but returned seconds later with a bag of red liquid. She handed it to me hesitantly.

I studied the bag of what looked like blood, wondering why it made my stomach burn. I gasped and dropped it to the floor when my canines popped down in my mouth. I was afraid I'd been in an accident, and they were about to fall out. I touched them carefully. They were sharp and firmly in place, right where they should be. My eyes found Edrea. She picked up the bag from the floor.

"You need to feed, Re. Otherwise, you'll be a danger to the family." She placed the bag back in my hands. I looked at her like she was crazy. It had to be a strange dream.

My eyes traveled down to the burgundy bag. "Is this cherry juice or something?" My stomach screamed at me, like I was famished and hadn't eaten in a month. How could I drink from it? It looked sealed. *It doesn't matter if this is a dream*, I thought.

I raised it to my mouth and pushed the corner between my lips. I bit down, and my teeth punctured the rubbery plastic. Warm silk flowed down my throat, bringing me to life. A growl rumbled from inside me as I drank the liquid, which tasted of sweet copper and iron. I had no idea why it tasted so amazing, but it caused a kind of frenzy that shot through my veins, a strange ecstasy I hadn't experienced before. Well, except for *that* kind of ecstasy.

I looked above the bag to Edrea, who watched me awkwardly, like she hadn't seen me for years, and I'd changed somehow. The bag finally flattened between my fingers, and I pulled it away. "Wow, I was thirsty. Why didn't you just bring me a glass?"

She took the drained bag from my hands. "Blood doesn't really come in glasses, Re."

Blood? For a moment, everything spun around me. Only in a dream would my sister give me a bag of blood, and I would freely drink it, right? I stood frozen in place, trying to decipher if this dream would turn into a nightmare and if I should wake up for real now.

"Do you want me to get Bassét?"

The name that left my sister's lips sent a pleasant chill through my limbs, like my flesh remembered him before my brain did. A handsome face brushed my memory. Dark eyes and hair. Tanned skin. A smirk that caused a tingle in my chest. I clearly knew Bassét, and yet the memory of him wouldn't solidify.

"Maybe he'll help you remember. I'll go get him."

She left me standing there. In the distance, I heard voices, most of them familiar. This was no ordinary dream, and I began to wonder if that was what it truly was. I went back to the bed and sat down, watching the door inquisitively.

A man stepped into the light of the moon, his face obscured in the darkness. I watched him come slowly toward me. He stepped into the shimmering light, and I saw that his face was the one I'd seen in my thoughts moments earlier. Strange that I knew his face but couldn't remember how I knew him.

"Are you Bassét? I'm sorry if I don't remember who you are. Actually, I don't remember who I am. I mean, I just drank a bag of blood. I'm clearly dreaming this all up. Either that or I'm completely crazy."

He stepped in front of me, looking down at me in awe, his eyes shining dauntingly red in the light of the moon. He lifted his hand and touched my cheek with his thumb. I grabbed his wrist and pulled it down ambivalently.

My hand still on his wrist, I stared into his strange eyes. A chill tingled down my spine the deeper I looked into them. It was as if I could see and feel his story. "I don't . . . I'm . . . I'm definitely dreaming."

I gasped as images came flowing through my mind, as if flowing from his mind to mine. They were like vivid memories, but not mine. I saw myself through his eyes, first at a nightclub dancing, then in a coffee shop, and then dangerously close to a mountain lion in a dark forest. I saw myself working in a lab with chimps, my parents in a dark cell. Every memory zipped by in fast-forward until they ended at a building by a river. The last image was of a woman shooting me. I grabbed my stomach when I felt the strange phantom pain.

My eyes widened. All the images seared into memories. Real memories. My memories. "Nadine?" I said, her name burning with hatred in my gut. "My parents and Liron. Where are they?"

Bassét took my shoulders. "They're here, Rena. We're in a safe place. We're at Mikale's house." His familiar French accent soothed me.

I looked up at him, a world of pain, rage, fear, and sorrow gathering behind my sternum but still not completely my own. "You . . . you saved me, didn't you?"

That was when I realized what had happened. This wasn't a

dream. That evil bitch had shot me. She had killed me after all. And yet, there I stood, flesh and bone. The bag of blood I'd just finished came to mind. My body stiffened, and I grabbed the edge of the bed. "You fed me your blood? I'm . . . I'm a vampire?"

He looked down at the floor and swallowed. His intense gaze turned up to me, his eyes glowing dark red. "Yes. A day-walker like me."

"Shit," I said wide-eyed. "And Nadine. Where is she?"

He looked off to his left, his eyes pained, like he had done something awful. "I shot her, but it was too late. She had already fired the gun at your sister. You stepped in front of the bullet. You saved her." He went to the window and froze, and I followed him with my eyes. "I imagine Nadine is dead now. The last I saw her, she was stumbling into the building on Mare Island."

It took everything I had to feel sympathy for his loss. The world would be a better place without her, but she was still his maker, and there was a bond between them, regardless of her wrongs. "I'm sorry, Bassét."

He looked at me. "Are you ready to see your family? We have to make sure you aren't craving blood. Are you satiated?"

The thought of fresh blood was disturbingly appetizing, but my stomach didn't ache for it yet. I nodded. "I'm ready."

Edrea appeared at the doorway. She opened the door wide and waited, sadness in her eyes. Bassét took my hand, and we left the room together.

When we stepped into the hallway, I had to squint because the light was too intense, and the walls were too white. They led me down a short stairway into a living room where little globes of dim light hung from the ceiling like dying suns.

My insides warmed and flowed through my frigid limbs the moment I saw my family, my human family. I stopped at the base of the stairs, afraid their life's blood would tempt me. On a large

L-shaped leather couch, my parents and Liron sat in front of a giant stone fireplace that reached halfway to the ceiling. Uncle Uri sat adjacent to them, staring into the fire, as if he hoped an old friend would be reborn from the flames. In a dining area to my left, Consus talked with the immortal everyone called the Nameless One. His lover stood in his embrace, his arms tightly around her waist.

I looked back into the living room. Mikale sat pensively on a blue chair across from my family, and Elias stood near the bookshelf, his fingers moving between the hardcover texts. Samuel wasn't there, and neither was Jule. I wondered where they were. I imagined it wasn't good. Even the air seemed heavy with sorrow and darkness.

I entered the room with slow heedful movements. I couldn't be too careful. A chill went down my spine when I saw the way my father looked at me, like I was no longer his child and instead a beastly thing come to eat him. My mother's eyes were swamped with tears. She held her arms out to me. I sat hesitantly next to her on the couch. When I was sure I could control myself, I snuggled into her bosom and let her wrap her arms around me.

It seemed everyone mourned my human life. Unless it wasn't only me they mourned.

"I thought I'd lost you," my mother cried. "Both of you," she said looking up at Edrea with awe.

Well, she kind of had.

My father reached over and touched the skin of my arm and then pulled back, like he had touched something ice cold. I looked at Edrea. She still stood at the base of the stairs with Bassét. Both of them looked uneasy next to each other. I doubted Edrea trusted him. I wasn't sure I did, not completely.

I turned my head against my mother's chest to find Liron. He had a dazed look on his face, like he'd been to war and back. I guessed he had. I sat up, feeling off, as if not quite settled in my new skin and not quite detached from my human life. I could feel, but I couldn't at the same time. It would be hard to explain to anyone but Edrea.

"Where's Samuel and Jule?" I asked warily.

The silence in the room seeped into the rest of the house. Even my parents stopped breathing for a moment. My mother took my hand. My father peered around the room like a terrified child. He was clearly in shock. Liron's chest rose and fell slowly. Images of him slicing off Victor's head with the samurai sword flashed through my mind. As they did, Liron shifted his body on the couch uneasily. He'd saved me too. Then I realized I must have seen inside his mind. I looked up at Bassét, remembering I'd seen inside his mind earlier as well.

"Samuel didn't make it," Edrea said finally with sadness in her voice. "He was shot with a poisoned bullet, a serum that kills vampires. We think Jule . . . we're not sure where she is, but we're doing everything we can to find her. No bodies were found. Not even Nadine's."

"Could Nadine still be alive?" Liron asked, anxiety filling his features.

"Only if she had an antidote to the serum," Uri said. "Mikale returned with Gus and Taralynn to Mare Island at sunset tonight. Day-walkers had already cleared out the bodies. There was no serum left behind either. If Nadine had an antidote, this is far from over. If she's alive, she's most likely gone into hiding. I'm sure she's aware I will go to the ISC about her crimes. It's too dangerous not to. The vampire world needs to know that we are under attack. All of us. I have to risk the ISC discovering we've broken the immortal code now that our human family knows of our world. I have no choice."

"What will happen now?" I asked, afraid my family was in

danger. "We can't just send them home unprotected."

"They will have to stay here for a few weeks, of course," Uri said. "We'll need to file a pardon with the ISC. I have the feeling they will understand after they learn Nadine forced us into it when she kidnapped your parents. I reckon they'll be more concerned with the new vampire race and the danger a biological weapon poses against vampires all over the globe."

"A few weeks?" my father said, looking around at everyone like we were the monsters ruining his life.

"Settle down, Abraham," my mother said.

I sank into the couch, feeling guiltier the more I learned about what Nadine had accomplished. I had helped her, working in the lab all year. Not only had I helped her torture animals, but I had also helped her test her weapon.

"I'm not feeling very well," I said. "I think I need some more rest." I turned to my family, who looked so fragile, so mortal. I had been just like them less than twenty-four hours earlier. "I love you, Mom and Dad. You too, Liron. You were all so brave yesterday. You're all safe now."

"I'll come check on you later," my mom said, as if I were still her little girl. Her daughter. I shot her a smile, but I couldn't quite feel the emotion behind it.

When I reached the stairs, Edrea wrapped her arms around me. "I didn't thank you, sis. You saved my life. That was so stupid," she said, a smile sneaking up on her.

I pulled away and smirked. "Now we're even," I said as I started up the stairs.

Bassét followed me, and I let him, knowing I would need his help.

The moment we stepped into my room, I closed the door securely behind us and went to the window. It was a two-story drop to the ground. That was nothing to a vampire, let alone a day-walker.

I felt one thing stronger than anything else, and that was guilt. I needed to repair the damage I had caused, and I knew exactly where to start.

* * *

I fleeted rather unsuccessfully at Bassét's side through the crisp night air, moonlight shining through the scattered silver clouds. I wished I could appreciate the world as it appeared through my new eyes, but I had to learn more about two aspects of my new life: fleeting and feeding.

We made it halfway between Mikale's house and the lab. The most challenging part was not hitting cars and buildings, let alone people, while going through the city. Once we made it across the Golden Gate to the outlands, I could more easily learn control while at vampire speeds. It was strange how time seemed to slow while fleeting. I would have thought everything would speed up instead. It had to be due to some theory in physics or relativity that I didn't understand yet.

Entering in and out of slow time, Dingo's wide smile appeared in the tunnel walls of my vision. It drew the distant blackness of sadness closer to my core, as if all my emotions existed behind a dam that would collapse when it reached its capacity. I wasn't ready for that yet. One emotion at a time.

We finally reached the hilly outskirts of the farm. The grass was damp and smelled of dew mixed with the sweet smell of eucalyptus. The intensity of the aromas consumed me until it was almost overwhelming. Standing on a high hill, I saw the sad oak tree that stood over my pet cemetery. I pushed away the emotions seeping through me as my eyes searched the premises for any vampires.

"I think they've abandoned the farm," Bassét said. "Let's

go save your friends."

He smiled, and I smiled back, not letting myself be drawn into the dark wonder of his eyes for too long. It would be distracting. Instead, I looked down at my phone and texted Edrea. I didn't tell her where we were, but she needed to know I was okay. All we needed was for my vampire and human family to think Bassét had kidnapped me. I put the phone back in my pocket and took his hand. Then we walked toward the grounds. We didn't fleet at first, wanting to be sure there were no guards lingering. We couldn't sense any movement or hear any voices nearby.

"Okay, let's fleet to the tree," I said.

We entered slow time, the curious tunnel vision surrounding both of us, low fog floating as if frozen outside our tubular passage. When the oak tree palpitated closer to the end of the tunnel, Bassét squeezed my hand, the cue to stop.

We stood for a moment at the base of the tree. I touched its cool bark with my fingers as my eyes passed over the little rock graves. I searched for the white flower. I was glad to see it still stood as vibrant as ever in its lonely paradise. Its white petals glowed a brilliant white under the moon, freshly sprung blades of gleaming green grass circling its stem like the rings of Saturn. There was an unforgettable beauty to it, even amidst that place of darkness, death, and sorrow.

We made our way to the large sliding doors of the barn. They squealed when we pried them open, echoing sharply into the distance. Both of us stiffened and looked around the grounds for any attention it may have drawn. Bassét was right. With Nadine dead or on the run, I would have been surprised if the entire barn and lab hadn't been wiped clean.

"Let's be quick about this," Bassét said, looking nervous.

We ran inside, brushing around the white van, and went straight to the door in the ground behind the wall. The first thing I noticed was the shelves that used to be stocked with lab instruments and equipment. They were empty, nothing but dust and sparse rusted pieces of tack. How did they manage that? It hadn't been much more than a day since I was there. Bassét didn't look surprised. He flipped the red oriental rug over and pried the door open, revealing those hellish stairs that led to the torture chamber. We made our way down step by step, listening for any noise. I put my hand around the cold handle of the lab door, worried about the death I might find behind it. I swallowed and pulled it open.

The screaming of chimps was like music to my ears, though at first, it was painfully sharp. I ran around the inside of the cages, my eyes traveling from the first cage to the last. The five of them looked relatively healthy. There was some food and water in the cages that would keep them nourished for the trip.

I looked around the lab, noticing all the instruments and serums were gone. "Why would they clear out the barn and lab but leave the chimps?" I asked, nervousness picking up under my skin.

Bassét flinched, his head turning toward the ceiling. "Someone's upstairs."

We ran to the right corner of the lab where we would be less visible. I hoped we wouldn't have to fight more vampires. We braced ourselves when the door opened slowly. Arnav came through the door, still wearing his white lab coat. I tensed when I saw a gun in his hand.

I took a few wary steps toward the seemingly exhausted vampire. "Arnav, what are you doing here?" It crossed my mind that this might be it, that he had been sent to kill us if we came back.

"Rena, don't," Bassét warned, grabbing my arm.

Arnav didn't make eye contact as he walked into the room. We weren't sure what he would do. Even the chimps waited in suspense. He proceeded across the lab and stopped with his back to us at the white countertop where his chemistry lab used to be. He placed the gun carefully on the surface in front of him. Then he turned to us, his eyes still focused on the floor.

"After you left last night, Nadine ordered me to dispose of any traces of the lab. To put down the chimps and bury them." His solemn dark eyes finally met mine. "But I'm done slaving for that awful woman. I knew you would come for the chimps, so I left them here for you." For the first time, a smile spread across his face.

"Oh, Arnav," I said. I fleeted across the room and wrapped my arms around him. He stood back, disgruntled, and took my shoulders, studying me. His smile disappeared, replaced by a look of grief.

"You're no longer human."

"Long story. Maybe one day I'll get the chance to tell you all about it. For now, I need to drive these chimps across the States to Florida."

"Florida?" he asked, bemused.

"There's a chimp sanctuary there. It's the least I can do, after everything."

Arnav studied me for a long moment. He reached into his white lab coat and withdrew a set of keys. "Take these, child. They're the keys to the white van in the barn. You should probably take the gun too. It will kill vampires."

Bassét appeared at my side. He took the gun and wedged it under his belt.

"Thank you, Arnav. You don't know how much this means to me," I said.

"Go now, Rena. There's no telling what else Nadine has up her sleeve."

"I have the feeling she won't be back for quite a while," I

said, "if she's still alive. Bassét shot her while protecting my family on Mare Island."

Bassét and I readied all the chimps and carried their cages up to the van. They screamed with what sounded like joy as we secured them on top of blankets in the back of the vehicle. We came down for the last one, and Bassét lifted the cage into his arms. I went to Arnav and kissed him on the cheek before I met Bassét at the door to the lab. I turned to look at the lab for the last time, for real this time. I gave Arnav a warm smile and then turned to the stairs behind Bassét, the chimp finally quiet in the cage.

"Nadine isn't dead. You can be sure of that," Arnav said behind us. There was guilt in his tone. "I created the antidote."

Bassét and I hesitated but then continued up the stairs, letting the door close behind us.

* * *

We traveled at night, as any vampire would do to avoid the sun. There was something so right about this journey, like everything had finally fallen into place. This time I had done the right thing. I would save the chimps after all.

We were on the I-10 East smack in the middle of Texas, a little over halfway to our destination, the Florida coast of the North Atlantic Ocean. Bassét and I stopped occasionally for chimp food and, of course, to feed ourselves.

As my maker, I couldn't have asked for a better teacher. He was a day-walker himself. We started our lessons in the precarious venues of local nightlife. We mostly hit nightclubs when the thirst grew in our bellies. We had met in one after all. We even got some dancing in, and that eased any tension we brought along the journey. The roads were occasionally stormy, but we trudged through. During the day we would find a bridge to park beneath or a secluded country road where we could hide the van under trees.

I missed my family. I missed my dog. I missed my human life. The emotions crept to the surface every day, that burning sun in the middle of my core ever expanding. When it got hard, Bassét was there by my side. My lover. My maker. My friend. But some things I had to hide for fear of hurting him. Things like Tony. I tried not to think too much about him, but it was difficult. He was part of the reason for this long journey. I saw it as a gift to him, maybe a way to say sorry for all I put him through. He would have wanted me to save the chimps. Bringing them to the same sanctuary he had brought me to years earlier was a sense of closure for me.

For there was a brand new life ahead.

The road to tomorrow.

Epilogue

Rena had disappeared once again. The good thing was, we had cellphones. Since her turning, our mind connection appeared to be momentarily severed. I hoped we could get it back. Then again, at the same time, I didn't. Too much sisterly connection was simply too much. As long as she was safe, I was happy. I mourned her human life, but I also saw that immortality suited her. She had turned into quite the woman, and if I may say, quite the badass. I expected she would stay away for a while until she faced all she needed to, learned all she dreamed to learn. When it came down to it, we now faced eternity together, however long that would be.

Jule, on the other hand, was still missing. It was like she disappeared off the face of the earth. Uri promised he wouldn't stop using all the resources we had to find her. That comforted me, but I feared the worst, and the thought she may never come back plagued me every day. She was an important part of my family and my life. I wouldn't be at peace until I found out what happened to her.

I was glad I had Elias at least. He was the progeny I never planned to make and the best friend any girl could ask for. I would try not to jump into some strange relationship with him because that would be awkward. I hoped he didn't think I was out to sire a mate into my life. And yet the secret kiss on Mare Island when we weren't sure we would survive the night tickled in the back of my mind almost every day. I wasn't sure what it meant, even if it only happened in our minds. It could have just been a reflex in a moment of heightened emotion. Then again, it could also be the next adventure.

There was no telling what tomorrow would bring for any of us at that point. We weren't alone in immortality anymore. There was a whole new race out there, a race that could be exceedingly dangerous. We were all worried, as was the ISC, according to Uri. The good thing was, they had pardoned my family and exposed any Décret they could find working for them who had followed Nadine. My family, both mortal and immortal, was safe for the moment, but I knew that wouldn't last. Not when such a dangerous weapon existed in the vampire world, and definitely not if Nadine was still alive to see that it was used to her advantage.

For the time being, we would look to tomorrow and take all the necessary steps to protect those we loved. We would look ahead, but we would never forget the ones we had lost.

Like our sweet Samuel. He was my teacher and my friend. He was family. I wasn't sure I could ever accept that he was gone. There was so much I had looked forward to learning from him. So many things he was meant to teach me. The memory of him burned like an eternal sun in my heart. Every single day I expected him to walk through the door with a pearly white smile.

He would always be a light amidst the darkness.

A white dove soaring free in the blue sky.

Dear Reader:

It's hard to describe what it means to me that you continue on the journey with Edrea and Rena. Their characters are based on a real sisterhood and their family on a real kinship. Even though the story takes place in a fantasy vampire world, the meaning behind the story trickles into our own reality. We all share the same pain, the same sorrow, the same love and joy, the same fears and even hatred. We all share one humanity. Together we can face both the beauty and the darkness that exist in our hearts and in our strange universe.

Hidden within the world of *The Beauty in Darkness* is a place where we can all relate and somewhere we can dream. It's a place where we can remind ourselves that even when the sky glooms over with a chilly melancholy, and the darkness consumes everything around us, we can always find warmth and joy when we keep those we love close. We can always find beauty, even in darkness, for the stars will always come out and shine.

Thank you again for your interest in this series. Don't forget to leave an honest review on Goodreads and Amazon, and let the world know what you think!

If you're wondering about the continuation to this story, book three is in the making! I'm so excited for what comes next and hope you return for the final chapter in the series. You can follow me on Twitter, Instagram, and Facebook for any news, or go to my website, https://leah-reise-author.sitelio.me.

The Real Rena and Trish, AKA Flo and Katie

Photography by Brooklyn Brat Images

Made in the USA
Monee, IL
01 November 2020